P9-CMT-834

GUILT TRIP

GUILT TRIP

A Lina Townend Mystery

Judith Cutler

This first world edition published 2012
in Great Britain and in the USA by
SEVERN HOUSE PUBLISHERS LTD of
9–15 High Street, Sutton, Surrey, England, SM1 1DF.
Trade paperback edition first published
in Great Britain and the USA 2012 by
SEVERN HOUSE PUBLISHERS LTD.

British Library Cataloguing in Publication Data

Cutler, Judith.
  Guilt trip.
  1. Townend, Lina (Fictitious character)–Fiction.
  2. Antique dealers–Fiction. 3. Aristocracy (Social
  class)–Fiction. 4. Detective and mystery stories.
  I. Title
  823.9'2-dc23

ISBN-13: 978-0-7278-8142-7 (cased)
ISBN-13: 978-1-84751-414-1 (trade paper)

All Severn House titles are printed on acid-free paper.

MIX
Paper from
responsible sources
FSC
www.fsc.org   FSC® C018575

Typeset by Palimpsest Book Production Ltd.,
Falkirk, Stirlingshire, Scotland.
Printed and bound in Great Britain by
MPG Books Ltd., Bodmin, Cornwall.

For Kam and Nutan Chudasama, whose shop, open all hours and all weathers, is the beating heart of Kemble.

Acknowledgements

This novel could not have been written without the help of Dr Ian Simpson and Dr Chris Goldie, the staff of the Gloucestershire Royal and Cheltenham Hospitals and especially Dr George Asimakoplous and the staff of Bristol Heart Institute; huge thanks to them. I am deeply grateful too to Rev Michael Sanders and Rev Paul Youde, for kindness beyond the simply pastoral.

Lastly, thanks to Steph Richardson and Shane Forkner, for their brilliant ideas for titles for this and, I hope, future Lina novels, and to Ivor Higgins, for his meticulous and generous oversight of the finished manuscript.

ONE

S ometimes you go to an antiques fair, take one look at what's on offer, and wonder why you bothered to turn up. Why anyone bothered, actually, whether they were punters or dealers like me. This particular fair was clearly a dud, though it was billed as a prestige event in what claimed to be one of Kent's premier hotels, the Mondiale, in Hythe.

They'd put out glossy literature and reduced space rental prices to entice dealers to the new venue. But we knew from the moment we set up our stall one Thursday morning in early September that we had made a mistake. There were very few old friends there. The newcomers seemed to be selling not good quality antiques, but stuff that I'd technically describe as tat, more suitable for a bottom of the market car boot sale.

Always keen to make people feel at home, Griff left me to finish arranging our goods and went round to say hello. He was soon back. 'I know I'm not to everyone's taste,' he said sadly, passing me a paper cup of overpriced and undernourished coffee, 'but there are so many stony faces that you'd think this was a tax office. Perhaps these mauve slacks were a mistake?'

'People are probably just scared,' I said, thinking of my first fairs with Griff, when I was little more than a feral teenager, in whom he'd seen something worth rescuing. 'Stage fright,' I added.

'All the more need for old-timers like me to greet them and make them feel at home.'

I hugged him. 'Nowt so queer as folk,' I said, in a dreadful attempt at a Northern accent guaranteed to make him wince. He'd started out, like many antiques dealers, as a professional actor needing to make money while he was 'resting', as he and his friends described being what other folk called unemployed, and could produce accurate accents at the drop, as he said, of a script. 'Now, are you happy with these lights?'

I prompted him. 'Or should I put an extra spot on that garniture?'

Head on one side, he inspected the trio of late nineteenth century Spode vases. 'To make them a little less vulgar?' He sighed.

He'd been very downhearted recently, though he'd denied it when I'd asked him if there was a problem. He might have been anxious because there was less and less trade around – at least, selling person to person, which he enjoyed more than anything. Now we made far more of our money selling on the Internet than in our shop or at fairs, which he found terribly unexciting and impersonal. There was always a chance that he was simply bored.

I'd better be upbeat as I tweaked a light. 'Or to make them more eye-catching? Some people like OTT, after all. There. They look positively glamorous.'

He rolled his eyes.

Ignoring him, I said briskly, 'Now, if you're happy, shall I go for a little prowl myself?'

It wasn't unusual for dealers to come across items that were good value but which didn't fit with their usual stock-in-trade. We specialized in mid-value Victorian china, but would stretch our dates if we came across something special. Once Griff had dealt mainly in treen, but while a lot of people brought me their precious china and porcelain to repair, I'd never learned how to restore wooden items to my satisfaction, so we'd decided to run down that side of the business.

I was keeping an eye out for people who might have set something aside for us. I was also sniffing out bargains they didn't know they had, like a water diviner coming upon water in a desert. Not that I always told them how good their bargains were. I might be a divvy, but I wasn't a saint.

As I mooched round, a familiar figure emerged from the shadows. Titus Oates. Even in a brightly lit room like this, he always managed to get the dimmest corner. He dealt in old books and manuscripts, nine-tenths of his stock absolutely spot on. I didn't ask about the rest. Ever. Especially as he employed my father to produce it.

Glancing around the room, he raised an eyebrow, turned down his mouth and shook his head. Never again, his face said. He didn't need to use words.

Neither did I.

Completely satisfied with our conversation, we drifted apart. But then he summoned me back with a minute jerk of his head. 'Sad about Croft. Bankrupt. Topped himself.' And he was gone.

Croft had made genuine reproduction antiques – never pretended they were anything else. Brown furniture was at an all-time low: maybe repro was as bad. Maybe with Griff in his present mood I wouldn't pass on the information. I cogitated while I continued my prowl.

An old friend who dealt in old linen had found a Victorian spectacle case I might like. It wasn't china, obviously, but we had a regular customer who'd come to prefer spectacle cases to our usual stock and would take practically any we could find; we were still hunting for an elusive Tunbridge-ware one for her. Another mate produced a scruffy little bourdalou priced at a tenner that really did not sit well with his collection of garden and other tools. Griff had dinned it into me that all our deals must be done with honour and honesty, and I liked the guy, anyway. In fact, it might have been his accent I'd mimicked earlier, come to think of it.

'Dave,' I said, checking the piece carefully, 'you do know this is Derby?'

'It could be Ashby de la Zouch for all I know about it. Just some sauce boat with flowers on.'

'Flowers, yes. Sauce boat, no. It's a sort of Portaloo.'

'You what?'

'His Lordship could nip out of his coach and pee against the hedge. Her Ladyship certainly couldn't. So she'd use one of these.'

It took him a moment to work it out. 'A posh potty? Bloody hell. So what's it worth?'

'On your stall, who knows? On ours, it might just fetch two hundred and fifty to three hundred pounds on a good day.'

His eyebrows shot up. 'Eh, for a little 'un, you know a lot, don't you?'

'Do you want me to sell it on for you – just take commission?'

'I said I'd sell it, and the price was a tenner. I can't go back on that.'

'We're stuck then. I can't take it at that.' Arms akimbo, we glared at each other.

He broke first. 'What say we split the difference, lass? And you can buy me a pint if you make more. Eh, now I can tell my dad I've done what he always wanted me to do: I've changed trades, and I'm into plumbing. He'll be right taken aback – same as when I said I was marrying Pat and moving down south. Mind you, being a Yorkshireman he quite likes the freebie holidays he gets down here by the sea.' He gestured, with a huge curling thumb, at the stall opposite Titus', in a corner as dark as his. 'Hey up, have you seen that load of crap over there? Go on, take a look. And smell. They've used modern glue and modern varnish. Enough to make your hair curl.'

These days a lot of people gutted old dressing-cases and writing slopes to convert them into more user-friendly jewellery boxes, but most dealers did their best to make the alterations sympathetic. Not these people. I tried not to look at the cheap ugly fabric linings; they weren't even stuck in neatly. On the other side of the stall, there were other boxes that mercifully hadn't been converted. Some were dreadfully battered, needing help to get them back to a little dignity. Others, including a couple of Edwardian mahogany dressing-cases, had had chips roughly filled and then been varnished to within an inch of their lives, so much that even the so-called hidden drawers – little flat hidey-holes in the base opened by pressing a discreet catch – were sealed shut. I didn't know whether to be sad or furious. These had been places where women with no privacy could hide things that were precious – perhaps a letter or so, or maybe cash or a keepsake. You could scarcely see them on a top-class box. You couldn't see them at all on these. The silver bottle tops were still tarnished – inexcusable – and one or two bent where they'd been forced in the past. Since silver's so soft, it would have been the work of minutes to press them back into shape.

What were they daring to ask for these poor orphans of some unknown storm?

The stallholder, glued to his mobile, had his back to the room, as if daring any customers to approach. So I checked the prices myself, only to be defeated by the code. Most of us used some sort of shorthand when we priced things, if only to tell us how far we could drop a price and still make a profit while making a quick sale. It was easy enough for another dealer to work out: if we keep an eye on other people's stalls when they're on snack or loo breaks, we need to be able to help possible buyers, after all. Those on this stall meant nothing at all to me. Nothing. But then, I didn't have any proper education to speak of, and probably someone like Titus would crack it in no time. I decided that I must ask him next time our paths crossed.

By now the stallholder, still talking down his phone, was watching me every inch of the way. I had an absurd suspicion he was even talking about me to whoever was at the other end. Shaking my head, as much to clear it of silly ideas as to show I didn't fancy anything he was offering, I stalked off.

Continuing my circuit, I checked another newcomer's stall. I introduced myself and said as many pleasant things as I could. The woman's response was cool to icy, so when I spotted a pretty Swansea cup and saucer for far less than I'd be able to sell it for next time we were in Wales, I didn't talk up her price for her.

Accusing eyes glared at me. Full of guilt, I turned quickly. Thirty heads and faces stared in my direction. It took me a moment to realize that they all belonged to busts and Toby jugs. I didn't mind the busts, but I really loathed the jugs, probably because we had a regular client who bought every one she saw, regardless of condition. I got to restore the whole lot, always under pressure because she wanted work done yesterday. Perhaps it was a rare Toby jug calling me on her behalf? No. No, I didn't think so. It was a dusty Parian bust, of all things, of a serious-looking man with a beard. It was always weird when I got summoned by something I knew nothing about, but that was what was happening here. Was that a signature there? And a date? Two dates? I coughed up the trade price the stallholder was asking, just twenty pounds, and took Beardie back for Griff's approval, just as if he were a new boyfriend.

But Griff was on the phone, talking with more animation than I'd seen for weeks. I tucked my purchases under the skirts of the counter to show them to him later.

By now Griff was sounding very regretful, shaking his head and repeating that he couldn't, simply couldn't. He was sorry, but no. And he cut the call, his mouth turning down dreadfully at the corners.

It would have turned up again if there'd been any customers to charm, but there weren't.

'Look,' I said, pointing at the empty room. 'I can fight off all these seething masses. We're only a few hundred yards from Waitrose. Why don't you go and see what you can find?' As he hesitated, I added, 'I bet the lunches they sell here are as bad and overpriced as the coffee. A nice salad and a fresh roll would go down a treat. And some of that nice Victorian lemonade, just to remind us that it's really summer.'

'Only just,' he said, adding gloomily: 'Autumn will be on us before we know it.' But he pottered off all the same.

Normally, I could phone Aidan, Griff's long-term partner – in the other sense – and ask him to suggest something to bring back his smile. A few days in London doing all the shows and catching up with old friends would have been ideal. But Aidan was in New Zealand, with his dying sister and the rest of his family, who, I gathered, simply assumed he was a bachelor about town and had no notion of his real relationship with Griff. They phoned and Skyped, but as I was all too aware, virtual people weren't the same as real live warm ones in the same room. Not at all.

If I let my thoughts drift to Morris, my boyfriend, who was currently on secondment from the Met Fine Arts Squad to Interpol in Lyon, I'd soon be as miserable as Griff. When he'd accepted the posting, we'd assumed he'd be able to get back to England pretty well every weekend, or that I'd go to him. But his bosses kept rescheduling meetings, and sometimes his daughter was ill, and . . . No! I wouldn't start resenting the fact that he couldn't always be there for me. He did his best, after all. But sometimes . . .

Perhaps a bit of lippie might cheer me up; it ought to stop other people asking what was wrong. But Griff had dinned it into me that no one ever applied slap in public. Ever. So reaching for a compact was off limits, although only a few punters had strayed in. They looked as if they'd missed the turning for the beach. I'll swear some were carrying towels and shrimping nets. None of them seemed to know what to do next. Not spend their ice cream money at Tripp and Townend's stall, that was for sure.

A nod from Titus in response to my lifted eyebrow told me he'd keep an eye open so, grabbing the bourdalou and shoving the lipstick in my pocket, I nipped off. Washed with the hotel's best water, nothing else, it came up even better than I hoped, the little blue and green sprigs and the gilt lines standing out beautifully against the white ground. I was so pleased I almost forgot the lippie.

When I returned to the hall, however, I was very glad I hadn't.

In the dead centre stood this tall woman, looking as out of place with her elegant clothes and exquisite shoes as the bourdalou had done amongst Dave's garden spades. She held one hand to shield her eyes, like an intrepid explorer scanning a distant shore. Gradually, her gaze moved from one stall to the next.

I had time to scuttle to ours, where I found myself standing, just like my colleagues, more or less to attention. We might have been servants greeting the lady of the house. None of us so much as fidgeted, though some of us might have wanted to curtsy. I certainly did, until I told myself that but for a quirk of fate I might have been a Lady, or something similar. At this point my chin went up, all of its own accord.

At last it was my turn to be inspected. But this time she stepped forward, her hands spread as if in disbelief. 'But where,' she asked the whole room, not loudly but very clearly, 'is Griffith Tripp?'

In the past I'd have squared up to her, asking, 'What is it to you?' Now some of my father's aristocratic genes must have made me say, without a single squeak, 'I'm his partner, madam. Can I help you?' My dignity might have been some- what diminished by the presence of the travelling chamber pot in my hand. Perhaps she didn't register it.

She glided forward, right hand outstretched, as if to shake mine, but she held it at such a curious angle that I had a terrible fear she might expect me to kiss it. I didn't, but I did place my new purchase safely on the stand before offering my own. 'Lina Townend,' I said as I did so.

'Ah, his protégée,' she said, moderating the volume slightly but giving each syllable its full value as she leaned across the stall to air-kiss me. Her scent was expensive, but close to I could see that her skin owed far more to very skilfully applied cosmetics than she'd probably have liked to admit. As for those huge diamond studs weighing down her ears, I'd have insured them as paste. Good paste, but paste. 'I've heard *all* about you!'

'She's my darling Lina – the granddaughter I never had!' declared Griff, startling her into a tremendous jump, only half of which was spontaneous. 'She's my dearest friend possible.'

He'd made an impressive entrance despite the three Waitrose carriers he was clutching – worse, surely, than my pot. He passed them to me as if he was bestowing a huge favour, and taking both of our visitor's hands, he kissed them in turn.

It was a good job I was holding all that food or I swear I'd have applauded.

So might the rest of the stallholders. Possibly the few punters thought all this came with their entrance tickets, a sort of indoor street theatre, because they formed a loose circle around the pair. Theatrical it certainly was. The woman fell to her knees, her clasped hands raised imploringly, like the model for a bad Victorian picture.

'Griffith Tripp,' she began, 'on bended knee, I beg you to take that part. We cannot manage without you. The part calls. The stage calls. Your public calls.'

A murmur ran round the room, as if the public was responding to its cue.

To my delight, Griff silently expressed extreme reluctance. One hand repelled her, the other called on the heavens for support. Both held their poses. What a tableau. It could have been a bad illustration for a scene from Dickens.

'Go on, mate, do the decent thing! Make an honest woman of her!' someone yelled, breaking the silence.

So Griff turned, both hands outstretched to take hers – a good job since I was pretty sure she couldn't have got up under her own steam without an undignified scrabble. 'Very well, Emilia. I will at least give you ear.' He cast a strange look at me (see, the language was catching!): was he asking for help or for approval?

'Why not go and have a coffee and talk it over?' I asked. The punters had got more than their money's worth and might be in a mood to buy. It wasn't just our business that had been suspended, after all.

For whatever reason, things seemed to improve a little. In half an hour I sold two pretty Royal Worcester blush egg cups and an elegant Edwardian Crown Devon jardinière going cheap because I'd restored extensively. And yes, I showed the buyer exactly what I'd done. A smattering of people were now carrying the bright lime green polythene carriers the fair organizers insisted we all used, so other dealers must have profited too.

Titus appeared a few yards away. 'Nice bit of drama, eh, doll? Acted like a dose of castor oil on the wallets, too. How much did he pay her? Though it looks more like she's going to pay him. Griff as toy boy. Who'd have thought it?'

He'd gone before I could reply. All those sentences from Titus. He must have made a killing on something.

Something was beginning to smell oniony. Something in one of the Waitrose bags. They ought to be in the van, but with so many people now milling round I didn't care to leave the stall unattended. Griff and this Emilia could have five more minutes, but then I'd call his mobile.

In fact, it was nearer fifteen minutes, because I was busy with a couple of the most frustrating sort of would-be buyers. They really liked one of our vases. But they'd seen something similar – well, not exactly like it – on a TV antiques auction show, where it had gone for much less than I was asking for it. Eventually, still managing a smile, I resorted to the lowest trick in my book, which worked almost every time. I put the vase into the woman's hands. It was like handing her a longed for baby. In her heart and head it was already hers.

Their cash was still warm in my bumbag when Griff reappeared.

I hugged away his apologies. It wasn't the first time I'd held the fort alone, and I was sure it wouldn't be the last. 'So what has this Emilia woman persuaded you to do?'

'Is it so obvious? My dear one, Emilia – Emilia Cosworth, you must have heard of her. No? Ah, me – she once had her name in lights on Broadway and in the West End. I'll tell you all about her later. What matters now is that Emilia owns and runs a tiny theatre in a converted oast house and wants me – she says to star, but really it's to be part of the regular ensemble – in a play she's commissioned.'

'Commissioned!'

'When she – like us all – had periods of resting, she taught creative writing. The play's by one of her former students. Not a household name, dear one.'

'We all have to start somewhere,' I said, not one to begrudge anyone the sort of luck I had. 'What's it called?'

'*Curtain Call*. One hopes it's not an omen. There'll be a run of a week at most. The downside is that most of the actors are amateur, so there'll be endless rehearsals. One evening a week, at least, plus Sunday afternoons,' he wailed.

Privately, I thought it was just what he needed. 'Many lines to learn?' If there was anything to worry about it was his memory, which he insisted was fading.

'Ah, that's the wonderful thing! I play an ageing Victorian actor-manager recalling his past triumphs as he writes his autobiography. So I can have the script in front of me! Not to read,' he added hurriedly, 'but to refer to, should I need it.'

'And when do rehearsals start?'

'They actually began two weeks ago. The actor who was supposed to be playing the lead pulled out quite unexpectedly and entirely without explanation. An amateur.' He shrugged. 'So they thought of me. That was the phone call. And then Emilia turns up here – so OTT . . .'

There was something he didn't want to admit. 'She certainly

put on a good show. Perked up everyone's sales no end. So when's *your* first rehearsal?' I asked at last.

Now he looked thoroughly hangdog. 'That's the problem. This evening. At seven.'

We didn't finish here till five. Then there was the packing up. But I managed a smile. 'No problem. I'll drop you wherever it is, go home, unload, and pick you up. How about that?'

'But it's miles – the oast's miles beyond Hawkhurst.'

'OK, so it's a bit of a schlep. But usually you'll be able to drive yourself. And when the nights draw in,' I continued, overriding his next protest, 'you'll be able to stay over at Aidan's. Tenterden's only spitting distance from Hawkhurst. OK? Now, I think we have a customer and I need to get these bags – what on earth did you buy? – into the van.'

TWO

Though I'd been upbeat about Griff's journey, when I picked my way along what our new satnav assured me was the best route to the oast house theatre, I felt less positive. Griff hated driving in the dark, and naturally these lanes hadn't a glimmer of a street light. Some were so narrow that there was room for only one vehicle, with passing places at intervals. When I finally reached a nice fast A road, the right turn on to it was really tricky, with cars belting round an almost blind bend like the proverbial bats.

The turn-off was signed to an industrial estate, of all things. As we nosed through it we saw a smokery, an artisan cheese-maker and a microbrewery – all of which had Griff rubbing his hands with glee – but also a lot of other unmarked work-shops, scruffy and down-at-heel. The oast house lay at the very far end of a badly surfaced road, with a car park so rutted that I'd have welcomed a four by four – I was worried stiff about our poor stock, being tossed around in the back. I'd swathed everything in acres of bubble wrap, of course, but hadn't expected it to have to put up with this.

Griff was tut-tutting and exclaiming. Any moment he might cry off. But I could tell even from the way he'd been sitting how much he was looking forward to acting again. Correction: *treading the boards*. Not that there were many boards to tread, as we discovered when we finally arrived at a longish rectangular building attached to the roundel of the oast. I think you'd call it a space, not a stage. The audience would sit on a rickety set of wooden platforms, looking down at the actors. Running halfway round the extension, behind the acting area, was a balcony. Apart from a fire exit, which was for some reason chained and padlocked, the only entrance and exit was via the oast, which housed a tiny bar and the two loos (I could imagine the interval queues already!). Goodness knows where the actors' dressing rooms might be.

Emilia, who was clearly running the whole show, waved me off dismissively, telling me that carriages were at ten thirty and not a second before. Were they indeed? But I didn't so much as grimace till I was out of Griff's sight, manoeuvring the van round in a tiny parking area so that I could head back to Bredeham via more of those horrible little lanes. There was no one around, so why did I feel as if I was being watched? Home, I told the satnav, quick as you can get me there.

I just had time to empty the van and stow everything safely before I had to set out again, this time in our smaller but still personalized van. There were times when I longed to nip round in a nice anonymous Fiesta, silver, just like everyone else's Fiesta. For some reason Griff, though addicted to other forms of protection – you should have seen our home and shop security systems, worthy of the Bank of England – stuck to the idea of advertising our business wherever we went. We'd even had rows about it, something we never did about anything else.

There were still lights on in some of the units when I turned up – clearly, running small businesses was hard work and time-consuming for everyone, not just us. One lot of lights went out as soon as I turned into the estate, but no one emerged from the building.

I pulled into the closest space to the oast house, next to a Range Rover with a flat tyre. Half of me wanted to go in and see what Griff and his friends were up to, and warn the owner of the Range Rover, but I couldn't trust myself not to be rude to Emilia if she got on her high horse again. The other half decided to text Morris; although he worked all hours, he might be free by now. But there was no network coverage, of course. So, locking the van, I went for a prowl, eyes mainly on the mobile's signal bars. The area was grimmer now it was getting dark, unlit skips and bins looming. There were a couple of pallets still shrink-wrapped in polythene. The brewery and smokery gave off predictable pongs. Another, unmarked unit smelt of chemicals and wood, the blend really sickening.

A signal at last. I told Morris I loved him, and for good measure I sent him a picture of me blowing a kiss through the gloom. Nothing came back. I'd just have to wait.

He was very good at keeping in touch, as he'd promised he
would be when he was seconded by the Met, but if it had
been hard when he was based in London, it was doubly hard
now. When he managed to escape the bosses who seemed to
delight in messing up our arrangements, he'd come as near
to a port or airport as he could and I'd nip over, even if it was
just for a day. Once or twice he'd brought the child he hoped
was his daughter, Leda, but only when her mother and the
man who also claimed to be her father were both working.
His access to her was such a problem that I tried really hard
not to complain when we were *à trois*, not *à deux* (see, I was
already picking up bits of the language). Leda was getting to
an interesting age, and I'd discovered a talent I never I knew
I had for making sandcastles on windy beaches. Even so, it
would have been nice if he'd needed me as much as he needed
her.

Why was someone watching me? It wouldn't be Toby jugs'
eyes this time.

Retreating to the van, I flicked the locks shut and sat tight.

Before I could get into a proper panic, however, someone
came round the side of the building, carrying a paper file that
I assumed held his script. A fellow actor as young and nice-
looking as that – he could have doubled for David Tennant
– and Griff would be in heaven. He looked a little surprised
to see me, but through the dusk flashed a gorgeous smile. Then
he melted away. I didn't see any activity from the other vehicles parked up, or even the light of a torch: he must have eaten
a lot of carrots to be able to see so well in the dark. Then a
door in the oast opened, surprising and delighting a whole lot
of insects, and Griff and his fellow thespians straggled out.
He headed my way deep in conversation with a tall rangy
man, for whose bulgy-veined legs mid-knee shorts did absolutely nothing. The man stopped when they saw the Range
Rover. Until I got out of the van I couldn't pick up everything
the man said, but to be honest, I didn't need to.

'It's unlike you, my child,' said Griff, settling beside me
as the man dialled so hard that I was surprised his mobile
didn't bite him back, 'not to have done something about that
poor man's car. I don't mean to change the wheel, heaven

forfend, but to come in and tell us of the problem. He could
have called the AA or whatever, and they'd have been here
by now.'

'Only just arrived,' I lied, not terribly proud of myself for
ogling the David Tennant lookalike. 'And I didn't know the
etiquette of interrupting a rehearsal.'

I didn't need to interrupt anything for the next five miles.
Griff poured out a series of what I can only call lamentations:
the cast, the space, the direction, the script itself.

'So you're going to give up, are you?' I asked,
tongue-in-cheek.

'I thought of it. I still do. But perhaps an actor of my
experience will help pull everything together.' When he
sounded the *r* in *actor* I knew he was smitten.

'If anyone can do it, you can,' I declared, concentrating
once more on the road ahead. We were trying a different route
back, if anything slower and more awkward than the outward
one. Why had no one ever got round to building straight east-
west roads in Kent, proper dual-carriageways, not these wiggly
diagonal things? Talk about all roads leading to Rome. The
only place to go to or from quickly was London. 'So tell me
about your part . . .'

'Ah, the final straight,' he said as at last we picked up a familiar
A road. 'But what's going on over there, my love?'

He pointed to what used to be an old-fashioned garage,
servicing cars and selling petrol, though naturally at above
supermarket prices, so it had gone bust. For months it had lain
idle until a couple of enterprising and quite gorgeous Eastern
European lads had set up their car wash business, which Griff
had made a point of using – anything, he said, to support
people trying to make a living. Now it seemed that they'd
gone too. There was a shopfitter's van outside, with people
obviously working away inside – even though it was now
nearly midnight.

'Tomacz never mentioned that,' Griff said.

I was busy overtaking an unlit cyclist. 'Perhaps Tomacz
didn't know. Perhaps someone sold the lease over his head.
Perhaps their little business wasn't even strictly legal.'

'We could stop and be nosy?' Griff was still obviously high on adrenalin; usually, he'd have been fast asleep by now.

'Let's pop back tomorrow – then you can have a good gossip with the workers.'

'My sweet child, I never gossip!'

All the same, the following morning, over breakfast in the garden, he reminded me of my suggestion.

'I'd love to,' I said, not very truthfully. 'But I've got to get that Worcester figurine back on her feet so the owners can collect her on Monday. Why don't you go on your own? But remember Mrs Walker's got a wedding dress fitting and can't mind the shop today.'

'Oh, I'll be back by eleven, never fear.'

When Griff was having a good chinwag, however, he tended to lose all sense of time, so I took my work things down to the shop. I didn't expect any interruptions, the way business was, nor did I get any till a large delivery van pulled up outside.

Cautiously, I unlocked the door, locking it behind me as I stepped into the sunlight.

The driver might have been Tomacz's designer-stubbled twin and spoke rather less English. He claimed to have a delivery for us.

'Antiques, Bredeham,' he insisted, jabbing the papers. He might have jabbed me too, if I hadn't sidestepped.

It was true that ours was the only antiques shop in the village. 'Let me see,' I said. OK, I was as nosy as Griff.

Eventually, he handed over the papers. I nearly whistled: he had a huge consignment of furniture, all listed carefully. Someone must have an equal mixture of capital and optimism.

'We don't sell furniture,' I told him. 'It's not for us. We only sell china.'

'Ah! China too!' He pointed at his list.

Yes, indeed. Twelve packing cases of china. More than we'd sell in a year.

'I'm afraid it's not ours, though,' I insisted. 'It's all someone else's.' But whose? This was antique dealing on an industrial scale. No one I knew would handle anything like that amount. And then it dawned on me where he might be heading – the refurbished garage. I sent him on his way.

So when Griff came back from his foray to the old garage, he wasn't the only one big with news.

'An antique shop – oh, they call it a centre! – almost on our doorstep!' he raged. 'I don't recall seeing a notification of planned change of use when I was there last. Tomacz should have mentioned it. Surely, they have to get permission from someone?'

'Seems they must have done somehow,' I said. 'And they've got a lot of stock to put in it.' Time for my story now.

'Twelve cases of china?' he repeated.

'Full-size packing cases,' I nodded. 'After all, they've got a lot of space to fill. What does it look like? Hard to make a garage look like anything except a garage, surely.'

'They've managed it. OK, it's only hardboard, I should imagine, but they've faked panelled rooms and low ceilings, and laminated old oak floorboards are going down even as we speak. Everything genuine fake,' he concluded bitterly.

'I wonder if the stuff they sell will be too.'

'If anyone can tell that, it's you, my love. Oh, and they're going to run a tea room and sell plants.' He sat down hard, as if his legs had given way. 'So they plan to ruin us and Sally Haskin and Midge Poulter. Antique shop, café and flower shop, just like that!' He snapped his fingers.

'Only if we let them,' I said grimly.

THREE

People acting on their own would probably be no more than flea bites, so I suggested group action, although it would be like trying to herd cats: Sally Haskin and Midge Poulter had had an argument years back, before I even came to the village, and had never spoken since. Wisely, Griff set off to talk to them separately. Knowing I wouldn't see him for some time, I resigned myself to further work in the shop: not on the counter, altogether too public, but on a small side-table that folded away when not in use. The light wasn't anything like as good as in my workroom, and I didn't have everything I needed within reach. But I made progress.

I was just wondering whether I dared flip over the 'Closed' sign and nip and get a coffee when we had one of those rare birds, a customer. He seemed impatient at even the few seconds' delay between his ringing our bell and my unlocking the door, but I didn't take it personally. His face had seen a lot of impatience, to judge by the pinch of frown lines round his mouth.

'Lina Townsend?' he asked, with what could have been a slight French accent, though I couldn't be sure. He laid a stylish black leather case on the counter. It might be just a computer bag, but it wouldn't have looked out of place being carried into the Ritz. Even so, I didn't like things being slung on the counter like that, so I raised a cool eyebrow. Without looking abashed, he opened it long enough to fish out a business card, before closing it and putting it on the floor. He pulled down the cuffs of his elegant suit, then dropped the card on the square of green baize we use to protect the counter from hard objects and vice versa.

'Lina *Townend*. That's me.' I wished it had been a better-dressed me, because though my T-shirt was clean, it was only workwear, after all. And you don't posh up when you're dealing with paint and adhesive.

He looked down at the Worcester figurine. 'Of course it is.' His smile took ten years off him; if I'd seen him like this the first time I might have thought him charming. As it was, I reserved judgement. 'I've heard so much about you,' he added, his face softening still more. 'And now I can see you in action.'

I smiled too, but regretfully. 'I'm afraid restoration isn't a spectator sport. It has to be done in decent privacy.'

'So no one sees what you've done?'

'Not unless it's work on your own property. But even then you don't get to watch – it'd be like having a patient's relative in an operating theatre,' I added. Surely, it was time for him to explain why he was here? I didn't have all day to waste on verbal sparring. 'How can I help you?' That was blunt enough.

'It's how *I* can help *you*.' He turned the card round so if I wanted I could read it.

'Help me?' Griff could have warned him that when I rounded my eyes and sounded little-girly, I was actually getting angry. Approaching furious, actually, when, the side of one lip curled, he looked round the shop as if it was some junk shop.

'I should imagine your workload is pretty patchy – heavy one week, then nothing for ages.'

He could imagine what he liked. Most weeks I had more than I could handle. For people who weren't my regular clients, there was a wait of a month or more. Which of them might have sent this guy here? Or was it a fellow dealer, genuinely impressed by the quality of my work?

'All self-employed craftspeople have good times and bad times,' I said, still managing to sound mild.

'How would you like to have good times all the time – a properly managed work flow, regular hours, paid holidays?'

'Self-employed people don't have lives like that,' I pointed out. So I was about to be offered some sort of a contract: the only question was who was offering it. At least one top-of-the-range dealer had already approached me, as had two museums. I'd turned down their offers and would do the same to any others. My place was here with Griff.

'But you could still call yourself self-employed. In fact, it might be advantageous were you to do so.'

Were I to do so! Any moment now I could be getting very bored with this smooth-talking city type.

'I like to call myself what I am. It's often easier to tell the truth.' I looked at my watch. I'd prefer to get rid of this man – Charles Montaigne, according to his card – before Griff returned. Why didn't the card give more detail, not just his name and a mobile number? Like what his business was? I was sure it was business. Curators of cash-strapped museums didn't run to suits like that. 'Being self-employed doesn't mean working part-time, however. And it doesn't mean you don't have to meet deadlines.' Charles Montaigne. How did I know that name?

'Cheap fifties Royal Worcester,' he said, pointing to the figure on my side table.

'Not so very cheap – a Freda Doughty. "The First Cuckoo".' I wished I didn't sound so defensive.

'Three or four hundred at most. You're better than that.'

'So I've been told.'

'Harvey Sanditon says you're the best.'

I'd been wondering when his name would crop up. He was far further up the food chain than Griff and me, but had taken a shine to us – OK, to me in particular – and put a lot of work my way. He'd once tried to lure me down to Devon, but when he'd been knocked back hadn't seemed to bear a grudge. In fact, I sometimes wondered if all the work he put my way from other dealers might be a sop to his conscience for flirting so thoroughly when he was married. But, hey, it was work, and who was arguing?

'He's a friend of Griff's.' That was the way Harvey preferred to play it, once his wife had found out he had feelings for me – which was well after I'd sent him packing, incidentally.

Montaigne's eyebrows rose, then dipped. 'Of course. So you don't want extra work put your way?'

'I'm always happy to consider work,' I said. 'But on an individual basis. And I do ask owners to agree a pretty tight contract – would you believe that some dealers try to pass restored work off as perfect?' I added sunnily. I reached a copy from a drawer under the counter.

He ignored it. 'How wicked of them,' he said ironically.

'Well, if you change your mind, all you have to do is call this number.' He touched the card again. With a final look round the shop, a bit of a sneer and something of a shrug, he went out, leaving me in peace.

Actually, I felt far from peaceful. Angry, patronized and – yes – rather intimidated, though I couldn't for the life of me have explained why.

But that was something I could keep to myself, I told the little figurine, apologizing for the shakiness of my hands. Griff was horribly quick at picking up my changes of mood, so I decided to pre . . . pre . . . One problem of having no schooling to speak of is forgetting useful words. I had to get my question in first – *pre-empt* him, that was it. 'How's the campaign going?' I asked, the moment he appeared, only half an hour late.

He rubbed his hands with glee. 'In train already. To my absolute amazement, the two old witches – and were it after six o'clock I might use a stronger variant of the word – are prepared to join a little action committee, together with the people from Spar and the pharmacy. Revolution! Tariq Ali, eat your heart out.'

I'd no idea who Tariq Ali might be, but to look at gentle Griff now, pumping his right fist in the air, I was sure he would.

'Oh, it'll be like when I was a young man, awash with the testosterone of rebellion! We may not tear up the cobblestones of Paris, but we might manage a protest in the market square,' he added with a self-mocking smile. 'We meet tonight. Watch this space. Meanwhile, my love, the items we took to Hythe – was it only yesterday? – are still in their packing cases. I suggest that since your morning's work was sadly interrupted by our pantechnicon friend, you leave that to me.'

He could see how little I'd achieved, couldn't he? Was this the moment to tell him about the other visitor? No, it'd only worry him to think I was turning down what he'd see as a good career move.

I nodded. 'Aren't we off to Sevenoaks this weekend? So I wouldn't bother taking the stuff out. We can just pack every-thing back into the van.'

He stared. 'Sevenoaks? But the play . . .!'

'No problem. We can both work on Saturday, and I can go

on my own on Sunday. Titus will be there so you needn't worry about me.'

'All the more reason to worry about you, loathsome man. No, to do him justice I suppose he believes there's honour amongst thieves. He'll provide muscle in both senses – probably more useful than me,' he added plaintively.

I didn't bite, largely because what he'd said was true. These days anything in the way of heavy lifting left him pale and breathless. So far I'd not been able to frogmarch him to see Dr Chapman, but any day now I'd make an appointment in my own name and simply grass him up. 'I need better light, so I'll take this little lady upstairs and work on her there.' Half-true, anyway – and the best I could manage. I slipped the business card in with all the others in a wicker basket Griff meant to sort out one day.

In the quiet of the garden, over lunch – some of the scrumptious end-dated goodies Griff had picked up yesterday – I asked him about his campaign. Ours, really, of course.

'The thing is,' I said, 'it's a case of David and Gollum.' When he looked puzzled, I added, 'You know, that guy with his Precious.'

'I think you mean the guy that David slew with a stone from his sling. Goliath, sweet one.'

'Goliath. And though David didn't exactly fight dirty, he had the . . . the element of surprise,' I said in a rush, quoting one of the BBC's Afghanistan reporters. 'Now, whoever set up this here centre will assume we're going to fight, but he'll also assume that we're going to fight clean. What he won't expect is a little stone from our sling.'

'And what little stone would that be?'

'I've no idea,' I admitted with a grin. 'But I know a man who might help find it. Titus Oates, of course.'

Predictably, Griff winced. 'A man so hard to like, dear one.'

In the past I'd had to walk down the village street to phone him. This time I was going to be upfront. I smiled grimly. 'But such a useful one.'

I waited till Griff had gone to mind the shop before dialling. Titus answered first ring.

With Titus, you didn't bother with all those polite things that usually start phone conversations. 'Who's behind the big antiques centre on the A road between here and Ashford?'

There was a silence. 'What antiques centre?'

'Arrived last night, courtesy of some shopfitters working overtime. And their stock arrived here a couple of hours ago. A big van, full of furniture and china.'

'Just like that?'

'Just like that. Plus it's got a tea room and plant centre.'

'Fucking hell.' The line went dead.

While I had the phone in my hand, I might make another call. For someone who made money with international transactions Harvey Sanditon was very slow at dealing with emails. He hardly touched texts at all. So it was a good old-fashioned bit of communication, especially as Harvey did like all the curtsies. No, not curtsies. *Courtesies.* That was the word.

'My dear Lina, what an unexpected pleasure. How are you? And dear Griff?'

Knowing he'd be interested, I told him about Griff's new campaign against the antiques centre. Only then did I lead into what I really wanted to know. 'Harvey, you know how generous you are putting work my way—'

'I put it your way not because I'm generous, but because you do such good work, Lina.'

Whatever. But I didn't say it out loud. 'I've been approached by someone who said you spoke highly of me—'

'Which I do to everyone.'

'Thank you. I was wondering what you know about this particular guy. Charles Montaigne.' At least, thanks to my trips to France, I managed not to mangle the surname too badly.

'Charles Montaigne? Never heard of him. No, actually, I have, but I've no idea where or in what context. I've certainly not spoken to a man with that name about you.'

'Oh.'

'Is that a problem?'

'Yes, actually. Why should he suggest he's best mates with you?' I answered the question myself. 'He was trying to sweet-talk me into working for him – full-time, by the sound of it.'

'Which you declined to do.'

'If I was ever going to work full-time for anyone, Harvey, you'd have first claim,' I said. 'Because I know you're honest. And this guy was somehow suggesting that I'd still call myself self-employed when I wasn't. He looked absolutely loaded.'

'Which could have been window dressing, of course. Did you check his car registration and so on?'

'He'd parked out of sight.'

'Which, dearest Lina, I hardly need observe, is suspicious in itself. Charles Montaigne . . . I will ask around – discreetly, of course – on your behalf. However, and it pains me to say this, the best source of information is probably that shady and laconic friend of yours.'

I knew *shady*, but not *laconic*. But I could have a good guess. 'Titus Oates?'

'Does he have a proper first name, or were his parents students of English revolutionary history?'

'If he has, I've never heard it. Thanks for the advice, Harvey. I'll call him.' Again, of course.

With Harvey, you couldn't just get what you needed and cut the call. You had to go through the same routine you'd started with. Or do I mean ritual? Griff always liked it, matching Harvey's twisting, turning sentences with some of his own, as if they were performing some complicated verbal dance.

If only I could have remembered any of the steps. Usually, I let Harvey get on with it, while I remained *laconic*. (Was that how you used the word? I must ask Griff.) But at last I was free to decide whether to do what he suggested: phone Titus. Again. On the whole I thought I'd wait for him to call me.

Meanwhile, I had the Worcester to finish.

'My child, I did hope you'd be coming to the protest meeting this evening,' Griff said, putting a cup of green tea on my work table. 'But here you are, still toiling.'

Managing to put the figure down safely, I stretched, hearing and feeling something clunk in the top of my back. 'What's the time, then?'

'Almost six. I popped my head round the door earlier, but

you might as well have had a *Do Not Disturb* sign hanging from your back, so I tiptoed away.'

'I'm sorry,' I said, reaching for the tea. 'I lost all sense of time.' Actually, I'd been hoping Morris might phone, as he sometimes did, and suggest a stolen weekend together. My theory was that if I sat and daydreamed, he wouldn't, but if I really got stuck into a job, he would. Sometimes it worked; sometimes, like today, it didn't. 'But of course I'm coming to your meeting. After all, it involves me as much as it involves you.' I cleaned away the adhesives and paint. I liked a nice clean space to start the next day.

'Almost but not quite, my love. After all, you could always earn a living with your hands.' He pointed to 'The First Cuckoo'.

Had he seen that business card? 'Could. But I'd rather do it as part of Tripp and Townend than on my own. And I don't like people who bend the rules others like us have to obey,' I added firmly, but under my breath.

The village hall was packed. Maybe some villagers had turned up because there was nothing worth watching on TV, but most seemed really keen to protect the shopkeepers who gave Bredeham what they called its 'character'. They passed a vague resolution promising not to patronize the new centre and to eat and buy more locally. I could see how that might help Spar, but there was a limit to the number of Doulton vases a family might want. And Griff would fall at the first hurdle. Spar had a wonderful range of cakes, but these barely crossed his radar, not while he could cook his own. As for the cheeses they stocked, they weren't much use to an unpasteurized man.

Perhaps that's why he didn't make the Shakespeare-laced speech I'd expected, but he did raise a little dust when he asked why none of our parish councillors was in attendance, as he quaintly put it. They'd not even sent their apologies, which made the handsome law-student son of the Bangladeshi takeaway owner declare that they'd all been bribed by the owners of the new centre. The vicar's wife insisted on adding all sorts of words like *conceivably* and *not impossible* as she minuted his allegation. The pharmacist, much more down to earth, said that the meeting was being held at very short notice, and we should hold another to which they were specifically invited. The motion was passed without argument.

All of which left us feeling rather flat. Me, at least. I wanted action, and I wanted it now. Specifically, I wanted action from Morris, of course, but there was no point in taking out my grumpiness on Griff. So when he suggested a late drink in the garden, so we could watch the overhead display by the birds and bats, I agreed.

'You're very quiet, my dear one,' he said as he brought out ice-cold Moselle and some posh nibbles. 'Light that candle, would you? We don't want bugs to drive us back in. An evening like this we should cherish – autumn will soon be upon us, after all. *Season of mists and mellow fruitfulness*,' he added sadly.

Autumn, with rough channel crossings and nowhere for Leda to play. Unpleasant drives across to cold church halls for antiques fairs that hardly paid. Probably ferrying Griff in the dark to this oast house theatre. It was a good job we didn't have a cat or I'd probably have kicked it.

FOUR

It would have been a very bruised cat indeed – if it had hung around long after the first assault – by the end of the weekend. Sales at Sevenoaks were brisk, but there was no reason for Griff not to leave me on my own for the second day and toddle off to his rehearsal. No reason at all, except a phone call late on Saturday night from Morris, calling from Paris, saying he might just be able to slip over for the day.

'I've got to work,' I whispered. 'At a fair up in Sevenoaks.'

'Can't Griff cope?' he asked reasonably. 'Or Mrs Walker?'

'She'll be in the shop, as usual, and Griff's booked elsewhere. So I'm doing it on my own. And no, much as I'd like to, I can't just skive off. It's a two-dayer. All our stuff's laid out already.' I was near to tears. 'You know how it is at weekends,' I added defensively.

'Of course.' He sounded as glum as I felt. 'What's this about Griff being booked?'

I reminded him about Aidan's visit to New Zealand and added, 'He's been very low recently. So when some woman from his past burst into a fair at the Mondiale and demanded that he star in her show, I encouraged him,' I explained. Then I added glumly, 'I didn't know about the Sunday rehearsals then.'

'Every Sunday?' His voice was so controlled that it was obvious he was close to losing his rag.

'Looks like it.' I tried to appease him. 'But, of course, we don't have fairs every Sunday.' And I didn't actually have Morris many Sundays, either.

'So on top of everything else, I have to try to juggle my free time to suit not just your work, but also some aged thesp's crappy play in a location no one's ever heard of.'

I hoped he meant Emilia, not Griff. 'I suppose if you put it like that, yes.'

'How else can I put it?'

He could have put it that I was stuck in the UK, with him swanning round Europe following a career choice he didn't have to make – he could easily have stayed at the Met. It was a six months' commitment, he'd said, maybe longer. We were nearly halfway there, and this was our first tiff – but it felt as if the next months would be very long.

Before I could say any of this in a quiet and reasonable way, as opposed to a half-sobbed scream of complaints, I heard a wail. He must be speaking from Leda's mother's apartment. I'd been the first to say that Leda should be everyone's priority. But I hadn't realized that appeasing her mother would be the second. Not to mention his job coming in as a pretty hefty third. Which left me . . .

It would have been easy to throw a strop and cut the call. Instead, I took a deep breath and asked how she was.

'Starting the terrible twos early,' he said. 'I think she's going to be an opera star. Lungs and attitude – a proper prima donna. I'd better go and deal with her before the neighbours start complaining again. Catch you soon, OK?'

And that was that. At least we hadn't ended on an open wound, but I had an idea that if I wasn't careful I might say something that would cause one.

The following afternoon I was just loading the last plastic storage box into our van and longing for a deep, bubbly bath, when the phone rang. Silence. Number withheld. And again, ten minutes later. And again. Each time I had to stop to check, of course.

And then Griff phoned.

'Have you had a good day?' he asked.

I'd worked out the answer to this in advance. If I said I'd been busy, he'd beat himself up for having deserted me; if I said we'd been slack, he'd beat himself up for letting me waste time I could have spent on my restoration work – I'd not told him about Morris's call and didn't intend to, in case he was sweet and sympathetic and I got all teary. Or hissing spitting furious at him for him indulging that overdressed old cow I'd never heard mention of before. I knew I'd encouraged him, but that didn't make it any better.

'We ticked over nicely,' I said. 'Fewer customers than yesterday, but about the same takings. I'm just about to set out for home, as it happens. Get the kettle on if you get there first.'

'Ah.'

So there was a problem.

'Emilia's invited me back to her home for afternoon tea, my angel, and a gossip about old times. So I may not be back until – say, sevenish? Maybe later?'

'No problem,' I assured him. 'But promise me you'll set out early enough to get home in the light. The nights are beginning to draw in already, remember.' And Griff didn't drive well in the dusk. Put it another way, he scared me rigid.

Meanwhile, I'd get to unpack everything and stow it safely. For some reason, I knew that any moment now I'd sound and feel like the younger angry version of me, the one Griff had transformed, who had lashed out and broken things. I didn't like all these feelings one scrap. Apart from anything else, they were illogical. After all, times out of number I'd shooed him out the way and done everything myself. But tonight I just seethed.

At last I could turn the final lock on our boxes of stock and go and run myself that bath. If Griff had been around, he'd have pressed a glass of wine into my hand. On my own I plumped for tea. And a slice of Griff's latest cake. I even flicked on the TV to watch the last overs of a cricket match I didn't care about and picked up the *Observer*, left in a mess, as usual, because as Griff finished with each section he dropped it on the floor. I ought to start supper, too. Cooking was usually his area, but after an afternoon rehearsing and the long drive there and back, he'd be knackered.

It had better be a quick shower, not that long deep bath.

Just as I got thoroughly wet, hair too, the phone rang. I had a stupid hope it might be Morris, saying he'd come over to Kent anyway and was just down the road. So trailing drips and letting the shower run, I dived to answer it.

It was such a quiet, embarrassed-sounding Griff that I swallowed my scream of frustration, disappointment and – yes – anger.

I did manage to tell him to call back in two minutes when I'd turned off the shower.

This time he sounded even more embarrassed. 'I've been boxed in, loved one, and can't move the van. I can't persuade a taxi firm to come out here and collect me.'

'Where's "here"?'

'Out at the oast.'

'I thought you were going to Emilia's.'

'And so I was. But two lorries have absolutely trapped the van so I simply can't shift it.' Actually, he sounded as breathless as if he'd been trying to push them away. 'I didn't want to call you on your mobile in case you were driving.'

'Police?'

'Private land, according to Emilia. She's terribly upset, as you can imagine – talked very briefly about driving me back. I can't even reach our overnight bags or I'd find a pub to put me up.'

'Give me two minutes to throw some clothes on and I'll be on my way.' I cut the call before he could protest and before I could scream aloud.

Whoever had manoeuvred those lorries into place really knew their business. They'd backed in at right angles to the little van, with about two inches between their huge tyres and our bumpers – one at the front, the other at the rear. Then they'd unhitched the trailers from the cabs, which had now disappeared.

The trailers couldn't have parked like that by accident, and no other vehicle had been singled out for such treatment. No other vehicle, however, was brightly painted in the colours of Tripp and Townend, Antiques.

'You see,' he wailed.

'I do indeed. Surely there must be something to say who these belong to?'

Griff's look told me that he might be old but he wasn't an idiot. He'd looked all right.

I took photos of the scene with my mobile, though I wasn't at all sure why. Perhaps because I couldn't see a single CCTV camera – weird in a place with so many small businesses in

need of protection. But I was still angry and needed someone
to be cross with. 'No Emilia?' I demanded sarcastically.

'I sent her home, of course.' Griff seemed surprised I should
even have asked.

'Some friend, to leave you stuck like that,' I snapped.

The drive home was an unnaturally silent one. Usually, Griff
chattered away about whatever he'd been doing. I'd expected
he'd treat me to a probably libellous account of his afternoon's
activities, spiking his fellow actors with barbed comments.

At last, as much to hear someone say something – anything
– as to know the answer, I asked, 'Did that guy get his tyre
fixed OK? You remember, the other night?'

'Oh, I believe the AA turned up eventually. He said something about it having been slashed, not just an ordinary
puncture.'

I shivered. Had that gorgeous young man done it? Surely
not – I hadn't seen him anywhere near the car.

'And you can imagine what tyres cost for a monster-mobile
like that. He's a solicitor – wonderful orotund delivery. The
trouble is, he's no idea how to turn a line. I rather expected
him to have a tantrum and depart in view of the attack on his
vehicle, but he's stuck it out. Half of me is relieved, I must
admit: we have a plethora of women of a certain age and a
shortage of men. No one under fifty, of course, of either gender.'

I didn't want to hear abut their casting problems, especially
with another alarm bell ringing: if the David Tennant lookalike
wasn't part of the cast, why was he there? Perhaps he was
one of the backstage people. 'I can understand anyone getting
away with slashing a tyre – all you have to do is creep up and
plunge in the knife. But two huge lorries like those! Great
noisy beasts. Surely, people must have heard them. Why didn't
anyone dash out and stop them?'

'Thrown themselves under their wheels in protest?'

'Not exactly. But asked the drivers why they'd done it.
Emilia could have gone down on her knees like she did
the other day. That would have wrung the hardest heart.'

He stroked his chin. 'Perhaps it happened when we were
looking at the so-called dressing rooms, the far side of the
courtyard on the other side of the building: Emilia marched

us over there en masse in our tea break. I hope to God it doesn't rain during any of the performances – we shall be soaked to the skin as we scuttle across. Imagine those Victorian skirts dragging in the mire – there are still traces of it having been a farmyard, with the usual occupants. In fact, I'd venture to say that our changing area might have been one of the milking parlours once. All we've got are wooden tables, a couple of benches and some pegs. Quite Hardy-esque. How fortunate I've still got my mobile make-up kit.'

Still got? It was surely one thing he'd never part from. Although from the outside it looked like little more than a battered leather attaché case, inside there was an Aladdin's cave of colour. The top tipped back to provide a mirror, complete with battery operated lights round the edge. I'd joked it ought to have a space for a vase, so admirers' flowers could be kept fresh. Griff had looked at me reproachfully: an artiste wanted far bigger bouquets than could be kept in a mere vase.

'Have any of the others had mishaps to their cars?' I asked.

'Not that I know of. Just someone's idea of a silly jape.' He reached across and switched on the radio. Classic FM. So he wanted to be soothed, not nagged or argued with. Feeling guilty myself, I let him get on with it. *Or perhaps*, in my head, I corrected myself, *I let him get away with it – again.*

FIVE

Someone else who was really good at getting away with things was my father, who phoned while we were heading back to the oast house to rescue our van from its strange imprisonment. Pa might be a noble lord, living in part of a stately home people paid good money to see, but he was also a mate of Titus, which damned him as much as anything. He'd also taken zero notice of any of his tribe of illegitimate kids, and paid, as far as I could work out, no maintenance at all to any of their various mothers. Now at least a trust fund was in place for my half-brothers and sisters, but apart from me, none was in touch with him.

Actually, I was getting quite fond of him, now he'd given up trying to get me to leave Griff and live with him in the wing of Bossingham Hall which was all the trustees allowed him. All! At least three families could have lived there without any sense of being squeezed in. But I didn't want to talk to him just now, even though we had a hands-free phone set-up.

'I'll call you back later, Pa,' I said, 'when I'm not driving.'

'You're not on the phone when you're at the wheel! Good God! That's against the law!' He cut the call in horror.

'I guess your friend Titus has been talking to him,' Griff said, adding scathingly, 'him and his butter-wouldn't-melt ways.'

'They keep him and Pa out of gaol, don't they?' I snapped, wincing as the van lurched from pothole to pothole in the road through the industrial estate. 'Heavens, this is as bad as Pa's track. Why don't the firms get together and have something done about it? And install a few cameras while they're about it?'

'Not everyone's as security minded as us, dear one. Ah! I've been set free!'

So he had. There was no sign of the trailers, which had departed without leaving so much as a scratch on the paintwork. He was just about to drive away when I noticed another little problem, however: both the tyres on the passenger side were flat. Slashed like the Range Rover's. We carried one spare, of course, but not two. I sent Griff off in the large van and phoned the AA tearfully, knowing they'd prioritize a lone female. I didn't sit twiddling my thumbs while I waited for them, of course. I had a good prowl round, hoping to follow the lorry tracks to one of the units, so I could go and offer several chunks of my mind. But there were so many ruts and the ground was so dry that it was hopeless.

The AA man, who turned up within forty minutes, might have wondered why I'd parked in the middle of nowhere, but he didn't ask any questions I couldn't answer. I'd worked out a few hints about a relationship with one of the guys working nearby, with the possibility of a vengeful wife, but didn't need them. Job done in virtual silence, we exchanged smiles and went our separate ways.

My route home could be adapted to go past my father's place; I called him to let him know I could drop in. I should have known it wouldn't be as simple as that.

'Are you anywhere near a supermarket? Because I'm low on quite a lot of things . . .' He dictated a list, including – miraculously, for a man once addicted to Pot Noodles to the exclusion of all else – such things as salad and fresh fruit. I assumed he wanted me to stay and lunch with him. Work apart – and how many hours had I wasted this morning? – I was happy to be away from Griff for a bit longer. Nothing would ever stop us loving each other, but we had snapped at each other a bit recently. Correction: I had snapped at him.

Waiting till I thought he should be home, I called to say I was stopping off at Sainsbury's and asking if he wanted anything.

'That means Elham's out of champagne, I suppose,' he said.

'It's on his list,' I admitted, trying not to sound cross – with either of them. 'And loo rolls and porridge oats. It's over a week since I saw him, so I'll feed him while I'm there.'

'But what about "The First Cuckoo"?'

'What about it? I've finished it.' I reckoned I had done all I could for the poor Worcester girl. Actually, for a double amputee, she didn't look at all bad. She'd never be absolutely perfect – and I'd put a note in her box to warn her owners that the porcelain was more brittle than I'd have expected – but she could grace a display cupboard again.

'But aren't the Harpers collecting her this afternoon?'

'You can do the biz, can't you? The invoice is in the box.'

'Well, I was thinking of . . . Oh, very well. I suppose I can see to it.' He sounded really pettish, not like himself at all.

I was almost ready to ring back and ask what was wrong, and even promise to get straight back, but for once I thought I'd put Pa first. And I might even return to Bredeham via Canterbury, where I could have a sniff round Fenwick's end-of-season sale.

Pa emerged blinking into the sun. Since his hands smelt strongly of soap, I assumed he'd been working on something for Titus I didn't want to know about and had had to scrub telltale ink off his fingers. He helped me ferry goodies into the kitchen he still managed to keep clean, nodding doubtfully as I produced a different flavoured green tea from his usual blend. But the heavily discounted cases of champagne produced a broad grin, and he stowed two bottles straight into the fridge, where a couple from a previous batch already lurked. It was the work of seconds for him to open one, pouring nice cold bubbles into a fine Georgian flute I really ought to confiscate and sell for him.

We ate the flan I'd bought, with a bowl of salad and some nice bread, which was a good thing because I found myself getting outside of another glass of fizz.

The routine was that before I left I would hunt around to find items to sell. I made a note of them, Pa initialled the record, and once I'd got rid of them, taking ten per cent, we both signed them off. The saleable pile was steadily diminishing, but I reckoned there was still enough china alone to keep him in champagne for the next five years. After that I'd have to bone up on other things such as silver and the odd antiquarian item.

He held open his front door for me – not the seriously elegant main one, of course, with the fabulous flight of steps

leading to it from the oval gravel carriage drive, but a side
one, originally meant for the steward, whose room Pa lived
in – as I carried a box of assorted Victorian figurines to the
van.

As usual, he scowled when he saw it. 'That shocking pink
– not really the thing, you know, Lina. Never liked it. Couldn't
you persuade Griff to have something a bit quieter?'

I tried to look at the van with his eyes. The fuchsia was
either eye-catching or vulgar, depending on your viewpoint.
'I've been trying to get rid of the small van altogether,' I
confided, feeling instantly disloyal. I never, ever criticized
Griff, especially to Pa. But I ploughed on, 'I thought a nice
little Ka or something.'

'I'll keep an eye open for offers on the ads on TV,' he
said seriously. 'I'd have thought one of these jobbies that
look as if you're going to drive across the Sahara would be
useful.'

'A four by four? Not very environmental,' I said. 'And the
only time I'd need it is when I come to see you. When are you
going to sort out this business with the trustees and get the
track fixed, Pa?' I stared glumly at the potholes.

·   'When you get something without your name blazoned all
over it.' He pulled a face. 'Wish you'd take the family name,
you know. Nothing distinguished about Townend.'

'I don't think Lina Elham would work,' I said, taken aback
by the offer.

'Wouldn't be Elham, you silly girl. That's the title. The
family name is Doughton, remember.'

'Lady Doughton?' I repeated stupidly.

'No, no – you'd be Lady Lina . . . I think. Lord, years since
I even held Debrett's, let alone opened it. Wonder where it
is.' He rubbed his hands over his face as he did when something worried him. 'Lady Lina – doesn't sound very good,
does it? You'd have to revert to being Evelina. And then I
think I'd have to adopt you first – they won't do wrong side
of the blanket courtesy titles.' He scratched his head, looking
more puzzled and confused than he ever looked doing the
killer sudoku.

'Look, Pa, I'm too old for anyone to adopt me.' Griff and

I had looked into it a few years back, and there was no chance then. 'In any case, I'm happy being straight Lina.'

'But you're not, are you? Happy, I mean. Look at you. You look as if you've lost a guinea and found a rusty button. Had a row with that old queer of yours?' He peered at me. 'No, it's worse that that. Dear God, Lina, you're not up the duff, are you?' He sounded as outraged as if he'd practised foolproof contraception all his life.

'No,' I said flatly, putting the cardboard box down so I could fish out my keys. Chance would be a fine thing, I added mentally. How long was it since Morris and I had had a nice uncomplicated night together?

He narrowed his eyes still more. 'Ah, that chappie of yours is still swanning off round Europe, is he? Why don't you tell him to get his bum over here?'

'Because he's working, Pa. And he wants to keep an eye on his little daughter, don't forget.'

Pa didn't do father-daughter relationships, not in the way anyone else would recognize. He certainly wouldn't have changed a nappy, and I didn't recall him ever building a sand-castle for me. In fact, my only memory of him was in the library in the main part of the house, giving me a priceless book to read while he had a row with my mother, long since dead. But something obviously twanged in his brain. 'That's all very well, but it's my daughter he should be worrying about. We did absentee landlords at school. Messed things up shocking they did. Absentee lovers are even worse. Remind him of that old proverb – *absence makes a fond heart wander.*'

I was just about to correct him, when I wondered if he had a point. What if Morris was neglecting me because he'd found some fabulous svelte Frenchwoman to love? And where did a horrible voice come from, that whispered in my ear it might be easier all round if he had? Suddenly, the idea of going to Fenwick's seemed less attractive.

Griff was wearing an apron and sporting his rubber gloves as he opened the door to me and my box of figurines. 'Oh, don't bother with that rubbish! Where did you find this?' Closing the door with his heel, he flourished something in his left hand. After the bright sunlight, I could scarcely make out what his treasure might be.

'This!' He held up the Parian bust I'd bought in Hythe. I'd forgotten all about it.

'Twenty quid from that stall with all the heads and Toby jugs,' I said dismissively. 'But what are you doing with it?'

'I was just about to clean it up for you, my dear one.' He turned to the washing up bowl.

I could see the detergent bubbles from where I stood. 'No! Put it down. Griff, for God's sake!'

'I beg your pardon?' He flushed bright red, as well he might, the tone I'd taken.

But I couldn't stop. 'You mustn't let it get anywhere near water. Not Parian ware! What the hell are you thinking of?'

'I just wanted to save you some work, Lina – you've done so much recently, and I thought—'

'China, yes. Wash all the china you want. But not in Fairy liquid, come to think of it. Oh, Griff . . . I'm sorry. I know it was only twenty quid, but—' I took a deep breath. We never argued about money, and here I was yelling at my mentor just as my teachers had yelled at me. 'I'm sorry. A good dust, that's all. You can do him all sorts of damage if he gets wet. Here, come to Lina, you poor thing. Diddums!' If I acted the fool, perhaps he'd forgive me and everything would be all right. 'Did the man want to put you in nasty wet water? Lina'll clean you up, won't she? With that funny tickly thing on the vac. And then you'll make Tripp and Townend a bit of money. I hope. You don't think twenty was too much?'

Griff was now as pale as he'd been red before, and he was breathing noisily. But he knew what I was trying to do and took my hand and squeezed it in his usual loving way. He managed a smile. 'Twenty pounds. Did you have to haggle?'

'I didn't have time. And it didn't feel too much.'

'Unlike you not to argue.' He looked at me over his specs. It took me a moment to realize his eyes were twinkling. At last.

I played along. 'Don't tell me I've been robbed. You'll have to take it out of my share of the week's profits.'

'I might indeed. Did you realize that this was a bust of

Ulysses S. Grant? Oh, Lina, you've never heard of him, have you?' he added, not exactly reproachfully because he was all too aware of the gaps in my knowledge. 'A US President, sweet one.'

'Ah!' That was good news. The American market was more buoyant than ours.

'And you've heard of Isaac Broome?'

I nodded doubtfully. *Heard of*: no more than that.

Griff clearly knew more and was impressed. 'This is his handiwork. Which I nearly ruined. Oh, Lina!'

'Well, what's twenty pounds? Anyway, you didn't. And you think it's worth more than I paid?'

'With luck . . .' He stripped off his gloves and took the bust. 'Well, Mr President, Lina can work her magic. And then we'll decide where to offer you for sale. I might just contact a couple of American colleagues for their advice. And I see, sweet child, that you found a sauce boat,' he added, deadpan, putting Grant on the kitchen table and holding up my Derby bourdalou.

'I did indeed. A hundred and fifty from Dave Hutton.'

He mimed strong shoulders. 'Big Dave from Leeds? So what was this doing amidst all his horticultural implements?' He put it back and dug out some stomach tablets from the nearest cupboard, quickly slipping a couple into his mouth as if he didn't think I'd notice. Since when had he been chomping those? He always claimed to have the digestive system of an ox, even when, having checked on the Internet, I'd pointed out that an ox had far more stomachs than he did.

'Looking lost. He didn't know what it was and hadn't even bothered washing it.'

'I hope someone had, before it went on sale!'

I ignored his lavatory humour. 'He only wanted a tenner, but I didn't like to take advantage.'

He tipped his head to one side. 'Soft hearts don't make profits, my love. On the other hand, I'd rather have Dave on my side than not, and we should still make a hundred or so profit ourselves. Excellent. What would I do without you, beloved?' He looked at me anxiously, as if it really was a question.

I hugged him as if it wasn't. 'More to the point, what would I do without you?'

'You'll have to one day, you know,' he said. 'My age – your age. But we must make sure you have adequate provision for the future. Absolutely sure.' He marched off to the bathroom without waiting for a reply – even if I could have given one.

He'd propped a letter addressed to me – standard A4, with a computer-printed adhesive label – on the mantelpiece. A French stamp? Morris! But all he'd done was enclose a picture postcard of Le Havre, unsigned. We'd spent a nice day there a month ago – perhaps he thought he didn't need to say anything to revive happy memories. Suddenly, I was happy again, despite Griff's ominous words.

SIX

'We've decided to skip the next couple of weekend fairs,' I told Morris happily, when he called about ten minutes later, knowing he'd hear the smile in my voice even if he couldn't see it on my face. 'So I'm free to hop the Channel any time you want.'

Actually, both venues were too far away to justify the fuel costs against the small returns we could expect, and Griff was getting twitchy about my doing all the driving and having to do most of the setting up on my own. But economics hadn't really weighed with me when I helped make the decision. I just wanted to spend my free time with Morris – and Leda too, if she had to be part of the deal.

There was a long silence at the other end of the phone. I could feel his sigh.

'I'm really, really sorry,' he said at last. And he sounded it. 'I've got to go to Kraków this weekend, and the chances are I shall still be there or in Budapest the following weekend. It's really manic at the moment. But at least it means my leave is stacking up nicely, so when the case is closed, we should have a good long break together.'

I think I made a joke about breaks and my job repairing them.

In which, of course, you didn't really take long periods off. People didn't stop taking chunks out of their best vases, and they didn't stop wanting them repaired in less than no time. But there was no point in telling him that, not really, so we nattered a bit until we ran out of things to say.

I forgot to thank him for the card.

Swallowing a lot of emotions I wasn't at all sure about, I arranged my face into something like its usual lines and, because I didn't want to spend the evening howling and tearing my hair, went along with Griff to the second indignation meeting in the village hall. This time we should hear what our parish councillors thought of the antiques centre.

The councillors were our neighbours – friends of a lot of us – but we bayed for their blood as if they'd helped decorate the new antiques centre themselves. To be fair, they did look dead shifty, especially when the vicar's wife raised the accusation, thinly veiled, that they might have made money out of the deal. But without hard evidence all we could do was huff and puff. However, one enterprising soul said that if they couldn't give us hard information, we'd have to go to the media, and all of a sudden they said that if we'd adjourn this meeting, they'd come back with all they could find next week.

If they overheard the muttered suggestion that we should keep them under surveillance so they didn't slip off to France, they didn't give any sign – apart from a dull flush on the cheeks of one of them.

So here I was with a weekend to kill. A wet weekend, too. I spent the Saturday dealing with some of the restoration backlog and hearing Griff's lines, reading aloud for him the speeches that led into his, so he could pick up cues. On Sunday morning was a rare visit to church – the village one, not one at which my friend Robin was vicar – and a skim through the Sunday papers. All the news was depressing. On impulse, as Griff started off for the oast theatre, I offered to go with him.

'My dear one, it'll be like watching paint dry.' All the same, I caught the note of relief in his voice at not having to drive. 'Now, where's that bag with my script and props?'

'I can mind the van. I might even go and have a look at some car showrooms, actually. We can't go on worrying about it, Griff, can we? We need the sort of car anyone could drive, with those complicated number plates no one would remember belonged to us.'

'But I've always had a fuchsia van.'

'You'd still have the big one. But think of the times we've had to hire anonymous wheels – it's time we bit the bullet and got a nice little hatchback, same as everyone else's. Heavens, if we got a low mileage second-hand one, we could even keep the van, if you insisted – there's just about room in the yard.'

He chuntered away for most of the journey, even suggesting

that it wasn't appropriate to swan into showrooms wearing jeans and trainers. I let him get on with it. It wasn't often I got the bit between my teeth, but now I had, no amount of sulking from Griff was going to make me change my mind. In any case, he was forced to agree that sitting in the awful car park watching rain trickle down the screen wasn't anyone's idea of excitement, and he certainly didn't want another episode with lorries or tyres.

I was just waving him goodbye and putting the car into gear when the phone rang. Titus. I preferred to give him my whole attention in case I missed anything, so I stopped again.

'That centre. Word is, the guy who's running it is well dodgy. Forgeries. You'd want to watch any cup of tea he sold, let alone the china it's served in. And I dare say his plants are plastic. So don't you go having anything to do with him, doll. On the other hand, don't go stirring shit either, in case you annoy him. Remember old Croft. Get Griff off that protest committee. Oh, make some excuse, doll. Safer not to attract any attention. Right?'

'What's his name?'

'Haven't got to that yet. Can't ask straight questions, now, can I?'

Not of the sort of person from whom he got all his information. 'So how did this guy get Change of Use Planning Permission?' I asked, sure, after the meeting, that I'd got the lingo right.

'Couldn't possibly say, madam,' he said, sounding as if he'd got an official plum in his mouth. 'Actually, I don't think it's your councillors that are bent. Think it's higher up. Just stay out of it, though – OK? Now, one more thing: your Pa says you're feeling blue, doll. Tell you what, ditch that bloke of yours. Shagging one of the filth, in-bloody-deed.'

'You can give me advice when you've sorted out the centre,' I said, with one or two other words Griff wouldn't have approved off, and cut the call. That felt better. Usually, it was he who hung up on me.

While I'd been talking, another couple of cars had pulled up, disgorging more wrinklies, with elasticated waists much in evidence, for both men and women. Hell, I'd never thought

of Griff as old before! But he must be pushing seventy-five.
Maybe more, since that was all he'd admit to. And he wasn't
old, not really. Just compared with me, I suppose, as if he
really was my grandfather. And he certainly didn't dodder,
like these old ducks. Not unless he meant to. And his eye still
gleamed when he saw eye candy, such as that David Tennant
lookalike I'd come across the other night. Griff had said there
were no young actors in this company, so perhaps he was part
of the backstage team – lighting, for instance. On impulse, I
decided to stay and check him out. The latest arrival, another
pensioner, had parked so badly that there was room for me
between her and the car she was nearest to, so I eased the van
in between them. If the vengeful lorries came back, they'd
have to box in a whole load of people, not just us, and there
were plenty of other tempting tyres besides ours.

Which was how I found myself sucked into the world of
Am Dram.

It wasn't dramatic in itself. I don't even think anyone noticed
I'd arrived, and in any case, all I was doing was casing the
joint in the hope that the guy with the gorgeous eyes was
somewhere around. But the moment I slipped into the rectangular room attached to the oast, I knew I had to stay. When
Griff and I read aloud to each other, he made people and places
come alive in a way I didn't know was possible – and certainly
my voice never did the same, no matter how hard I tried. None
of these people was in the same league as Griff, and to be
honest very few were even as good as me. But they were
trying to manage without scripts, and if I couldn't remember
words when I needed them, how on earth would I manage whole
speeches? Besides which, the play was cast. And there were
no roles for young people. And definitely no sign of the good-
looking bloke. So I might as well fall out of love with the
whole thing and go car hunting instead.

But I stayed.

I should probably have coughed and drawn attention to
myself. Instead, I just stared.

Griff – still in his everyday clothes, of course, but somehow
looking different – occupied the downstairs acting space, sitting
behind a couple of planks that were meant to be a desk. By

the light of a very twenty-first-century reading lamp, one of
those bright spotlights they advertise in the papers, Griff was
using the props he'd brought. Apparently, he was reading a
diary, a thick pad, the binding of which I recognized as an
old tooled-leather *Radio Times* cover which he'd bought for
a pound the other day, the sort of thing a fifties stockbroker's
wife would buy to conceal an everyday item she thought was
a tad vulgar. Since he'd already learned his part, he could
pause and look around and generally bring this actor-manager
guy to life.

Emilia, his twenty-first-century equivalent, was with the rest
of the cast up on the balcony which ran round half the space.
She was hopping into and out of role like a flea, hamming it
up as Griff's wife or mistress – it wasn't clear which – then
trying as director to extract a modicum of feeling from their
'son', the man whose tyres had been slashed. Three or
four other middle-aged to elderly women were staring at their
scripts, mouthing their words silently as they tried to learn
them. Someone was picking his nose and inspecting the results
before stowing them in a hanky.

None of them, of course, realized they had an audience.

To put it another way, that someone was spying on them.

I'd better leave as I came in – very quietly indeed. And if
anyone spotted me I could pretend to be slipping in – a message
for Griff or something. As I edged towards the door, however,
I noticed Griff doing something that definitely wasn't in the
script. He was rubbing a spot in his chest, as if it really trou-
bled him, and he reached for an indigestion tablet. The tablet
didn't seem to be doing any good, either: his face said he was
in pain as he rubbed again. In an instant, I had him suffering
with terminal stomach cancer. I almost called out. But, like
the guy fielding his bogies, he was unaware of my presence.
So I couldn't simply ask him over supper what was up – not
without admitting what I'd been up to.

The rain had given way to watery sunshine, but I'd been so
long eavesdropping in the theatre that there wasn't time now
to go car-hunting. Too restless to go back to the van – still
with its tyres intact and still free to move – I headed off for
a walk around the estate, dodging puddles and stepping over

stuff someone should have cleared up ages ago: half pallets, swathes of bubble wrap, the inevitable supermarket carrier-bags. It would never have been a beautiful area, but it offended me to see a place in the middle of the countryside looking as tatty as this. In fact, I grabbed a polythene sack that had once held animal feed – though we were a long way from anything four legged unless it was being smoked – and stowed as much rubbish as I could cram inside.

'Proper little Goody-Two-Shoes, aren't you?'

It was hard to tell the attitude of the speaker. He wasn't the gorgeous bloke I'd hoped to see, just a weather-beaten man of about fifty, baseball cap pulled down over his eyes, wearing overalls spattered with sawdust.

'Point me to a vacant bin,' I suggested.

He jerked a curly thumb towards the side of what looked like a derelict Nissen hut. In your dreams. Out in the open or nowhere for me, after that nasty sense of being watched I'd had the other night. After a mutual shrug, we went our separate ways, not, on my part, with the feeling that we'd be friends for life. I found a skip near the oast and was about to drop my spoils into it. But it was full of wood, and I didn't want to spoil the recycling value. Only as I thought such a virtuous thought did I register what sort of wood it was: oak and mahogany. Nothing recognizable – just odds and ends. However, this time I smelt not cheese or smoke, but a large rat.

I was ready to reach in and investigate further when I remembered that sense of being watched. Felt it again, actually. If I'd looked round furtively, it would have been a very bad move. So I pretended I'd got some problem with my foot and retied my trainer. Then I carried on walking, still carrying the rubbish.

Thank goodness I found something to walk towards. Those must be the dressing rooms Griff had complained about. He was right about their inconvenience and right about the yard – it still had slippery signs of the previous users. And a hint of a smell. Griff must have wanted the role very much to put up with this.

There was no sign of anyone.

I turned suddenly, as if I were playing Grandmother's Footsteps. Yes, although against the sun it was hard to see who it was, someone was standing next to our van. And it wasn't Griff, let out early for good behaviour, but that guy with the lovely eyes. Once again he melted away behind the oast complex, but I was left with one very clear impression – he very much preferred my room to my company.

I counted sixty elephants, then followed. He almost seemed to be heading for the dressing rooms, but at the last moment he veered off past a pile of rubble and old beams ripe for a bonfire and disappeared. I padded after him. Why not? Anyone could go for a walk. But when I saw him and Overalls Man together, having a conversation neither of them seemed to be enjoying, to judge from the quite violent gestures, I stopped dead, taking cover behind the dressing room block. It was too far to hear what they were saying, of course. But from the way they both pointed, I had a feeling they might have been talking about me.

There were voices behind me. The rehearsal was over. I slipped back towards the cars and was in the van when Griff appeared, most unusually for him, laying down the law to a woman in her late forties who didn't like what she heard. I leaned across to open the passenger door, which put an end to the argument.

Wrong. Griff got in, but was silent and huffy. He'd obviously wanted the last word. At last, possibly hoping I didn't notice him chomp another Gaviscon tablet, he launched into an account of his afternoon, starting with the woman I'd seen him with. It turned out that in addition to her small part, she'd offered to look after costume and make-up but didn't have a clue where to get the one or how to apply the other.

'Just in case you think I'm blowing things out of proportion, other people in the company have had cause to speak to her too. Talking during rehearsal, not paying attention to direction, arguing with Emilia—'

'You mean you don't?'

'Oh, some of her ideas are so OTT. But she's the one in charge, angel heart, so if I remonstrate, I try to do so in private.'

'I bet she doesn't like even that.'

'A bit of an autocrat is our Emilia – always was, I suppose. But she was beautiful when she was young, truly beautiful, and could simply play on her looks to get her own way. I sometimes think that beauty can be a two-edged sword. When it goes off as you age, you still try to play your old tricks and all they do is irritate people.' He glanced at me. 'You're pretty, my love, and I know you turn heads wherever you go, but part of the reason for that is the energy you give off. I'm afraid, much as I love you, I can't say your bones are as good as hers.'

'Sounds as if that's a good thing.'

Perhaps he hadn't heard. 'Even languid, even in repose, Emilia . . . she was as lovely as a Greek statue. Heavens, when they come to write her obit, they'll need a couple of paragraphs just to list the men with whom she's been associated. Or rather more.'

'Any pistols at dawn?' I asked idly.

'Oh, indeed. And there may be more. Gerald, the man with the injured Range Rover, locks horns with Denis, the nearest we have to a juve lead, every time they speak. If only they could manage such dramatic skills in fiction as in real life . . .'

'It's weird,' I told him, when I could get a word in edge-ways. 'Your words say you're bored and wish you'd never got involved. But – apart from when you're slagging off your colleagues – your voice says you're having a whale of a time. Which should I listen to?'

'Both, dear one. I love the acting, but, alas, not the Company – most of whom couldn't act their way out of a paper bag. Learning lines is a terrible fag, as I'm sure you'll have gathered from the hours you've spent with me, but most people have had their parts longer than I and are still glued to the text. How they'll fare – how we'll all fare – when we're told to work without scripts, I dread to think. No prompt, of course. As for props . . . Thank goodness I could provide some things of my own, but I truly cannot be responsible, as I told Emilia, for equipping everyone, nor for making sure everything is in the right place at the right time.'

'Tell you what,' I said, trying to sound grudging, 'if Morris is in Budapest or wherever next weekend, I could come and help out a bit. If you don't think anyone would mind.'

'Mind! They'd fall on your neck, angel heart.'

He slipped into a bit of a doze. He'd forgotten to ask me what I'd been up to, and this didn't seem the moment to tell him.

SEVEN

Tuesday saw us going off to a house sale in Hastings. The house, overlooking the town, was at the top of a long flight of steps, which soon had my fellow dealers moaning about their knees. My own pulse was racing, not with the exercise, but at the sight of Griff clutching at his chest as if trying to undo a belt round the ribs and then reaching for a stomach tablet. Stomach indeed.

'What're you doing?' he gasped.

'Calling an ambulance.'

'No! No, please don't fuss. I shall be fine,' he gasped, proving quite clearly that he wasn't. 'Just let me catch my breath.' He tugged at his shirt as if it was too tight.

I took his arm and, elbowing aside someone too busy with his BlackBerry to notice, thrust him into a chair. Refusing an emergency ambulance was one thing, but I'd have him at the doctor's tonight even if I had to tie him up and carry him.

Or would I? My phone call, made from the top of the offending steps, wasn't promising.

'Dr Chapman's on holiday till next week,' the receptionist told me. It sounded like the new one, not the one who gave Griff tomato plants in exchange for geranium cuttings.

'I know. But isn't Dr Baker available?'

'Mr Tripp is Dr Chapman's patient.'

'He's been to both doctors,' I said truthfully.

'But he's registered with Dr Chapman. And it's practice policy for patients to see their own doctor.'

'But I told you at the start, this is urgent. Mr Tripp's having severe chest pains after exercise.'

'I can give him an appointment at eleven ten next Thursday.'

'You can give him an appointment tonight,' I said, definitely not yelling. 'With Dr Baker,' I added, in case she hadn't got it.

Her sigh practically blew my ear from the phone. 'You don't understand, do you?'

No, I bloody didn't. But Griff had taught me that icy calm sometimes worked best. 'I understand that you're telling me that a man in his seventies with chest pains can't be seen for a week. I hope I don't have to repeat this conversation to the coroner. Or would you like to find Mr Tripp an appointment this evening?'

She did like.

I wish I hadn't spoiled everything by bursting into tears when I'd fixed it. Mopping up and hiding the worst evidence meant I missed a couple of lots I'd really wanted to bid for. But that gave me time for a proper mooch round, checking out other lots I'd never have dreamed of touching, not even with the proverbial bargepole. At last I slipped in beside Griff and took his hand.

'Are you well enough to hang on just a few minutes longer? I want lot three hundred and seventy-three.'

'A bedroom suite, angel heart? That disgusting fifties bedroom suite?'

'The same. Actually, if I bid it might make folk think it's worth having. I'll get Big Dave to do it. He owes me a favour, after all. Don't move till I've paid our debts. Then I'll bring the van round for you.'

'I'm not an invalid!' But he handed over the paperwork I'd need without a squeak.

Dave was happy to take the roll of notes I pressed into his hand and, since he was hanging on for the garden tools, right at the end, didn't mind bidding for me. He earned a kiss when he promised to load it on to his pickup truck and bring it back to Bredeham for us on his way home to Herne Bay. And then I was more than happy to leave: watching me from the far side of the room was none other than the guy who'd run the treen stall back at the Mondiale in Hythe. And he didn't seem any keener on me than he had then.

'All this fuss over a touch of indigestion!' Griff moaned as I settled him in his favourite chair and brought him a glass with some aspirin dissolved in it. Whether it would do him any

good, I hadn't a clue, but maybe it wouldn't do any harm –
unless it really was indigestion, of course.

'You're worth making a fuss over. Anyway, you're seeing
Dr Baker this evening. Five thirty. OK?' I shot him a sideways
look. 'If you don't promise to tell him the truth, the whole
truth, etc, I shall come with you myself.' When he didn't
protest, I added, 'Do you want me to? I'll certainly run you
down there if you don't feel well enough to walk.' His silence
was frightening. 'Are there any other symptoms you have to
tell him about?'

He sighed. 'Don't nag, Evelina.'

Evelina! He'd only once called me that when I was
being truly vile. So now I was scared. And terrified, when he
agreed to have a nap before he set out.

'What on earth made you buy a load of crap like this?' Dave
demanded. His pickup sat in our yard, looking embarrassed
by its load. 'Here's your cash – it only set you back a fiver.'

'One man's crap is another man's collectible,' I reminded
him with a grin, pocketing the notes without even checking.

'Collectible! I don't know that I'd even house my hens
in it!'

'You've got hens and they'd like a home? They can have
this!'

Arms akimbo, he stared. 'You spend a fiver on something
and want to give it away? Been too long in the sun, Lina?'

'Give me a hand up, will you? Thanks. This is what I
wanted, not the poor, ugly stained wood.' Standing in the back
of the pickup, I opened the door with a flourish.

He was tall enough to peer inside without having to do my
gymnastics. 'Clothes!' His voice oozed disgust.

'Yes, clothes. A load of fifties and sixties clothes. Retro's
big at the moment, Dave. And I might not want to sell them
all – I like wearing them myself.'

He pulled a face. 'I know. I've seen them, and very pretty
they are, some of them. Don't do anything for me, mind – they
make you look like some doll Griff's dressed up. You're young,
and you've got a nice figure. You should be dressing young.'

I couldn't think of anything to say. I grabbed armfuls, with the hangers, and passed them down. 'There. You can have the rest for your hens.'

'Might want to check the dressing table drawers, too, while you're at it. Unless you mean that for my chooks, too.'

Although I was fairly sure he was joking, I did check – nothing. But then I turned back to the wardrobe and its big long drawer. It was held down with one of the many ropes Dave had used. He looked at his watch as I tugged.

'Don't want to embarrass your hens, Dave.'

For the first time he was less than gracious, chuntering under his breath. And then he had to jump up on the truck with me to yank the drawer free. A load of paper slipped out into the body of the wardrobe. Old Vogue and Butterick dress pattern envelopes! I squealed with pleasure at seeing them and fury at having them disappear in front of my nose.

Even Dave couldn't reach them all. 'Tell you what, Lina, I'll bundle everything else up and drop it by next time I'm down this way. How would that be?'

He obviously wanted to be on his way, and it was time I shunted Griff down to the surgery.

'Brilliant,' I made myself lie. 'But don't let the hens anywhere near, will you?'

'You're a right funny one,' he said, making one last sweep and coming up with a few more. 'First you buy a potty, and then you collect paper fit for nothing except to wipe your arse on. But each to his own, that's what I always say. And it may not be chooks, Lina – this lot'll do well starting my wood-burning stove, if it's all the same to you.'

'So long as you get the Bakelite handles and knobs off – Mary Penney might make a bob or two on those.'

'You sure you weren't born in Yorkshire, lass?'

'You mean I'm as tight as a tick? I just don't like wasting anything, Dave, and that's the truth.'

Griff insisted he could walk to the surgery and got quite angry when I argued. In fact, he wasn't happy about my part in the whole business, so I resolved to stay out of the way, lip buttoned, till he wanted to talk to me. Making any start on preparing supper was a no-no – he regarded that job as his, and I only helped by invitation. But there were emails to check, the china he'd bought to wash – and when I'd done all that there was the huge treat, which I'd saved up, like a bar of chocolate, of sorting through the dresses I'd acquired.

As you'd guess from the paper patterns, some of the dresses were home-made – not that this meant they were any poorer in quality. But there were some Marshall and Snelgrove's own lines, a sixties Mary Quant to die for, and even some Rayne shoes. Heaven. Pity they were way too large for me. I hung the garments up to air in the big cupboard in the shop with others I wasn't sure whether to keep or sell on. All of them, even those in my size. Was Dave right? Did wearing vintage clothes make me look odd? No one had ever questioned my appearance before. Well, jeans and top or trousers and top were pretty well uniform for women my age, weren't they? And I only wore vintage on special occasions. I must ask Morris when I next Skyped him. I could even put one of the dresses on. But my joy in them had gone.

Maybe it was because however much I tried to occupy myself I was really listening for Griff's return, which drove all thought of them out of my mind.

'Tests!' I squeaked as I passed him a glass of wine.

'Oh, you know what they say about Dr Baker – he'd even test head lice to make sure they're nits. And he's given me some pills and a little spray.'

'What sort of tests?'

'Oh, things down at the surgery . . . He said he'd get the nurse to contact me with an appointment.'

The nurse. That didn't sound too bad, then. I'd had visions of his being whipped off in a private ambulance to Harley Street, courtesy of Aidan's millions. But I mustn't sneer. Aidan loved him as much as I did. I didn't think he should be kept in the dark if Griff was ill. I knew he had a lot to bear at the moment, but loving and being loved gave rights as well as responsibilities. Maybe, just maybe, at the back of my mind lurked the thought that he might insist on imme-diate, private treatment, and that if he did I'd be eternally grateful.

I was sure that, left to himself, Griff would say nothing. Not to him or to anyone. Should I grass him up?

Before I could make any sort of decision, the office phone rang. I scuttled to answer it. There was a long pause before anyone spoke, and I was just about to deal with nuisance callers in my usual way – a piercing whistle – when a man spoke.

'Charles Montaigne, Ms Townend. Or may I call you Lina? I was just hoping you might have reconsidered my proposal.'

'I don't remember any proposal,' I said. There'd been hints, but nothing concrete. I took a breath. 'Why don't you put it in writing, and I'll give it some thought.'

'Writing!'

'Would you go into anything blind, Monsieur Montaigne? No, I thought not. Good evening to you.'

I may have sounded cool, but all the same my palms were sweating as I headed back to Griff, now in the kitchen happily consulting a recipe book. He looked up enquiringly.

Shaking my head, I put on a fake American accent. 'Congratulations! You have won a holiday in Florida! Or not,' I added in my normal voice. 'Anything I can do?'

EIGHT

E ven if I hadn't wanted to get involved with Griff's play, there was no way I'd have let him drive to the oast and back in Thursday's weather. When a week ago he'd gloomily observed that we were heading for autumn, I might have insisted we were still in summer, but this evening I would have said we were heading into an early winter. Global warming? Hardly. But climate change? Spot on. They said we'd get more storms, and rain bringing floods. Tonight we got enough rain and wind to make me believe them. Whoever *they* were.

We were still in the small van, but not for much longer. Griff had point-blank refused to contemplate something he considered as *infra dig* as a Ka, though where he'd got the idea he had any dignity to lose I wouldn't know. At least, when I'd dragged him along to a veritable paradise of car showrooms just outside Ashford, he'd conceded to a shiny suited salesman that a top of the range second-hand Fiesta might do.

Top of the range! After a van! But so long as it came in silver with one of those forgettable sets of registration numbers and letters, it was fine by me. Actually, I'd lost my heart to a magenta one, but since we were aiming to be invisible, not instantly noticeable, I'd had to let my head take over. I couldn't wait to take delivery. And I don't think Griff could either.

Once again, I managed to park between other vehicles. Griff came round to the driver's door to ease me out, as if I were royalty, though actually I was so anxious I was afraid I might be sick. Pre-stage fright, perhaps. Crazy.

'Remember,' he said quietly as I zapped the central locking, 'that you have skills they need, my loved one. No one else was prepared to take on the irritating task of props, and no one was saintly enough to sit through every single perform-ance of this damned production with ears and eyes open at all times. There will be people who carp and complain – that you're too quick with a prompt or too slow, too loud or too quiet. But if they need you it's their fault – remember that. If they had the lines, you wouldn't need to intervene. As to the props, do as that dear dead BBC reporter did – count them out and count them in. With your unparalleled eye for detail, you'll know exactly where they should be put each time.' He squeezed my hand reassuringly.

'I might make notes anyway,' I said, returning the pressure as he pushed open the door. The place was blacked out, with only the stage lit up. No one stood under the lights, preferring the darker seating area, where they stood virtually invisible to anyone coming from outside.

'Ah! Griffith's darling child!' Emilia declared, surging up to me and air-kissing both cheeks. 'Welcome. Thrice welcome.'

Blow me if once again I didn't want to curtsy. 'Thank you. As you can see, I've brought along a box of items Griff thought would be useful, ready for when the cast need to use them.'

She wafted them away, although Griff had assured me it was high time that the actors were getting used to handling fans and so on. 'Oh, in the oast itself, I suppose. We'll discuss them during the break.'

Discuss? What was there about fans and smelling salts bottles to discuss? I caught Griff's eye. He raised his eyebrows to heaven and mimed slitting her throat. It was easier to do as she asked, so grabbing the box I elbowed the heavy door open. There was a stack of plastic picnic tables in the middle of the roundel, and I plonked my burden on there. Dusting my hands, I returned to the others.

'Vina, you could sit over there,' a woman in dun trousers declared, pointing to the furthest point from the stage. Brilliant idea. Or not.

'Lina.' And then, because I needed to know the actors' names too, I repeated it more loudly, smiling around the loose knot of people watching the little scene. There wasn't much response. It was as if they were afraid I'd nick their parts.

'Are you sure she's capable of this?' another man demanded of no one in particular in what I suppose was a stage whisper. It certainly meant every single person in the space knew that he doubted my skills. I knew his, of course – picking his nose.

'Absolutely. My darling Lina can do anything. She has never, ever let me down in anything,' Griff declared, in an equally carrying voice.

'It's a matter of timing,' Nose Man muttered, not quietly enough. 'Sensitivity and timing.'

Though I was ready to throw the script that I'd scanned and printed for myself at him, I smiled and confined myself to recycling Griff's earlier comment to me. 'If you actors know your lines, then you won't need either from me, will you?' Armed as Griff had suggested with pencils, a rubber and even a little torch, I tucked myself into a corner. I was still fizzing – mostly excitement, I think, though a bit of anger lurked too.

'Dear Griff – such a clever child,' Emilia said, almost ready to pat my head as if I were a pet dog.

'But what about the warm-ups?' a voice demanded. 'They're so intimate, so private.'

Emilia permitted exasperation to flit across her fine brows. 'But Evelina is now part of the company. She may wish to join in.'

Griff hadn't mentioned anything about intimacy or privacy. I shot him a look.

'I have yet to hear of a prompt needing voice exercises,' another voice said.

'I should have thought they were exactly what a prompt needed – no point in the girl whispering, or we won't hear her.'

I caught Griff's eye. 'Maybe if I come back in ten minutes?' Not waiting for a reply, I headed out. Now the fizz was definitely anger.

Head down against the rain, I strode round the worst part of the industrial estate, not even bothering to dodge puddles. The litter could stay where it was too. There was no sign of either of the men, though a smile from the one with the gorgeous eyes and soulful expression wouldn't have come amiss. In fact, a smile from anyone would have been nice. A large van drove off from what seemed an empty unit, the driver negotiating the potholes as carefully as if he was carrying a load of cut glass. I fancied he turned his face away as he passed me. But there was no time for speculation. If I was late back it would look as if I'd had an attack of pique.

Griff was already in place at his plank desk, though there was no sign of anyone else. By the sound of the thunderous thuds from the roundel, they were climbing the stairs to the gallery. Whatever exercises they'd been doing, walking softly wasn't one of them.

Lights, camera, action – or whatever.

What had all seemed so glamorous when I'd peeped round the door now seemed desperately slow. No wonder Griff got frustrated with his fellow cast-members. He knew, instinctively it seemed, how to turn a line, how to make the right gesture and when. Emilia did too, even if I found everything she did a tad exaggerated.

Even with their scripts, the others missed lines, fumbled for words, waved their arms round vaguely. I chipped in once or twice.

Puncture Man turned on me. 'Why should you think I need a prompt, when I have the script in my hands?'

'Because you turned over two pages at once and missed half a scene.' How to win friends, I don't think.

Come half-time – or was there a technical term? – someone produced glasses and wine. A glance at the bottles told me they weren't worth risking my licence for, so I slipped off to the van to find the bottle of water I always keep handy.

And practically ran into the David Tennant lookalike, standing remarkably close to our van. Again.

'Can I help you?' I asked, not as if I thought he needed help.

'Yours, is it?' He didn't look guilty – not even slightly fazed. And I liked his voice, which was a nice light baritone.

'Yes.' Usually, I say which half of the partnership I am, but not this time.

'You had a bit of difficulty the other day.'

It was hard to tell whether he was being sympathetic – not much warmth in those eyes of his.

'Brilliant manoeuvring by the truck drivers,' I countered.

'But they didn't need to slash the tyres.' When he said nothing, I added, 'I lost a whole morning's work sorting that out.'

'Work?' he repeated, as if the concept was strange to him.

'Yes, work. No work, no breakfast.'

'But surely all you do is stand in a shop and take people's cash.'

'Yes, but you need to have the shop open for that. And saying I stand there all day taking cash is rather like saying all a doctor does is look down people's throats.'

His eyes gleamed briefly. 'Six years of study, a mountain of student debt?' He made a 'this high' gesture over the top of his head.

'Apprenticeship and learning on the job.'

'Learning what?'

'Try social history, history of art, furniture, porcelain.' For some reason I didn't want to mention my restoration work. In any case, why was I putting up with all these questions? It felt more like a cross-examination than a conversation. 'And you? What's your area of expertise?'

To my surprise, the question, more formal and aggressive than I'd intended, brought another brief twinkle to his eyes. If I knew what was amusing about it I'd try again. When he smiled he really was as attractive as I'd first thought.

'Oh, this and that.'

Not interested in either, I reached into the van for the water bottle and zapped the locks again with the extra pressure on the button that set the alarm.

But he hadn't finished. 'So what's going on in there?'

'Amateur dramatics.'

Now the skin round his eyes crinkled nicely. 'Are the public allowed to buy tickets?'

'I should imagine the answer is: *Yes, please.* You put on a show, you want an audience.'

'When's it on?'

I clapped a hand to my mouth. 'No idea!'

We both collapsed into giggles. 'Isn't it rather important to know when you're going to perform?'

'Might be if I was. I'm just prompt and props. And it's time I went and laid a few out,' I fibbed.

'Will you be here every Sunday?'

What if he was asking all this so he could try to break into our premises, in the belief they must be empty? Bring on those anonymous wheels. Or what if he was casually going to run into me again? I tried a sideways approach. 'Assuming I can find someone to take my place in the shop again, yes. And will you be knocking around here this-ing and that-ing?'

'Assuming I'm not toiling to pay off my student debt.'

With that I had to be satisfied. And guilty. Setting up a flirtation with another guy. Not good. Sorry, Morris. But it was so good to have a bloke look at me as if he appreciated me, not just my skills in building sandcastles for his daughter.

'Only, next time we'll try it with props for us *all*, dear ones,' Emilia declared, wrapping up the session. 'Theresa, is there any hope of those drapes you thought you might find? Oxfam, was it?'

Theresa, the woman with whom Griff had had that falling out, had been way too busy. 'Surely, she should be doing it,' she said, nodding at me.

She? The cat's mother? But finding props was what I had volunteered to do, so I produced a smile from somewhere and jotted. 'Any particular fabric or colour?' I asked.

'Velvet, a nice dark crimson for preference,' Griff said. He looked worn out, but obviously he wasn't too tired to remember we'd acquired some heavy curtains exactly like that in a lot we'd wanted.

'Budget?' I asked, pen poised.

Emilia's eyebrows went walkabout, at least as far as they could, post facelift or Botox or whatever. 'Darling, I've no idea how much things cost.'

'Neither have I. So I need to know how much you authorize me to spend. Do you want receipts?' I studiously avoided Griff's eye.

'Darling, you make this sound like a business! It's not as if I haven't known Griff for ever – I know he's not going to swindle me out of thousands.'

Did she, indeed?

While she and the others chuntered away about budgets, I

got on with stowing the few props they'd used, most of which
had found their way on to the planks that formed Griff's desk,
which I had to take apart, propping the planks behind the
boxes they stood on. Planks? No, something much more interesting. I held Griff back as the others drifted away. 'Where
did you get the timber?'

'No idea. It was here when I took up the role.' He asked
with what seemed an effort, 'Why?'

I pressed on all the same. 'Did you ever look
underneath?'

'My dear Lina, why should I? How could I?'

'Look at the patina.' I stroked them like other people stroke
cats. 'I don't know much about wood, Griff, or furniture, but
I can feel when something's old and top quality. And this is
both.'

'When have you ever been wrong about such things?'
Managing a smile, he touched my cheek with pride. 'Am I
right in thinking that there's more of the same around somewhere? More planks like this, and maybe some legs?'

'I wouldn't be surprised. If they aren't part of a sixteenth
or seventeenth century refectory table I'll eat them for supper.'
I added more seriously: 'The thing is, Griff, I'm not exactly
the flavour of the month round here, am I? So maybe it's you
who might just ask where they came from.'

I had a pretty good idea, of course. From a skip not far
from here. It struck me that another walk round the estate at
a time when they wouldn't be expecting me, courtesy of the
good-looking man, might prove interesting.

I grinned. 'I've found out when the smokery and cheese
factory open, by the way.' He needn't know when I'd found
out. 'We must come over one day . . .'

NINE

Monday's weather was as lovely as the previous day's had been vile, made even better by another card in an envelope from Morris – Le Touquet this time. But after breakfast in the garden, Griff drifted about as if he had all day to fill with nothing. If I knew him, he was trying accidentally to 'forget' the appointment he had with the practice nurse. Perhaps this involved her taking a sample of his blood; he was so squeamish that he always wittered on about being likely to faint. But I was on to him. 'If you don't set out in the next five minutes, I shall have to drive you down, shan't I? And then I can ask the nurse what they're looking for.'

'I do wish you wouldn't nag me so, Evelina. I'm just looking for my glasses.'

'Here.' I passed him his case. 'Reading glasses, unless you've put the wrong pair in again. Scoot.'

He scooted, oozing resentment.

What did he think was wrong with him? Something he didn't want me to know about. Had he confided in Aidan? I could scarcely email Aidan and ask, because any secret wasn't really mine to tell, and simply asking would reveal there was a secret. What if I looked his new pills up on the Internet? I might get some clues there. But then what would I do with the knowledge? If I taxed Griff with it, he'd know I'd been spying on him, something we'd both sworn solemnly never to do. For years the pact had worked: I didn't want him to know every last awful detail of my past life – no more than he could guess at, anyway – and he was very reticent about the details of his relationship with Aidan, for which I'd been really grateful, though I was a bit less prissy these days.

I stood outside his room, biting a stray hangnail. How would I feel if he rooted about in my things, to check on my contraception, for instance? Or to see if my father had ever given me any goodies I was keeping private? As it happened, I was hiding just one thing, a photo of Pa's mother, my grandma, and I couldn't for the life of me think why. After all, on posh occasions I sported the Cartier watch Pa had given me, and from time to time I let slip that Pa still hadn't run her engagement ring to earth, though he very much wanted me to have it. But I think hiding the photo was as much to protect Griff as anything – the less I was involved in my past, his theory ran, the more I'd be locked into his present.

Even though I stretched my hand out, I couldn't push open his door and hunt for tablets, or even that mysterious spray. Just couldn't. I'd simply have to try harder to make him tell me all about his appointment and ask what he'd told Aidan.

The office phone rang. I ran down to answer it.

The person at the other end didn't wait to hear who'd picked up. He said immediately, 'Have you thought any more of my proposition, Lina? You'd be very unwise not to, you know.'

Deep breath time. Perhaps if I sounded as pompous as Aidan, who people never argued with, he wouldn't pick up my terror. 'Monsieur Montaigne, I told you I would consider any offer you put in writing. None has so far arrived.'

He cut the call.

The phone rang again. I nearly wet myself. Then I realized the voice at the other end was altogether more gentle and measured.

'First ring, eh, lass? Must have known it were me. Now, I shall be passing not far from your place in about half an hour. If you fancy getting that kettle on, I'll drop the rest of your property off. Can't say fairer than that.'

Big Dave sank on to the garden bench as if he'd been toiling for the last five or six hours. Perhaps he had: perhaps his hens woke him early. Or perhaps his kids had. He wrapped a huge hand round the biggest mug I could find. The thick slice of Griff's latest cake looked so inadequate that I pressed the rest on him.

'Nice spot,' he said, looking at the garden, Griff's pride and joy, full of colour and shape, as one type of flower gave way to another, with shrubs and trees joining in. 'Like the Tardis. You'd think, looking in from the outside, you'd only have a pocket handkerchief – one of those chic spaces full of decking and minimalism, if you can be full of minimalism, of course. But this – this is like the cottage gardens in jigsaws I used to do with my gran.' He drank deeply and sighed. 'Another tradition gone. My kids play with their computer games, and their grandma is off in the Caribbean with her toy boy.'

'Which worries you most?' I said, before I could stop myself. Dave was a Yorkshire man, after all, and didn't do emotion.

He set down his mug on the little table. 'Hard to tell. Any road, our Lina, you'd best have those patterns you wanted. Some looked like tat, and no more, to me, but I brought everything anyway, every last scrap. Our recycling bin was full, you see.'

I followed him to the pickup truck he'd left in the street. On impulse, as he passed down a cardboard box, I asked, 'You keep your ear to the ground, don't you?'

'You could say that. But I'm not like yon Titus – hears the rumours before they've even happened.'

'But you might know things – people – he doesn't. What do you know about some guy called Charles Montaigne?'

He stared. 'Having me on, aren't you, lass? More your line than mine. Be seeing you – right? Oh, and the chooks say thank you kindly for their new extension.'

'Right. And thanks!' I spoke to a cloud of exhaust fumes – you could almost feel those nasty little particulates hurtling into your lungs – and went back inside, remembering, of course, to lock up, so I could pore over my booty. But what had he meant about Charles Montaigne? I was so puzzled that I stowed the mugs in the dishwasher and washed and drained the now empty cake tin before I opened the goodies.

There were more standard patterns, Simplicity and the like. But then there were some ordinary large envelopes, complete with stamps. My fingers shook. Could these be Spadea patterns? These had never come in the traditional packets that home dressmakers bought at haberdashers (what a lovely word – another to thank Griff for). You had to order them from the factory, which then posted them to you. They consisted of an illustrated instruction sheet (or sheets) and unprinted pattern pieces which were pre-cut at the factory

to your exact size. Very rarely, a collector'd get the bonus
of the envelope the factory had sent it out in. And here were
two. Even though there was no one to hear, I squealed with
delight. And then sat down with a bump. One of the patterns
was a design by Charles Montaigne. None other than the guy
who wanted to seduce me from Tripp and Townend – I don't
think.

Did this sinister man know so much about my tastes that
he'd deliberately chosen this name to mess with my head like
this? In which case, what else did he know about me I'd rather
he didn't? And where had he got his information from? Before
I knew it, I was crouched over the loo losing my breakfast
and cake.

I'd done no more than wash my face when I heard Griff's
key in the door.

'Well?' I demanded, still only halfway down the stairs.

'Well, now I'm in their clutches, they're not going to let
me go. They're talking about yet more tests, would you believe?
And the NHS is supposed to be desperately short of funds.
Heavens above! Do I smell coffee?' He looked at me. 'You
look as if you should be the one down at the surgery. My dear
one, what's the matter?'

I ignored the question. 'What are they looking for, with all
these tests?'

'Who knows? They don't tell you anything – just that they
want one more look at the next thing. They say I'll get an
appointment through the post. Meanwhile,' he added with a
grimace, '*keep taking the tablets.*'

'But—'

'Your nagging really is getting more than a little tedious,
dear one. Now, let me have my coffee, and you may get on
with your work.' He turned his back on me as if I were an
awkward employee.

I was shaking too much with a whole variety of emotions to
contemplate the fine restoration I should be doing. Griff had
never spoken to me like that before. We might never have shared
confessional secrets, but we shared love. We had done ever
since we'd walked into each other's lives. I might have pushed

him away once upon a time, but he'd never, ever shut a door in my face like this. Dimly, I think I realized he wasn't angry with me, but with something else. Possibly himself. Possibly the part of his body that was letting him down.

If only I could have turned to Morris. If only I could have been encircled in nice comforting arms and told everything would be all right, even if it wouldn't. But that would mean admitting that Griff was ill, maybe very ill, maybe – but he couldn't die. He couldn't leave me. He mustn't. I almost shouted aloud that he must get well. Must.

I don't know how long I sat on my bed, trying not to cry. Eventually, I thought I'd better do as I was told. Get back to work. Though I couldn't risk handling china, at least I could deal with any Internet business that had come through. First, however, I idly checked my personal emails – I got so few, I didn't bother more than a couple of times a week.

There was the usual rubbish wanting details of my bank account – as if – and nothing much else. I nearly deleted the one from New Zealand on the grounds I knew no one from there. But I opened it – to find it was from Aidan. I might have known he wouldn't do email talk.

> *My dearest Lina,*
>
> *I trust you will forgive me for intruding on your valuable time. However, when you know the reason I'm sure you will understand my reasons.*
>
> *Though Griff is usually the most regular of correspondents, I have hardly heard from him recently. Any communications have been terse to the point of abrupt. I wonder if you might tell me if I have offended him in some way. As you can imagine, this is not a request I make lightly, as I suspect that even if I had, he would be unlikely to confide in anyone, even – or perhaps especially – in you, whom he loves so devotedly. Furthermore, I would not wish you to break any confidences you may have shared.*
>
> *As you can imagine, life here is not easy: the delight of seeing spring arrive is more than tempered by the knowledge that my sister is entering prematurely*

*into the winter of her life, and not enjoying the
companionship I have relished for more years than you
can imagine is making life even less bearable.*

*I would be grateful, more than grateful, if you can
cast light on the situation in Bredeham.*

Your affectionate friend,
Aidan

It must have cost him so much not to be able to reach for his
favourite pen and sign with a flourish. But this time I didn't
take any joy in mocking his pretentiousness. If it was possible,
I felt sorrier for him than for myself.

So what did I say in reply? Griff was still holding forth to
Mrs Walker, no doubt, but I guessed the subject was more
likely to be her wedding than his health.

Dear Aidan,

*I'm so sorry you're having such a bad time. I wish I
had some hard news for you, but I haven't. Griff's never
said anything to suggest any problems between you. He
does seem . . .*

The first sentence might have taken a couple of minutes to
type, but then I slowed down.

*. . . to be suffering a lot from indigestion recently. Maybe
he's stressed out after the arrival of another antiques
shop in the village. It's not just any shop, it's a huge
affair, with more stock than we could imagine handling
and a tea room and plant centre. Griff's joined an action
committee to get it shut down. He's also joined an
am-dram group with really poor amateur actors. There
have been troubles with people parking there – slashed
tyres and so on.*

*I wish I could tell you more. Why not organize some
Skype time and try to pin him down yourself?*

Love,
Lina

Phew. Half an hour of head scratching just to write a couple of short paragraphs. Somehow I'd have to tell Griff that he was treating Aidan badly without letting on we'd been in touch. Hell, more pretending, but from me this time.

TEN

Chichester was a bit of a schlep for a one-day event, but we had promised the organizer, one of Griff's old theatrical friends, a long time ago, and Griff simply refused to consider pulling out. It was an early start, so we packed the large van on the Monday evening. He'd shown the barest interest in the dress patterns, although I'd have expected him to be as delighted as I was. So I'd not told him about the dresses, still lurking in their cupboard. I might sell them as a lot to a specialist dealer, or see what I could do online. As for Ulysses S. Grant, although he looked very good after his thorough dusting, Griff hadn't reported on progress selling him and, in his current mood, reminding him wasn't an option.

I relied on the satnav for the journey, switching it on without bothering to consult Griff. Really, this was the weirdest behaviour for both of us. All I wanted him to do was let me hug him and comfort him, in the face of whatever illness he was afraid of, and if I knew anything about him, what he really wanted was a good cosset. Well, he had the cosset, in that I'd done all the lifting and packing, but it was a cold, silent one, because he simply didn't respond when I tried to be my usual self. Clearly, we needed a miracle.

What we got was the usual crowd of dealers, which was much more comfortable for Griff than the newcomers we'd met in Hythe. Without a backward glance, he left me to set up our table while he went round meeting and greeting as if he was royalty.

Eventually, I too was greeted by Mrs Crews, a woman who Griff insisted was in her eighties but looked a spry seventy. She had a small but good collection of Meissen figures and always made a beeline for us. I was just about to say we'd nothing of interest for her this time, but, almost in tears, she produced a shoebox.

'I broke the poor girl's arm last week,' she said, unwrapping

a figure of a woman feeding birds and a separate, smaller
package containing half a tiny arm. 'I was going to contact
you, but I thought you'd be here and you'd be able to save
her. See, it broke just below this flounce.'

I gave what I hoped was a reassuring smile. 'That'll make
it easier to hide the repair. I'm afraid she'll never be perfect,
Mrs Crews, but she won't have to keep her arm in a sling for
the rest of her life. Do you want a written estimate for your
insurance company? It's done serious damage to the value,
after all.'

'It's all done by phone, Lina. But they say they'll want the
paperwork later.'

'They'll get a fully itemized account of the damage, my
work and the new retail value,' I promised her, adding doubtfully, 'but I've got a stack of work already in the queue.'

'Your house must be like A and E, all these bodies wanting
treatment,' she said. 'And how is dear Griff? Oh, my dear,
have I said something I shouldn't? I have, haven't I?' She
fished in her bag, a jolly Radley, which I'd always coveted,
and produced a tissue.

It was easier to take it than to make a fuss.

Putting her hand on mine, she asked, 'Have you two had a
falling out?'

'No. Absolutely not. It's just he's not well, and he won't
tell me what's the matter.' There! All blurted out. To someone
I hardly knew. A friend of his. The ultimate betrayal.

'And he gets horribly tetchy when you press him? My
husband's the same. A little head cold and it's man flu, but
something that could be serious, and you have to drag him to
the doctor. Do you want me to have a word?'

I shook my head so hard my hair flew. 'Absolutely not.
Please, please, please. I shouldn't have even mentioned it.
He'd be furious. And that seems to make whatever it is worse,'
I added, in for a penny and in for a pound.

She nodded slowly, as if working out the implications. But
then Griff headed closer, so she said clearly, 'I'll entrust her to
you, then, Lina. Though I don't know whether to hope that
triage means she needs early and immediate treatment or if
she can wait her turn. It's not as if she needed brain surgery,

is it, Griff?' She held up the figure with a whimsical smile.
'And how are you? Would you take pity on an old woman and
take her for a proper cup of coffee? I can't bear these paper
cups, can you?' Taking him by the arm, she drew him away.

As I packed the Meissen, I became aware of eyes on me.
Just like I had at that industrial estate by the oast house. But
I couldn't see anyone obviously trying to catch my eye, or
even, if you see what I mean, obviously trying not to. I
exchanged a flicker of an eyelid with Titus, who seemed to
be coming towards me. He changed his mind, however, as a
customer approached. A sale must always come before
a gossip, even the silent sort Titus sometimes indulged in.

And it was a good sale. I don't really like the texture of
Wedgwood, but I can see how people might like the colour
and the little classical figures. And I certainly liked the cash
price this punter paid for a blue Jasper ware cheese bell and
stand. He was surprised when I gave discount for cash and
insisted on having our card and giving me his in case we came
across anything else he might like.

As I waved him from the room, I realized who'd been
watching me earlier.

Charles Montaigne was on the far side of the stall.

He smiled as he approached. Not a smile I liked or
responded to. 'You're a good woman, aren't you, Lina? Honest
to a fault. Loyal, too. Loyal to shits like Harvey. Loyal to an
old codger like Griff, whose business is going nowhere. Loyal
to an alcoholic father. Loyal to a guy with whom you're stuck
in a long-distance relationship, even though he thinks more
of his daughter than he does of you. Isn't it time to break
out?'

Refusing to be scared that he knew so much about me, I
smiled as I parried his words back. 'If you want to make a
purchase, Monsieur Montaigne, I'll be happy to attend to you.
But I tell you, I should want cash. I don't like dealing with
people who hide behind . . .' The bloody word went. I dived
in for another: 'Behind other people's names.' Suddenly, it
came back. 'And you might want to try a more original alias
next time.'

His face told me that the joke was on me. He knew not just

about my friends, but about the clothes on my back. I refused
to let my voice shake. 'Good day, Monsieur Montaigne.'

With an exceptionally graceful bow, he scooped up his case,
looking at the box with Bridget Crews' Meissen in it and then
at me. 'It's a shame when pretty arms get broken, isn't it?
And hands,' he added regretfully, looking at mine and turning
away to merge with the punters as effectively as if he were
Titus.

All I could manage was to lean on the counter, trying to
steady the pounding of my heart as I did my best to think.

How much of this conversation should Griff know? None,
if I could manage it. It would leave him as it had left me:
clammy-handed and stiff-faced. Why should anyone want to
go to all that trouble to find out about a china and porcelain
restorer?

Sitting watching my hands tremble – they had my permission now – wasn't the answer to anything, was it? I needed
to consult someone. The obvious person was Morris, who was
one of the people the so-called Montaigne had clocked, after
all. But there had to be other ways of killing cats. I didn't
even have time to break a china kitten now, however, as we
had a little knot of customers all eager for service.

I might have smiled and talked a lot, but I still managed to
work out a plan, and by the time Griff drifted back, with the
sort of wordy apology I'd have expected of Aidan, was ready
to put it into operation.

Heading off, apparently to the loo, I caught Titus' eye. He
nodded, drifting towards the exit, where we gestured each
other through at the same time. As if apologizing, he said,
'Didn't see the bugger's face, but I saw yours. And I didn't
get his car number either, but it was a nice motor – black
Seven Series BMW.' And he was gone.

At least I had a story ready for the security staff, two of
which were handy. Which should I approach? The young one
with zits or the guy who looked like a fat version of my father?
Spreading my hands, I looked helplessly from one to the other
and got both. I decided to keep the talk well away from
antiques.

'Look, I know I shouldn't be asking you this, but I don't

know who else could help me.' I blinked hard, as if my eyes were smeary with tears. They both seemed to be soft-hearted, so I pressed on. 'Thing is, some guy backed into my car the other day. It's only an old banger, so no harm done. But as he got out of his car to grovel he dropped something. I didn't notice till after he'd gone. A wallet of photos. I bet he's missing them like hell. And I think I saw him earlier. My friend says he's already driven off. I don't suppose you've got any CCTV footage of the car park, have you? So I could check his registration?' Wide blue eyes. Big innocent smile. What a lying toad.

They even shared a brew of tea with me as they checked the footage.

'Seven Series?'

'Yes. Black.'

'Could that be him?' A warty finger pointed at a grainy image. Zits and warts: some folk didn't stand a chance, did they?

His mate zoomed in. 'There's the number. But now what'll you do with it?'

Writing it down, I wrinkled my nose. 'The police, I suppose,' I said – truthfully, this time. After all, I had not just Morris to call on, but someone much nearer home, who fancied she owed me a favour.

First of all, I'd got to get through the rest of the day being heart-breakingly polite to Griff, who was even more courteous to me. We might have been strangers meeting up after a long absence neither minded. Even a dreadful tailback on the A27 and the sight of accident wreckage which would normally have had us clutching each other's hands in horror didn't do more than have him reach for Classic FM.

ELEVEN

Detective Chief Inspector Freya Webb's bulge was scarcely visible over her desk. She might not have been pregnant if it hadn't been for me. Well, that's claiming a bit too much credit, I suppose. The thing is, I'd been with my vicar friend Robin, a very ex-boyfriend of mine, when they met. When I could see the chemistry between them, I shoved them together a bit. But soon things went pear-shaped, and at one point he spoke about going over to Rome and becoming a celibate priest. A bit late, I told him, for that. She'd actually booked into a clinic for a termination, but he threw himself at her feet in the middle of a police budget meeting, apparently, and told her he adored her. Then these sensible, career-orientated people had decided they didn't want their baby born out of wedlock, and they'd married by special licence in one of the churches in his parish. Big *Aaahs* all round. So far, so fairy tale.

But Freya was having, in her words, a totally crappy pregnancy. The sickness had gone on much longer than in the textbooks, and she was still looking totally exhausted at a point in her pregnancy when all her friends had told her she'd be full of beans and bursting with energy. Not many of them were senior police officers, maybe, DCIs expected to work more hours than God expected humans to work, including the Sabbath, when, of course, Robin was also working his surplice off. He had to keep his eye on some six or seven churches. At one time I'd thought he was cracking up under the strain, but Freya had grounded him and made him clean his kitchen, in whichever order. But even before I'd introduced them, my relationship with Freya had been touchy – definitely without *feely* to follow. She and Morris didn't get on either, as she was inclined to pull rank. I sometimes thought one of the reasons he'd agreed to work for Interpol was to get promoted to the same level and not have to call her Ma'am when she felt like it.

I'd popped over to see her at Maidstone Police HQ, the day after the Chichester trip, at about seven in the evening. Griff was still being too polite to chunter, and in any case he'd always pressed me to make more friends of my own age. Freya must have been a good fifteen years older than me, but she more or less qualified. We'd agreed to go on to eat in Maidstone, to find a restaurant that catered for whatever craving she was enduring at the moment. Robin would be at two PCC meetings, one after the other.

'Business first?' I suggested as she waved me to a seat the far side of a mass of paper files.

'Always,' she said. 'If I can stay awake long enough, that is. Nothing personal,' she added, not quite as if she meant it.

I filled her in on the story of Charles Montaigne as best I could. It didn't take long before she started taking notes. 'And since he knew all about my family and friends, not to mention my taste in clothes, I thought yesterday's words constituted an actual threat,' I finished, bravely dipping into jargon.

She rocked her head. 'There's always gossip in a profession like yours. Take your father: it must be common knowledge now that you're related, and equally well known that he's an alcoholic. You and Griff – well, you're not exactly top of the range Burlington Arcade dealers, are you?'

'True. But me and Morris and Leda?' I'd not mentioned the most vicious details about the pecking order of love and didn't intend to, not to Freya.

'That's a bit more worrying, especially if they know he has a daughter.' She found a dusty looking Polo mint in her in tray and chomped on it. 'You kept that business card of his? Haven't touched it, have you?' Blinking hard, she peered at the little piece of card in its freezer bag, the best I could do for an evidence bag.

'Only by the edges.' I didn't like to add that it had been sitting in Griff's filing basket and might have been pawed over by him.

'You and I both know that even though the guy who gave it to you has changed his name, he wouldn't be able to change his fingerprints, would he? Or his DNA?'

'You're taking this seriously?' I didn't know whether to be relieved or scared.

'I don't think a guy who finds out that much about you just wants to send flowers on your birthday.' She rubbed her hands over her face. 'Who else knows about this? Morris, of course? No? No!'

'I didn't like to worry him, since he's the other side of Europe and or worried about Leda.'

She threw me a funny look, rather spoilt by a yawn. 'Griff?'

'He's not well, and stress seems to make him worse.'

'Even so . . . After all, Mr BMW might not regard him as his favourite person. Griff's got something, after all, that he wants.' When I looked blank, she raised her eyes heavenwards. 'You, of course. At least you've got that security system to beat all security systems.'

'Which has taken these photos of Monsieur Montaigne.' I passed her the disk I'd saved the best images on to. 'And this is his car number. Please don't ask how I got hold of it.'

She jotted, raising an eyebrow. 'Anyone else?'

'Harvey Sanditon.'

'The man Robin calls a pretentious prick?'

Not very clerical language, but I didn't argue. 'The same. I phoned him when Montaigne first said I should work for him, to ask what he knew. Which was zilch. He said he'd ask around. Actually, he suggested I ask another antiques dealer who knows most things.' I knew she wasn't going to like the next bit of information, so I made her wait for it.

'Who is?'

'A guy called Titus Oates.'

For the first time she sat up straight. 'Oates! Now if you could help us to nail him—'

'He's a mate,' I said flatly. 'So I wouldn't even try.' I didn't complicate things by saying he was a mate of Pa's, too.

'I didn't hear you say that. And Oates said?'

'He knows no more than Harvey. But he did help me out yesterday, when Montaigne came over. He saw I wasn't enjoying the conversation and tried to tail him for me. He managed to ID the car. Then I sweet-talked some security men and got that number for you.' She started tapping the registration into one of her two computers.

'Oh ho,' she said at last. 'Oh very ho, in fact. You're sure this is the number? Yes? Then it sounds as if, not satisfied with inventing a name for himself, he invents his own vehicle reg too. Shit.' She sat back as if everything was too much for her.

'These are the organizers of yesterday's fair – that guy there's an old friend of Griff's.' I fished out an advertising flyer and dropped it on her desk. 'One of them – any of them – might know something about him.'

She peered not at the crumpled paper but at my bag. 'What else are you going to pull out of there? A whole warren of rabbits?' She stopped grinning. 'It's not like you to have passed up the chance of digging this information out yourself, Lina.'

'It's the company I keep – turning me respectable.'

'And?'

I didn't want to pour out the whole Griff business again, so I looked at my watch. 'What time did you say you'd booked that table? It's nearly half seven now.' No wonder she looked so tired if she regularly worked so late.

'Let me just get all this straight in my head,' she said, checking over her notes, point by point. She made a special effort to look at the note and the paper I'd given her. 'If I don't do this it all goes,' she said apologetically. 'My memory's disappeared out of the window. I go upstairs and forget what I've gone for. And then I think, well, I might as well have a pee, anyway, because that's the usual reason I go upstairs these days. Thank goodness Robin's place has a downstairs loo.'

'How are the plans going for you to move in?' I asked. Yes, they'd turned the usual pattern on its head: they married before they lived properly together. Weird. But that was Robin for you. And I suppose the schlep from Stelling Minnis to Maidstone cop shop wouldn't be much fun if you had to factor in morning sickness as well as the traffic on the M20.

'Not good. But then, there's talk about him applying to move to another parish nearer Maidstone. Only one church in this particular benefice, thank God, unlike his present one. Is it seven or eight churches he's supposed to keep an eye on . . .?'

The Thai Palace isn't actually near a palace. It's at the top end of Week Street, unpromisingly near to the station, County Hall and prison. Freya was too hungry for the longish walk, so she'd led the way in her new Peugeot. Had she been trained in pursuit driving techniques? I could hardly keep her in sight. But at last I pulled in beside her in a car park in Brewer Street. Then there was a scamper to the restaurant in the next street – a scamper for me, at least. She, with her long legs, could make more elegant speed, despite the bulge.

'I'm surprised Griff let you out tonight,' Freya said, tucking briskly into the Thai prawn crackers – our second portion.

'Oh, he's on some village committee. A new antiques centre appeared just outside Bredeham the other day, just like that, selling teas and plants and goodness knows what else by now. A lot of livelihoods are at risk.'

'Yours included. Are you sure you don't want to finish these?' Her hand hovered over the crackers basket.

'I'm not eating for two. Though I have to say, bulge apart, you don't seem to have put on an ounce.'

'Not supposed to at my age. Supposed to watch all sorts of things, including blood sugar. Considering it's a natural process, there's an awful lot of scientific monitoring.' She scooped some more sweet dipping sauce. 'Whose baby is it?'

I blinked.

'This centre – whose baby?'

'No one seems to know exactly.'

'It must have a name.'

'Bredeham Antiques Centre doesn't give much away.'

She sighed. My stupidity always made her sigh. 'The Internet, of course. It should be registered, with the names of the owners, at—' She broke off, eyes wide, at the sight of our shared starter. 'Doesn't it all look lovely! Now, end of shop. Absolutely no more work-talk, for either of us.' By the way she tucked in, she meant it, so I didn't dare ask where I should look for information. But no doubt the action committee would

know anyway. Eventually, having crammed food down her
throat as if she was one of those geese, she asked, 'So what
– in the absence of Morris – have you been up to? New bloke
yet?'

'Why should I want a new bloke?' I didn't give her time
to reply. 'Actually, I did come across this really dishy guy the
other day. The first time we met, he looked at me as if I was
the last person he'd ever want to meet. And the next. But last
time we got chatting – he seemed quite nice. But keener,' I
added slowly, watching the last spring roll disappear, 'to learn
about me than to tell me about himself, if you see what I
mean.'

'Just as it should be – a bit of flattering interest. Where did
you meet? Next to some suit of armour in a junk shop?'

'Outside a converted oast-house, in the middle of an industrial estate over in Sussex. Griff's starring in some am dram
piece. And I'm prompt and props,' I added, with a touch of
pride.

'Poor cow. Worst job in the world. Worst *jobs*. Props – you
put in hours hunting round for stuff the cast immediately lose
or break. Prompt – you have to be there for every single
rehearsal, even when the actors who aren't in that act get the
evening off. Someone saw you coming, Lina.'

Although she was only saying what Griff had already told
me and what I now knew for myself, my joy in the job disappeared as quickly as the prawn I'd been hoping was mine. I
grabbed a beautifully carved carrot fish. Perhaps it was
supposed to be there simply for decoration, but I was going
to grab every scrap of nourishment I could, especially as, if I
knew Freya, we'd be going Dutch. Money wasn't an issue. If
it'd had been Robin I'd have treated him to the meal and as
much booze as he could tip down his thirsty throat, no argument. But all her regular hints that since I was a partner in a
business I must be some Kentish oligarch had irritated me
ever since Morris had told me how much his promotion to
DCI would be worth. And it was a great deal more than I ever
took from Tripp and Townend, even with all my restoration
work.

'So what did you say the eye candy did?'

'This and that. And there's such a wide range of individual units out there, from cheese to carpentry, it'd be hard to guess which this or that. It's a horrible, scruffy place, with badly maintained roads, tatty old buildings and rubbish everywhere. And yet it's got this little theatre in the middle.'

'And does Lover Boy's this and that extend to acting in this theatre? Oh, Lina, that's why you agreed to dogsbody, isn't it?'

'He's nothing to do with the theatre. He's just a guy.' And I had a sudden, unpleasant memory of him talking to the man I'd encountered when I was picking up litter. And a weird memory of sawdust and a skip full of wood . . . and another of the lovely old planks that had become Griff's pretend desk. Something else was flying right at the edge of my memory, too. If only I could catch it.

But as the waitress removed the platter that had once held the starters, now with not so much as a lettuce leaf left, Freya said, 'That's what you should be wearing. That sort of thing, anyway.' She nodded at the fitted jacket and severe skirt. 'If not in shot silk. Imagine looking in the mirror and seeing that.'

'Imagine being able to afford to wear that much silk. Oh, thanks to Griff and his eye, I've had the odd bargain at that gorgeous Thai shop in Tenterden, but it's not exactly the sort of thing I could wear for work. Or you,' I added, beginning to wish people would keep off the subject of my clothes. I wanted to grab my top and ask, 'Is Traidcraft Fair Trade good enough for you?'

'Better than going round looking like Heidi. Didn't you read it when you were small?' she added, when she realized I hadn't a clue what she was on about. 'Classic children's book, for God's sake. Shit, I'm not supposed to say that. Anyway, her clothes: just like all that retro stuff you insist on wearing. All you need is white socks and Mary Jane shoes – oh, and possibly a ribbon in your hair.'

'Retro's big at the moment and getting bigger, thanks to *Mad Men* on the TV. So I'm actually at the cutting edge of fashion.'

'And looking like Heidi.' Her eyes swivelled to the right. 'Wow! Are we supposed to get outside that lot?'

Our main course had arrived – no wonder they called it a feast for two.

For quite some time, there was no more talk – either shop or my fashion sense. I ate what I could and was grateful.

At last she slowed down. 'Tell you what,' she said as she signalled for more water, 'tomorrow I'll get one of my lads to go with you to this here antiques centre. Pretend you're setting up house, so act in love.'

'Setting up house means furniture – that's not really my thing.'

'Come on: you can tell a hawk from a handsaw.'

When she turned to quotations, she always took the wind out of my sails.

'Yes, but I'm china, not—'

'You're also a diviner, Lina – and though people like Morris have the facts, you've got the flair. Just go and do it. Hell, you know you're itching to get into the place, and what better cover than one of my lads? Wayne Langland would do. Right. Normal dress, please, nothing like your Alice in Wonderland look – jeans or something. And shades. Get Griff to make you up to look different – a wig'd be good. Oh, I'm sure an old thesp like him'll have something. Phone me at about ten to remind me, though,' she added, although she was making a note on her phone. 'Now, what about dessert? We could share, or we could have something individual?'

I plumped for something individual. But even then she finished it off for me.

TWELVE

Actually, asking Griff to fix my make-up was a brilliant idea, though Freya couldn't have known of the coolness between us, which would have been even frostier if Griff had known about my early morning call to Titus to warn him about Freya's interest in him.

'Ah,' Titus had said. Just that. No wild swearing, just that one syllable.

Now, rubbing his hands with glee, Griff scrambled into the loft – aided, I'm afraid, by his puffer spray, though he did his best to hide the quick dose he needed. The spray might go into his pocket, but a sweetish chemical smell hung on his breath. He came down with a bin liner. When he opened it, it looked as if he'd been a member of a successful scalping party – red hair cut short, blond hair in ringlets, dark hair in a long cascade.

I tried on one after another and posed like a small cartoon model.

He wiped tears of laughter from his cheeks. 'Dear one, if only there was a female juve lead in this play of ours. You'd be so wonderful . . . But for this more serious venture, with CCTV cameras, not spotlights, trained on you, we have to make sure that everything looks natural. We have to consider your natural colouring. So I think the auburn must go. Your skin isn't pale enough. And although we could fix the face, we couldn't disguise your arms and hands. What will your policeman wear? You need to be compatible, after all.'

'You may have to make him up too,' I said, enjoying a hug.

When Wayne Langland turned up, Freya having remembered to send him without any prompt from me, he didn't need any of Griff's skills. He was Mr Average, from his trainers to the tips of his gelled hair. He could have been anything. He nodded approval at my appearance, which, under the tousled black

wig, hinted at goth in its pale make-up and dark eyes and lips.
But only hinted. Nothing to scare the horses, as Griff said.

Wayne plainly hadn't heard the expression. He jiggled his
car key impatiently.

'If we take the car, their security system will record the
number,' I said doubtfully.

'But if you don't, they'll wonder how you got there,' Griff
objected.

'And only the police are allowed to check numbers on the
DVLA database,' Wayne said.

Absolutely deadpan, I said, 'Of course.'

'OK, so there are some leaks in the system. I wonder what
DCI Webb would want us to do.' He bit his lip.

'To act on your own initiative, I should imagine,' Griff said
crisply.

As we drove down to the centre, via a very roundabout
route, we agreed our backstory. We'd inherited a house, if
anyone should ask, a late-Victorian end-of-row villa in
Maidstone. So we wanted to furnish it cheaply with stuff that
wouldn't look out of place. Since the bottom had dropped out
of the brown furniture trade, this all held together. We sketched
a few rooms, about the right size, and had on our wish list a
dining table and chairs, some bookshelves and a chiffonier.
We decided we might argue a bit about any pictures we saw,
but do nothing to draw attention to ourselves.

'It'll all be good practice,' Wayne said as he crossed the
main road, 'for when Livie and I set up for real. After we've
paid off our student loans, saved a twenty per cent deposit
and survived redundancy, that is. Nice place you and your
grandad have got. Worth a mint, I should think. All right
for some.' He parked, not very well, in a completely deserted
car park, pulling on the handbrake with a vicious tug that felt
strangely personal.

It was too much trouble to explain about Griff and my father.
In any case, the odd reference to a grandfather sounded pretty
convincing.

'Is he leaving it to you? Or is there anyone else in the
family?' he continued.

'Just me.' He'd always assured me he didn't have any issue,

to use his term. But what about Aidan? He might have a claim on the cottage, if not the shop, in which I was a proper legal business partner. But I couldn't imagine Griff wanting me turfed out of what had been the only settled home I could remember, and to do him justice I didn't think Aidan would either.

Wayne whistled. 'Lucky cow.' And then started chuntering about how brilliant it must be to be in my situation.

Yes, with a great hole in the antiques market and cash-strapped museums which couldn't afford my restoration services. But no doubt he just meant my housing situation. If so, I didn't think telling him about Pa's place would help the conversation. Changing the subject, I said, 'If I stop next to anything and start saying how pretty it is, it means I think it's dodgy.'

'You mean nicked?'

'How would I know that? I mean it's a fake, or at best has been cobbled together from other old pieces.'

'And how would you tell?'

'Years of experience.' It was one thing arguing with Freya, another admitting a lack of expertise to anyone else – particularly someone I was coming to dislike as much as Wayne. Besides which, I'd sat up till the silly hours reading every book on fake furniture I could find on our shelves.

'But you're only a kid.'

'Whatever.' I was getting rattled now. 'I was taught by a brilliant master, who told me to use my eyes. They probably taught you the same thing at police college, so why don't we see how you get on? OK, smile for the CCTV camera.'

Whoever had set up this instant old emporium had done a pretty good job. Outside it might betray its origins as a service station; inside there were low beams and panelling and dim lights. You might almost have thought yourself inside a genuine barn conversion, if that's not a contradiction in terms. Hang on: I knew the proper word. An oxymoron. I grinned.

Wayne thought I was admiring a pretty whatnot. I didn't explain. But he didn't need to know how hard it could be for me to recall the right words. Just in case you're wondering, a whatnot is the correct name for a little set of Victorian shelves, not me scrabbling round trying to recall what it's called.

Whatnots aren't usually expensive unless they're unusually
delicate, so I didn't expect this rather chunky one to have
problems.

'Do you want a photo?' he demanded. 'Evidence,' he added
much more quietly.

We'd attracted the attention of a CCTV camera, which I
really didn't want. Taking a photo might attract human attention. 'Not a lot of point. It wouldn't fit in the living room,
would it?' I added clearly. 'Much more sensible to have a
chiffonier like that so we could put things in it and close the
door on them.'

'God, you sound more like my fiancée—' he muttered until
with what I hoped looked like playful affection, I punched
him in the midriff.

'I said I wanted a chiffonier. Always did. The trouble is,
this mahogany one or that pretty rosewood? Have you got
your tape measure handy?' I pointed at the more expensive
one, apparently Regency. It was an eye-watering seven thousand pounds, about twice what I'd have expected them to ask
for a perfect one – though I had seen something similar in a
top-notch shop in the Cotswolds for twelve thousand, and that
one had even had a SOLD label on it, which must prove
something.

'It'd be a lot out of our budget,' he said, back in role, thank
goodness.

'But it's very beautiful,' I countered, quite sincerely, squat-
ting down to stroke the lovely wood. The feet were right. The
drawers looked good. The brass inlay was spot on. So why
wasn't I happy? Something to do with the fact that it had been
placed firmly against a wall, so I couldn't see if the shelved
back married up to the lower section, with its drawers and
grille doors.

Since the place wasn't exactly bustling, my interest had
attracted the attention of a saleswoman so chic on her ultra-
high heels it was clear that asking her to turn the chiffonier
round wasn't an option. Actually, asking her to do anything
more difficult than slotting a credit card into a terminal wasn't
an option. So I tucked my arm into Wayne's, shaking my head
regretfully and dragging him towards a nice set of glass-fronted

bookshelves, just over a metre high. Victorian. Except they weren't quite right. Not with those feet. They'd been added later.

I looked inside. 'Ah, here are the peg holes that would have fastened the shelves to a bureau underneath.'

Wayne peered too. 'Black mark against the centre?'

'Possibly. Possibly not. Not many modern houses have ceilings high enough to accommodate both the bureau and its shelves. But they could have done a better job with those feet. Talking of feet, take a look at that Victorian card-table. The inlaid one.'

'The one on the fancy stand?'

'Yes. It's called a pedestal. And it's Victorian Gothic – see, it looks like a mini cathedral. Tell me what you see.'

'It's a different wood from the top?'

Slightly different shape, too, but I'd make him sweat a bit. 'Go on.'

'And the top looks as if it's been patched?' He ran a gentle finger over a section that no one without the sharpest eyes could have spotted. At last he inched up in my estimation. He jotted figures on the back of an old envelope and made a show of totalling them, sucking his teeth and shaking his head.

'And it's quite a different style. So we won't buy it for our dream home.' I tucked my hand into his arm and moved to another piece, a mahogany Victorian extending table with, we found when we opened it out, a middle leaf from a slightly different table.

There wasn't anything I'd have touched; I'm sure not everything was dodgy, but there was enough that was to make me suspect the rest. There were old dressers with new drawers, dressing tables that were actually desks with added mirrors. There was a lot of high end stuff I'd have loved to look at, but that might have blown our cover, especially as Ms High Heels was now definitely tracking us. There was no point in looking around for other customers who needed immediate help – the place was still empty. All that stock and no clients. Since they must have relied heavily on passing trade, no doubt they did most of their business at weekends.

Wayne pulled me into the crook of his arm and turned us

to face her. 'It's all just a bit out of our price range,' he said. 'We hoped we could get a table and chairs and a pretty dresser or a little sideboard thing.' He gave her a winning smile. 'And madam here wanted a nice bedroom suite too. Looks like we'd better head to IKEA, Kaz. Kaz?' He jabbed a hidden finger in my ribs.

So I was called Kaz, was I? Hell, what a pair of idiots not to have sorted names out earlier! 'There must be something,' I whined. 'Look, there's some sort of coffee place over there – let's go and do some sums.'

Ms High Heels smiled earnestly. 'If you were buying any sort of quantity I'm sure we could come to some accommodation. Why don't you give me a ballpark figure and I'll see what I can find?'

Wayne jabbed again. 'I think we need to talk it through properly, thanks. And we've got to buy a birthday present for Kaz's auntie, so we'll be looking at the china, too. Just give us a few minutes. Cheer up, Kaz.'

To do the place justice, the coffee and cakes were spot on, and not expensive. A loss-leader, maybe. We might have had our very un-lover-like talk but for the presence of several cameras. As it was, we maintained our roles. Wayne did a very good job of working his way through a column of genuine figures, while I argued about each item.

For someone wearing steel tips on the end of her shoes, the saleswoman made a remarkably silent approach. I'd have squeaked when she spoke if Wayne hadn't gripped my wrist to warn me.

'I saw you looking at a draw-leaf table earlier. What about a Victorian Pembroke table – for some reason they're not so popular these days, and we could offer one at a very favourable price? And if you could have three pairs of chairs, not six matching, that would come in much cheaper. And a sweet mahogany chiffonier, probably about 1850, has just come in – we haven't got it out of the stockroom yet.'

She knew her stuff. For the sake of argument, we went and had a look. Nothing wrong with any of them as far as I could tell, but of course they were all bottom of the range.

Fortunately, Wayne thought on his feet. 'They weren't quite

what we had in mind. Look, how about we write down the dimensions and then I take a few photos, so we can imagine what they'd look like in our new place? After all, we're not in too much of a rush.'

She pursed her lips. 'At least you asked,' she said slowly. 'We had some man here the other day who started taking pictures left right and centre without so much as a by-your-leave. We had to ask him to delete them and leave – security, you understand.' Wayne did a very good job of looking extremely puzzled and wanting an explanation, but she simply continued, 'So I'm sorry, but no photos. And I can quite see that you want to check the dimensions in your rooms – I suggest cutting pieces of paper to the same size and laying them out where you'd want the pieces to go. That'll give you a good idea. But don't leave it too long to make a decision. Furniture of this quality at this price doesn't hang around, you know.'

I bit my lip, as if I believed her and was anxious not to lose a bargain. But Wayne led me away, in a very manly fashion, and suspecting, no doubt, that the saleswoman or the cameras might still be on us, kissed me comfortingly on the forehead.

I clicked my fingers. 'Don't forget the china. Auntie's birthday, remember.'

He slapped his forehead. He really ought to have been in Griff's am dram group. 'Auntie Jackie! Of course!' He propelled us into the area devoted to smaller items. We were joined by an elderly couple who squawked every time they saw something they recognized from their youth and loudly regretted having given whatever it was away. Then a woman in her thirties paid using plastic for what she thought was a Martin Brothers bird. I could see from three metres that the makers' mark, supposed to be incised, was moulded. Ugly and a fake. Not a good combination.

Ms High Heels might not have followed us, but I've an idea a camera did. So I didn't risk a detailed examination of anything, despite having some very bad vibes. At last I alighted on a Victorian papier mâché spectacle case inlaid with mother of pearl at only a couple of pounds above its proper value. If

I sold it on to our collector customer, we wouldn't be able to mark it up to make a profit, but at least we'd break even. 'Just right for Auntie Jackie,' I announced. 'She'd be able to use this every day,' I added, as I was sure a Kaz would.

'It's a bit precious for that,' Ms High Heels said, appearing from nowhere.

'She likes pretty things, and she's got a lot of vases and stuff. My mum's always on at her to sell them,' I said. As she wrapped the case, I added, 'I don't suppose you'd be interested in buying some?'

For the first time, she looked flustered. 'Oh, I couldn't say. That's the owner's area, not mine.'

'Some of it's really nice,' I pursued, trying to sound downhearted. 'What's this guy's name? The owner? Then she could contact him?'

She made a great show of looking for something I suspected wasn't there. 'No, I can't see any of his cards here. But she could always phone us: the number's on your receipt.'

'Knowing Auntie Jackie she'll never get round to it,' Wayne grumbled. 'OK, Kaz, ready for a spot of lunch? And then we'll go measure,' he added, making it sound a big adventure as he grabbed my hand and led me to the car.

Since – I presumed – Ms High Heels was still watching, he gave me a smacking kiss before we set off.

'Remember to take the Maidstone road,' I muttered as it turned into a mini-snog.

As it happened, there was no need to worry about that. We were going back to Maidstone anyway, to report to Freya, surely too senior an officer to be involved at this point in such a lowly activity as debriefing a constable. However, she was multitasking, eating a huge home-made salmon salad out of a battered plastic box once occupied by ice cream. She despatched Wayne to the canteen for sandwiches for us.

'First off, no sign of the so-called Charles Montaigne,' I said, accepting a plastic glass (if you see what I mean) of her bottled water. 'The assistant was edgy when we asked about the owner – we wanted to sell some of my pretend Auntie Jackie's china. Edgy enough to see us off the premises – or maybe she was just a good assistant. She certainly worked very hard for an imaginary sale.'

'I trust she didn't guess it was imaginary.'

'She didn't let us take any photos. Security. Reasonable enough. And she said some man had taken some before and they'd made him delete them.'

'Two questions.' She speared a prawn from under a chunk of salmon. 'Who would want to take pics? And why make him delete them?'

'As I said, security. Steal to order. A lot of it goes on.'

'Fair enough. Ah, Wayne – what have you got?'

He looked nonplussed. He'd been sent to get food for us two, after all, yet here was a predatory – and very senior – hand reaching out for his goodies. 'Two sorts of sarnies – cheese salad and tuna salad, ma'am. And some crisps.'

She took the crisps and flipped him a fiver, which he pocketed before she could change her mind.

'Lina reckons a lot of the furniture is well dodgy, ma'am,' he said as he opened the tuna sandwich pack. 'But some might have been OK.'

'Do you want us to buy any of the pieces?' I asked. 'Or maybe Wayne could phone to say the sizes didn't work? Ms High Heels – you should have seen them, Freya, they were this high! – worked very hard for a sale, and I know from experience you want to know why people don't do the deal.'

Freya shook her head indulgently, as if I was a five year old asking a particularly silly question.

'I think Trading Standards could take a look,' she said. 'Their thing more than ours. Or, of course, the Met Fine Arts Squad, if it's still managing to stagger along without the famous *DCI* Morris.'

I ignored the dig and said, 'But neither of them until I'm completely forgotten, thanks very much,' I said. 'Wig or no wig, I felt vulnerable.' As always, I slightly stressed the *l*, to show that I knew it was there. 'I live only a mile or so from them, remember. And Montaigne is not the sort of guy I'd want to annoy further.'

'We need some good reason to find out who really owns the place. Companies House says it belongs to Chartham

Holdings, and it lists three directors, none of whom is called Montaigne,' she said through her crisps, which she alternated with her salad. 'But that doesn't mean a thing.'

'It means whoever's chosen the name knows my passion for vintage designer clothes,' I muttered, before I remembered what she thought of my wardrobe.

'Quite,' she said, in the voice of my least favourite head-mistress when she meant to stifle any more comments.

'We bought a spectacle case, but that was all,' Wayne said hurriedly, as if to head off any unpleasantness.

'No china?'

I shook my head. 'There was plenty I'd have liked to look at, but the CCTV camera was on us the whole time. Prices high, quality low, I'd say. And there were some objects so badly repaired that I'd have liked to strip them down and repair them again. Which might just link it to Montaigne, though he can't be the only one with cracked vases.'

'Quite. Now, assuming this is part of a scam, we don't want to go in too early. If they're faking furniture, we'd want to take out the carpenters too.'

'Cabinetmakers really,' I amended, wrinkling my nose. 'They may be fakes, but they're adequate fakes. I wonder why they've suddenly appeared. I don't suppose someone with those skills has just left prison or returned from abroad?'

Freya's eyebrows shot up. 'Teaching your grandmother, eh, Lina? Well, Kent police have been sucking eggs for some time, thanks very much.' She looked osten . . . let me get this one right – *ostentatiously*, not *ostensibly* – at her watch.

'What about the spectacle case, ma'am? Is it OK for Lina to keep it? Or—'

'Did she pay for it? Yes? Right, keep it. No "ors" about it. It's no good sending it off for any sort of forensic tests, Wayne, because the world and his wife will have had their sticky mitts all over it, won't they?' At least she got tetchy with other people too.

Wayne had to run me back to Bredeham, of course, but on Freya's orders he chose a different car from the pound and I shed my wig, for which I was duly grateful – it was very itchy under there.

I let Wayne in via the shop, so he could see what a real antique shop with guaranteed timelines should look like. To my surprise, not Griff but Mrs Walker was behind the counter. Mrs Walker took to him enthusiastically, pressing him to take tea and have some of Griff's best scones.

I let her get on with it, with only one thought in my mind: where had Griff gone without telling me?

THIRTEEN

I was no wiser and a great deal more suspicious when Griff insisted on changing his shirt and putting a load through the washing machine that evening. He didn't tell me where he'd been, fending off every question with another enquiry about my doings down at the antiques centre.

'I hope and pray that Freya didn't suggest you contacted that dreadful Montaigne person and agree to work for him,' he said at last. 'Just to flush him out.'

'To be honest, I'm quite surprised she didn't. There's still time, of course. What, off to bed already?'

'A little tired, dear child. And we'll have a long day tomorrow – it's rehearsal day, remember, and we still need to run some of those props to earth.'

'So we do. Shall I risk hanging the washing out overnight?'

'Why not? The forecast's good.'

I got on with it, thoroughly worried, because he often behaved as if he was the only one on God's earth who could peg a shirt. Was it time for me to talk to Robin, to see what he could get out of him? Or to suggest to Aidan that he should press him a little harder? The only consolation, I mused as I gave the washing whirligig a goodnight twirl, was that – secrets apart – at least we seemed to be friends again.

Although I was supposed to find all the props required, my restoration backlog was so bad that I gratefully accepted Griff's suggestion that he should run them to earth, preferably from our stock – not the items destined for the shop or the website, but the stuff that was waiting to be consigned to charity. Often we'd want a single item from an auction lot, and the rest was simply useless – as far as we were concerned, at least. So there was a well-beaten trail from our place to the Heart of Kent Hospice shop at the other end of the village.

I was just checking the last brush stroke on a Rockingham teapot when I heard Griff calling up the stairs, more excited than I'd heard him for a week.

'Angel heart! Dear one!'

I still remembered to put everything down carefully before I popped my head out of my workroom. 'Are you OK?'

'These dresses! When did they arrive?'

'Big Dave dropped them off. You remember that sale when I bought a bedroom suite? He had the furniture for his hens – no, don't ask: I don't know either – and he brought over the contents when you were out one day.' I could have pointed out that he was at the doctor's but didn't want to rock the very fragile boat. 'There are paper patterns too. I thought of eBay. And for the dresses too.'

'But they're your size!'

Coming down to join him, I pulled a face. 'People are saying they make me look like Heidi, whoever she is. And I don't think they're being complimentary.'

'I think they may in part be alluding to your relationship to me, my love. Heidi is a fictional character who lived with her grandfather. I'm sure you'll find a copy of the original book in the library, though it may be in the children's section. But forget Heidi! Look at the fashion pages of today's *Times*!' Taking my hand, he pulled me into the living room. 'What an investment you've made! Look!'

I looked. Fitted bodices, nipped waists and full skirts were all over the place.

'You'd look so good in them, it's a shame to sell any of them – oh, except some may not be your colour, of course.'

'Then let's try and sell those first, shall we?' I said, non-committally. 'By the way, how are you getting on with Ulysses S. Grant? Got a buyer yet?'

His face fell as quickly as if he'd slapped on that mask of tragedy, mouth really turned down. 'Dear Lord, I'd forgotten all about him!' Turning from me, he used his spray, I was sure of it. In fact, there was that funny chemical smell on his breath when he faced me again.

'Not a problem,' I assured him. 'Antiques don't exactly go bad, do they?'

'But *carpe diem*, Lina, *carpe diem*. I'll get on to it now!' he declared and toddled off. He turned back. 'Don't forget we have to pick up our new car this afternoon!' He even managed a little skip of pleasure.

I took some photos of the dresses that I really didn't fancy and posted them on eBay. I was just about to start work again when Griff summoned me down to lunch. Salmon salad. All these people and their oily fish.

Griff fell in love with the new-old Fiesta, no doubt about it, playing with the various knobs and buttons while I finished the paperwork and flirted mildly with the salesman.

He was practically skipping with delight when I emerged. 'I've tested every bell and whistle, dear one – did you know we had air conditioning? And fog lamps? And – look – you can open and shut the passenger window from the driver's side. Now, will that dear young man tell us how to use the radio – and fix all these preset buttons? Oh, even a darling little mirror in the sun visor! Bliss indeed . . .'

It was fish of a different sort from our lunchtime salmon that I smelt out at the oast that evening. No, nothing to do with the cast or the play. Kippers. The smokery was going full out, and on top of all the other unlovely things about the industrial estate, now we got a burst of fish every time anyone opened the oast door.

And it stayed. It didn't just linger, it actually seemed to get worse, as if someone was grilling kippers, as one of my foster-mothers used to do for a totally vile Saturday breakfast that lingered on your skin and in your hair even if you didn't eat a mouthful. I would have pointed this out if Emilia had given anyone else a second to speak. But she was tragedy-queening all over the place and even produced a tiny bottle of what she announced was very exclusive perfume to spray the place. She got quite hysterical with one of the actors who held the door wide open for a colleague carrying a wine box and some glasses. In her place I'd have told Emilia she wasn't going to get any of the booze in the interval, but the offender just whispered an apology and scuttled off to her place on the balcony, leaving the wine on the table in the roundel en route. Maybe she turned up the heating too: it certainly got hotter and hotter as the evening progressed, whereas it had been cool to bloody cold on previous occasions.

Although I didn't have a part, I had to say far more this evening than any of the actors, who were supposed to be managing without their scripts. And failing. I tried to be tactful with my interruptions, but they had to be made. You'd have expected Emilia to have said a few strong words, but as it happened she was one of the worst offenders, actually stumbling over the words herself, and I'm sure that when she said she was checking her script for marginal notes on stage directions she was really mugging up her lines.

Meanwhile, the smell was getting worse and worse. Not to mention the heat. If I hadn't had to concentrate so hard, I'd have fallen asleep.

During the break, because I didn't fancy the contents of the wine box and in any case was going to be driving a still strange vehicle, I slipped outside. By now it was too dark to see much. If I asked myself what or who I wanted to see, I quickly told myself I was simply breathing in good fresh air. Actually, there was still just a hint of smoke in the air, but it was nothing compared to the fug inside the oast. It was also chilly, cool enough for me to need to huddle into my cardie. After a quick check on our nice new Fiesta, beautifully anonymous in the middle of the row of other actors' vehicles, I scarpered back inside. I'd never been inside a smoking shed, but it must have been something like this, smell-wise at least. But there was no smoke in here at all.

Back to the door. Half in, half out, I compared smells. Far, far worse inside.

'For heaven's sake, you stupid child, close the door!' Emilia yelled. A bit more than yelled, and a few more words.

Behind her I could see Griff's eyes rounding in alarm. He must have seen my face tighten, my knuckles turning white.

Turning outside again – no way was I hauling the oast air into my lungs – I took a deep breath. If I reacted to Emilia as I wanted, it would hurt Griff more than it hurt her – which would be a very great deal. Breathe out, breathe in. And smile.

Even though she was still screaming about the door. Well, I suppose she must have thought I was simply being insolent when I disobeyed her orders so blatantly. Now I did worse. I propped open the door. Stepping back inside, I folded my arms so I couldn't flail with my fists and tried the smile again.

'Emilia,' I said as quietly as I could, 'I think you're mistaken. I think the smell's coming from in here.' I had to repeat it a couple of times before she registered I was arguing with her. No, not arguing, disagreeing.

Griff managed to smile at me, nodding encouragingly.

Still keeping my right hand clamped under my left armpit, I raised my left hand palm forward like a traffic policeman. Definitely not like a school kid asking for permission to speak. Don't think that for a minute.

Emilia moved closer and closer. She must have been a terrific Lady Macbeth. The trouble was that her neck had got scrawny with age, and her hissing reminded me of nothing so much as a bad-tempered goose on the field where we stored our caravan. So I did the unforgivable. I laughed.

As she got ever closer, I allowed my other hand to free itself, but I didn't ball it into a fist. Now I held both hands palms out. 'Hang on. Emilia, just hang on and listen.' I started to laugh again. When I heard a couple of murmurs from the actors, I thought I might have them on my side. 'This fish. It's in here somewhere. Not out there. Go and see for yourself. Lovely fresh air. Cold and fresh. No more than a hint of smoke.'

She didn't move, but a couple of the others did, returning with puzzled faces.

'She's right,' said Wine-Box Lady, with the terrified air of someone telling Emilia that someone else had just won the Oscar she'd been shortlisted for. 'I really think she is.'

Within moments, accusations were being hurled around about the contents of the actors' shopping bags. I would have loved Emilia to be caught out, but she appeared to carry nothing but expensive cosmetics, one of those crazily expensive leather-bound diaries, an address book to match, and two lace handkerchiefs, one of which she seized to mop her eyes. I hoped for the linen's sake that her mascara was waterproof.

For some reason, when everyone's secrets had been revealed – someone hoarded rail tickets, someone carried a Swiss Army knife with every blade going, to judge by the size – they all turned to me as if I was the fount of all wisdom.

Griff winked at me from the back of the room.

'First of all,' I said carefully, looking at the flushed faces and undone top-buttons, 'could we turn the heat down? And prop the doors open? All of them? Thanks, that's better.'

'What idiot turned the heat on?' Emilia demanded. 'We have to pay for it, remember. We agreed not to use it till October, if my memory serves me correct?' Having taken centre stage again, she looked around accusingly. Not surprisingly, no one owned up.

'What if it wasn't one of us?' I suggested as she pushed her blazing eyes within inches of her friends' faces. 'What if it was the caretaker? Or someone else?'

'There is no caretaker!' she declared.

The solicitor whose four by four tyres had been slashed shook his head, but, looking at Emilia, said nothing. Then he took a deep breath. 'Someone's got to be responsible for the upkeep and maintenance. But before we find out who, there might be another option.'

I was ready to revise my opinion of him, despite having first seen him wearing totally unsuitable gear for a man his age.

'Do you not all agree that there has been sabotage?' he continued. 'Many of us have suffered damage to our vehicles. I wonder if the same malicious person has now turned his – or her – attention to the theatre itself.'

'Exactly.'

He beamed at me. 'It might not be generally known, but one of my partners is a distinguished, as well as a notably discreet, divorce lawyer. Occasionally, he regales us with stories from his professional journal of the antics some divorcing parties get up to. One is what he has come to refer to as the prawn gambit.'

Someone muttered a correction. 'Surely you refer to the *pawn* gambit, Gerald.'

'I am in the habit of saying precisely what I mean. One of

the parties is so incensed by the behaviour of the other, who happens to be the one retaining what was once their mutually owned property from which he or she has now been excluded, that subtle revenge is exacted.'

I threw him a smile: I had a very good idea what was coming next.

'The person cast out from the property inserts into hidden places – I believe curtain rails are popular locations – a quantity of shrimps or prawns, which smell particularly unpleasant when they rot. I am wondering if instead of prawns we have smoked mackerel or herrings?'

'In a heating vent rather than a curtain rail?' I suggested, looking in the direction of Mr Swiss Army Knife. Surely, there must be a screwdriver amid all those implements? Yes, there was.

By the time we had located the fish – probably well past its sell-by date before it was smoked – it was far too late and everyone was far too ruffled to continue with the rehearsal. Gerald, the solicitor, called a quick meeting to discuss who might feel such hostility towards the troupe.

'What's happened before might have been construed as simple vandalism. This feels more like an attempt to make us quit the premises altogether,' he said. 'Does anyone know why someone should make such an attempt?'

Since their troubles had started before I even came on the scene I kept quiet – there might, after all, be other useful information coming my way.

'Of course we don't,' Emilia declared. 'Do we? As you so wisely said, darling, it's just some stupid yobs who should be horsewhipped. Now, throwing open all the windows and doors has made the place very cold, and it's quite clear you all just want to go home.'

There was a loud murmur, some of which might have been agreement. She took it as such, gathering up her things. So it certainly wasn't the moment for me to ask where the planks used for Griff's desk had come from, or, something that I was now beginning to wonder, why the actor previously playing Griff's role had quit so suddenly.

But we hadn't heard the last of Emilia. 'Rehearsal on Sunday will start an hour early and continue an hour later. Do I make myself clear? We simply cannot afford to lose time.'

For the first time – and probably the last – I found myself in absolute agreement with her.

FOURTEEN

Having been out of touch for longer than I cared to think, Morris phoned horribly early next morning. He said he'd got good news, bad news. Why was I surprised that there was bad? The good was that he was just about to fly to London for a meeting. Was there any chance I could meet him, just for a couple of hours? The bad news was that he had to fly out again the same evening – operational reasons, he said. Which might or might not mean Leda, I supposed. Even as I let the thought form I hated myself. How could I be jealous of a toddler?

For Griff, the only problem was my getting back from London. He was talking about meeting me and taxis and so on before he even gave a thought about what I should wear. I more than made up for his failure.

What with one thing and another, when we met in the nice hotel where he'd booked a room Morris and I didn't have much time for the sort of conversation that anyone else would be interested in. Then he waited outside to despatch me in a taxi to Victoria before getting in the cab behind. He was heading for the City airport for a flight leaving soon after eight.

I had never yet put my head down in a taxi and cried, but I felt like it now. Passion was all very well, but leaping from your lover's arms and heading home without so much as a nice wind-down coffee afterwards makes you feel curiously cheap. Soiled. It did me, anyhow. I spent the train journey home wondering . . . No, how could I tell him the relationship wasn't working? Griff apart, he was the only decent human being who'd ever loved me. How could I break up with him? He'd even given me what he called sorry presents – chocs and perfume. Not to mention another bloody teddy bear.

Sorry, Tim Bear – but he knew what I meant. I'll swear he

put up the teddy bear equivalent of two fingers to the trio of posh Steiffs as he snuggled into bed with me.

Fortunately, an urgent item for repair had been couriered over at much the same time as I was setting out from Bredeham the day before, so I was able to avoid Griff's compassionate glances more subtly than he was avoiding my anxious glances at him: I was in my workroom before nine and didn't leave, apart to refuel, until six that evening. By then I'd not only rescued a fine piece of Coalport, though there was still a lot of fine-tuning to do before I could call it repaired, but had also worked out a story that would account for my morning grumpiness. In the event it wasn't needed. An old acting crony of Griff's turned up out of the blue, and dear old Griff was so busy conjuring a feast for three from a meal for two that he didn't have time to cross-question me. It was my job to prepare the table (*lay* would be far too basic a term) with flowers, the best china, some fine old glasses and linen napkins. Oh, and candles. Of course.

Somehow Griff's feeding of the three had the same results as Jesus' feeding the five thousand: though you would have thought there would be a shortage of food, miraculously there was a load left over. Not a lot of wine, however. In fact, even Griff was so concerned for his old mate's driving that he pressed him to stay over on our sofa. However, I suspect Barrington – never Barry, he assured me, even amongst his intimates – had wanted a bit more than a solo night on a put-you-up bed, and he turned out into the night, even spurning extra coffee, as grumpy as a child whose goody bag had disappeared.

It was Griff's turn to be grumpy on Sunday, largely because of Emilia's unilateral decision to extend rehearsal hours. We would have to leave Bredeham before noon, which was, as Griff pointed out, far too early for lunch. But he certainly couldn't survive until seven that evening without sustenance – and I wouldn't argue with that. He wasn't diabetic, not quite, but had some pre-diabetic condition so he was supposed to maintain a steady flow of food.

'Easy,' I declared, feeling better after a steady stream of
texts from Morris beating himself up for the miserable date
we'd had on Friday. Perfunctory was one of the words he'd
used, which I thought was a good one. I committed it to
memory.

'Easy?' Griff prompted.

'Picnic,' I said. 'There must be somewhere near the oast
house where we can park up and party.'

'It's threatening rain.'

'We eat in the car. And I vac up the crumbs later.'

'What a pity those lovely lads have been forced out of their
valeting work,' he mused. And then looked alert. 'Have you
heard anything from Freya about your trip to the centre with
young Wayne?'

'Not a word. But she did imply that the whole investigation
might take some time and involve not just the police. But
that's between you and me, and certainly not for your "Ban
the Centre" committee. So, are we on for a picnic? No
spreading checked tablecloths and swigging champagne, I
know.'

'Of course. In fact, why don't I pack individual portions,
in some of those new plastic boxes I found in Lakeland?'

By the time we reached the Sussex border it was raining in
earnest.

'To hell with a view,' Griff said. 'We know we can park by
the oast.'

'Good idea.' Actually, that had been my hope all along –
what better for keeping an eye on things than parking up in
our anonymous car and eating a packed lunch? Though in the
event I decided to park a hundred metres or so away from our
usual spot – we could move closer when there were other cars
to merge with.

'Tell me,' I began as we opened his new airtight boxes
and armed ourselves with forks, 'how many of the cast have
had problems with their cars and so on? Not just us and that
lawyer guy.'

'I think Gina – that's the nice woman who brought the wine
box on Thursday – mentioned unexplained scratches on her

car. But no one took much notice, because she tends to park by touch, as it were.'

'What about the man you replaced as lead?'

'Andrew Barnes? I don't know.'

'Do you think you could find out? A man wouldn't sacrifice a nice juicy part without a really good reason. And questions would come better from you than from me – you can do the nosy gossip tone, whereas after my run-in with Emilia the other night it might sound more like an interrogation.'

'Very well, ma'am.' Eyes twinkling, he gave a mock salute. 'Any other enquiries I should pursue?'

'Actually, yes, there is another line – and I think it's more important. We've talked about it before, but never got round to finding out: when did the planks you use for your desk appear? Who provided them?'

'My dear child, we both know they're old.' He shot me a much shrewder glance. 'You're trying to see a conspiracy, aren't you?'

'The fish might have been meant to smoke us out,' I said, labouring the pun. 'And all the other events might have just led up to it.'

'But if the planks are part of the conspiracy – a reason, I should say – then why did whoever got in to put the fish in the heating ducts not simply remove them at the same time?'

When he separated his negatives and turned sentences round like that it always took me a moment to catch up.

'I don't know. I accept I have a suspicious mind, Griff – which is why all this pill-taking and puffer-spraying of yours worries me.' There! I'd managed to spit it out. 'Not to mention all these tests,' I added, in for a penny, in for a pound.

'My child, I didn't want to worry you, that's all.' He stared at the rain trickling down the windscreen. 'I've just been having a touch of angina. Quite normal for a man my age. But Dr Baker is such a keenie-beanie that he set me in train for all sorts of tests. And each time you've had one they find another you have to undergo. Such a bore. Especially since the next one involves an overnight fast and an appointment at the William Harvey at nine o'clock.'

'I'll take you.'

He hesitated. I'd been expecting a flat refusal, so I waited. At last he said, 'You know, if you're not too busy, I'd be terribly grateful. It's a different part of the hospital, and you know how hard it is to find your way around. But it'd mean your losing a morning's work I fear. Just to sit and do nothing. No! I lie. You could go and investigate the Outlet – you might pick up a bargain, and goodness knows it would be cheaper than paying for hospital parking!'

I managed a smile, as if I thought a discounted shopping trip was a brilliant idea when all I wanted to do was hold his hand. 'You're on. When?'

'Oh, not for a few weeks, I should imagine. It's not urgent, you know, dear one – just routine. Someone's research project, I dare say. Nothing more. Some fruit, my precious?'

'An apple, please.' I took one and a big, deep breath. 'There is just one thing, Griff – I know you think this discussion's closed, but it isn't. There was this story in the parish mag the other day. I know you never read it, but I do. You never know what nice words you'll find. Anyway, this story. A couple went on their hols and phoned back to see how their family was coping without them. And the daughter said, "The cat's died." Just like that. So the father said, "You should always prepare people for bad news. Why didn't you tell us that the cat was on the roof and you couldn't get her down? So we'd have been aware of a problem." Well, next time he phoned home, his daughter said, "Grannie's on the roof and won't come down . . ."'

He gave a perfunctory snort of laughter. 'The moral of this tale being—?'

'If one of these tedious tests found something you didn't like, something you really had to worry about, it'd be a terrible shock for the people who love you. At least I know the cat's on its way up the drainpipe, but Aidan ought to too, you know.'

'Aidan! He's got enough to worry about.'

'Even so. I could tell something was troubling you, Griff – don't you think he can't?'

He started to laugh. 'Very well, I will tell Aidan about the tests. Reluctantly. To please you.' He clasped my hand. I think we were both crying but neither wanted the other to know. After a moment, however, he added, 'And one day maybe you'll tell me why your relationship with Morris is causing you such distress.'

'Yes. Promise. But not now. The first of the actors is here.'

He peered through the fug that had built up on the new shiny windows.

'No! Don't wipe it with your hand! Use this duster!' I squeaked. 'You'll have it all smeary. And no one to valet it, remember, except me.'

He took the duster and polished. 'It's not one of us. Who could it be?'

It could be – and was – that young man with the gorgeous eyes. Come to think of it, his bum was gorgeous too, as Griff obviously noticed, because he polished the window as if his life depended on it. All the young man did was mooch up to the oast and peer in at a couple of windows. He didn't even go round the back; instead, stuffing his hands in his jeans pockets, and hunching against the wind, he strode towards the workshops. I was out of the car, equally hunched, in a flash.

'If anyone asks, we've had a row and I'm in a strop and walking it off. OK?'

Bewildered, Griff nodded.

I shut the door on any questions he might have.

I'd find out where Gorgeous Eyes worked if it killed me. No. Stupid expression. Even thinking of the consequences made me drop back a bit further. But I could still see him lope past a couple of wood-filled skips and towards the workshop which had attracted my attention my first evening here when someone had killed the lights but not emerged, leaving me with the sense that I was being watched.

Although the driving rain meant he was unlikely to turn round, it also meant I had to squint as it blew on to my eyelids – nasty, thin, needly stuff. My hair streamed. But at least I saw him let himself into a unit, and the lights went on, so he must be intending to work. They also meant someone outside – me, for instance – could see what someone inside was doing. The answer was nothing in the room that was lit up. But someone could just be watching me from an unlit window.

And with Griff in his present state, I couldn't do brave and foolhardy, much as I might want to.

I hunched more deeply and ploughed on, trying to make sure I kept turning in the direction of the oast. At least by now there'd be people there to protect me, if I needed to take to my heels and run.

FIFTEEN

'That all went surprisingly well, didn't it?' Griff said as we settled into the car four hours later.

Now we didn't need sun, we'd got it, loads of it, low late-afternoon stuff, dazzling on the wet roads. Fortunately, we were heading east, not west. All the same, I popped on my sunglasses. 'I got all the credit for the props when it was you who organized them.'

'Which is only fair, since you'll never get any credit at all for being a good prompt. And you are, for all some people grumble that they were just inserting a dramatic pause. Or that they'd rather make their memories work themselves. And it was kind of you to offer to read Megan's part when she's away next week. It means Emilia can keep to her rehearsal schedule. At least that's one thing she didn't have to moan about.'

Starting off as carefully as if I was taking my driving test all over again, I asked, 'Has she always been like that? What I'd have called a spoilt brat, even if she is sixty if she's a day?'

'Sixty? She's well over seventy, my love. She's had a lot of work done on her face, as you can see in a good light.'

'All the same, she's beyond rude.'

'I know. It worries me. Yes, she was always tempestuous, in a pretty, girlish way. A typical Gemini: up one moment, down the next.'

'This isn't pretty or girlish.'

'No. It isn't. Actually, she's so possessive of the play, so resentful of criticism, that one or two of us have speculated that it might be her work, not that of her creative writing protégé.'

'That would explain,' I began slowly, 'why – shit! Put your head right down as if you're reading a map. Just do it!' I put the car into gear and drove off as unobtrusively as I could. I'm not sure I breathed till we'd got off the industrial estate.

'And what, dear heart, was all that about?' Griff asked mildly as I pulled on to the main road.

Deep breath time. It was hard to lie to Griff, but I had to fillet out great chunks of my explanation – and make sure he didn't notice.

'It can't have been an ex-boyfriend?' he prompted.

'Not this time.' We shared a laugh.

He wasn't put off by that, of course. 'So it was—?'

'Some guy's been pestering me to do some work for him. He was talking of a lot of regular work. Much too much.'

'More than Harvey Sanditon sends you, I gather?'

'Quite. So I told him no.'

'It's most unlike you to do what I can only call a bunk when you spot someone you've clashed swords with.'

Turning right on to the A road was like embarking on a ritual suicide, what with the quantity of really fast traffic in each direction and the now brilliant sun. After what felt like five solid minutes I swore, risked the wrath of the driver behind me, and turned left. The satnav got ratty, but told me it was checking a new route. Good. That was what it was paid for.

'I was saying you were usually brave to the point of fool-hardiness – though I applaud your decision not to try to turn right there. So why avoid that particular man?'

'Because I didn't like his choice of alias. Charles Montaigne.'

Griff was silent for longer than I liked. Eventually, he said, 'I can see why you wished to avoid him. Such a choice suggests he knows your tastes in vintage clothes, my love, doesn't it?'

'Yes. Which is why when I was talking to Freya Webb I mentioned him to her.'

'And her response?' Out of the corner of my eye I could see him reaching for his spray.

'She's taken note and will get him checked out.'

'But she doesn't know his real name, does she?'

I was really anxious now, but I replied lightly, 'I'm sure she has ways and means.' More brightly, I added, 'She's got his business card for a start, and that's got a phone number on it. Freya's good – you know she is.'

'I know she is when she's not *enceinte*, sweet one. Pregnant, that is.'

'I've seen the word in one of your Georgette Heyer novels,' I said.

'Some women become terribly forgetful at such a time. I hope she's not one of them.'

'I can't imagine her forgetting anything. Though she did make a point of writing things down . . . and she did say something about her memory. Perhaps that's why she eats so much. The pregnancy, not her memory.' We approached an island. 'OK, satnav – over to you.' I obeyed its instructions. 'Did you find a moment to ask Emilia why your predecessor had jumped ship?'

'Andrew Barnes? I did indeed, while you were occupied in the gallery with your props. At first she was inclined to bluster, but when I pressed her she admitted that he'd complained of things happening to his car.'

'The same sort of things that happened to that solicitor's car – and to our van, of course?'

'Possibly. The more I asked, however, the less she wanted to tell me. So I did something I wasn't proud of but which you, being more streetwise, might applaud. I checked in that ultra-smart address book of hers – how much do people pay for paper and leather, just because it's got a trendy name on it? – and found Andrew's address and phone number. We're old acquaintances, no more, but I am quite prepared to contact him and ask exactly what unpleasantness he experienced.' Then he caught me off guard. 'That was a very attractive young man you pursued, my love. Is he an object of desire? In which case trying to accost him when your hair is drenched into rats' tails is not the most sensible of moves.'

Drat and double drat. 'I've spoken to him a couple of times when I've been waiting for you. And yes, he is very attractive. Lovely big eyes, cheekbones to die for. Nice bum, too, as I'm sure you noticed. I was interested to see where he works, that's all.'

I did not intend to tell Griff that when I'd popped out for air during the break he'd swung by, oh so casually, and suggested that being nosey wasn't always the safest option. He'd really looked concerned – not the sneering sort of false sympathy I'd got from Montaigne when he'd talked about my hands – and he'd had an air of taking a risk himself, just to speak to me. He'd ended what was hardly long enough to be a conversation with a few interesting words, however: 'See you on Thursday evening – right?' And then he'd sloped off.

'No. it isn't. All, of course,' Griff said. 'You might just as well tell me, you know. This infernal machine says we won't be home within the hour, and I do so like a good narrative.'

'Your other bit of information first, then. Where did those old planks come from?'

'Ah, I failed there. I'd clearly irritated Emilia enough. She threw over her shoulder some remark about Andrew which despite my miraculous new ears I failed to pick up.' He patted his hearing aids. 'Which reminds me, loved one. Emilia isn't happy about my wearing them – not authentic.'

'Of course they're not. They had ear trumpets in those days, didn't they? But they're pretty well invisible, even in the best light. And in the dim lighting she's promised, no one'll see. You could always grow your hair a little longer to make sure – or agree to that white wig she's been bullying you into trying. It's actually quite fetching, you know.'

'In a Worzel Gummidge sort of way.'

'You know who it does make you look like? That composer you say was a randy old bugger with a wonderful profile he liked to show off. Wrote music for pianists with twenty fingers, you said.'

'Liszt! Well I never. I suppose I should be flattered – though, given his proclivities, pretty obliquely,' he added as dryly as he could given that he was trying not to shake with laughter.

It was time to cut him down to size. 'Besides which, if you don't wear your new ears, you won't hear half of what your colleagues are saying – none of them speaks very clearly, you know. I don't know how the audience will manage. Some giant communal hearing aid, perhaps . . .'

Often I have to remind Griff about such things, but when we got home he toddled off to phone Andrew Barnes while I put the props in the storage area of the shop. Mrs Walker and her fiancé had done well with sales this afternoon – perhaps the rain had driven people indoors. At least they were still patronizing us small fry – or perhaps the sheer quantity of stuff at the new antiques centre had confused them. New antiques centre – was that another oxymoron or a simple state-ment˙of fact? If I remembered I'd ask Griff, who always laughed so obligingly at my jokes. What wouldn't make him smile was a note from Mrs Walker to say that a well-dressed man had come in asking to speak to me. He'd not left a name or a card, but said I'd know who he was and that his offer was still open. Just.

I didn't like his tone – not one bit. MW.

No, nor did I. On the other hand, he couldn't be in two places at once, and I'd certainly clocked him out on the industrial estate. But that was quite late in the afternoon, well after Mrs Walker would have closed the shop and gone home.

Phoning Freya on a Sunday seemed a bit OTT, but I'd certainly call her first thing. And if she didn't seem a bit more involved than she had before, then I might be forced to do something absolutely against my will – raise the matter with Morris.

Griff was looking very sober when I found him in the kitchen, unpacking the remains of our picnic and thinking about supper. 'I find I can raise no enthusiasm whatsoever for a *réchauffage* of yesterday's baked meats.'

'Oh, they've done very well. I think it's time to give them a rest in the bin or the compost heap,' I said, sorting animal from vegetable as I scraped. 'There. That gives you a nice clear run.'

He still looked grim when I came back in from the yard. 'Did you make sure you put the lids back tightly? We don't want another visit from that fox.'

Seven-foot walls, and they still got in. It was a good job humans weren't so lithe. All the same, it wasn't animals that were worrying him, I was sure of that.

'Are you OK?' At least I could be blunt now we'd managed to have that little conversation. I pointed at his chest.

'Oh, that's fine. The tablets really are helping. No, I'm worried – because I can see you won't let me prevaricate any longer – as a result of my conversation with Andrew Barnes. He declined to say anything over the phone. Anything at all.

In fact, we seemed to be having two quite separate conversations.'

'Perhaps there was someone else in the room.'

'Exactly. Someone who got to hear that it was a long time since we'd met and why didn't we have a quiet drink together one day soon. I was afraid that that was all I'd get out of him, so I suggested he email me with a few dates. Then I went further: I asked him for his email address so we wouldn't lose touch. Before you ask, it's a valid address, I've already had a reply and we're meeting at the Granville on Stone Street tomorrow. I'll book a table, just to make sure.' He grinned. 'To be sure of a table, but not him turning up, of course. Now, I've found some tuna in the freezer: would you like it crusted with herbs or with saffron mayonnaise?'

I pointed to the pots on the window sill. 'Whichever is better for your cholesterol, of course.'

At least I had important things to talk about when Morris and I Skyped later that evening.

'He just goes from one test to another,' I said, 'and each seems more serious than the last.'

'At least he's started to tell you. He's probably more scared than you – after all, it's his heart they're interested in. My father simply wouldn't tell my mother what was going on. In the end, they were at a petrol station and while he paid she drove off. Wouldn't come back for him until he promised to explain.'

'And what happened to him?'

He laughed. 'Well, if I tell you he's off hillwalking in the Lake District even as we speak you'll know there was a happy ending. He had to have surgery, which was actually worse for Mum and me than for him, I suspect, and there was a longish convalescence, but he's fine now. You know the only reason you've never met them is that they're always jetting off somewhere.'

'So you're thinking Griff may have to have an operation!' My voice broke.

'Sweetheart, don't panic! That's what all these tests of his are for. To find out.'

'He keeps saying they're because of some research programme. Not that he needs an operation.'

He pulled a face. 'We both know Griff, Lina. Maybe he's right, maybe he's wrong – but the dear old NHS is pretty good once you're in the system. They won't do anything that isn't necessary, though.' He narrowed his eyes. 'You're worried sick, aren't you? Why didn't you tell me before? Or at least say you were worried – I'd have spoken to him myself.'

'It was better for him to confess. And we haven't really had much time to talk about anything, have we?' I added. I didn't want a long-distance row, but having persuaded Griff to tell the truth I might as well try it myself. Any moment I'd get on to the Charles Montaigne issue.

He bit his lip. 'I wish I could tell you I was hopping on a plane right now and could spend next week with you. But I'm up to here in work. We know there's someone exploiting rich people's gullibility by selling them tat at hugely inflated prices.'

Good luck to them. 'I thought you were over there to sort out Interpol communication or lack of it,' I objected.

'I was. I have.'

So he could come home! My smile soon faded, however. He'd not finished speaking.

'But when a French government minister is defrauded – no, I really must not talk about it. I'm sorry. Not even to you, Lina. Though I tell you, I could do with your divining skills. And you. Oh, Lina—'

At this point the conversation at last took on a more personal tone, and I went off to bed feeling a lot happier. That was what I told myself, anyway. Though I still hadn't told him about the problems with Gorgeous Eyes and Charles Montaigne, had I?

SIXTEEN

S ince I couldn't raise Freya on either her landline or her mobile, I emailed her the details of my sighting of Charles Montaigne and the apparently friendly warning from Gorgeous Eyes. Until I'd seen Mrs Walker, who took Mondays off, there wasn't much point in saying anything about the threatening customer.

The email went through, and I got her out-of-office standard reply. I tried her home address too, but there was no reply at all. Of course, she could have been cleaning her teeth or hanging out the washing or a million and one things. All the same, considering what Griff called Her Condition, I found myself worrying. Not much, just enough to try her mobile. I had to leave a message. For a moment I thought of contacting Robin and asking if everything was OK, but since Monday was one of his lighter days, it occurred to me – at last! – that they might be doing something nice together.

I wouldn't be nosing anywhere till Thursday, of course, so I told myself not to be a wimp and to get my head down and work. I obeyed so thoroughly that I hardly came up for air, working on several highly rewarding repairs simultaneously. It sounds impressive, but in fact all I was doing was getting them to the point where they had to rest for at least twenty-four hours before I started the next stage.

I managed to finish one spectacularly ugly but very precious Victorian vase on Tuesday morning. But then there was Griff's lunch date with Andrew to think about.

I offered to drop Griff off at the Granville and collect him later. It meant he could have a glass or two of wine – he was now religiously drinking red, even when he was eating white meat or fish. Thinking I could kill two birds with one stone, I phoned my father to offer to bring over some lunch and do any shopping he needed. For a moment he sounded flustered, so he obviously had company, but he very audibly took a deep

breath and said he'd love to see me, but not to bother shopping en route.

'As a matter of fact,' he announced as he greeted me, 'I
thought on a nice day like this I might come shopping with
you.' He patted his sports jacket, worn with his better trousers.
He'd shaved, too, and remembered to brush his hair.

Catching sight of Titus' car tucked deep into the overgrown
shrubbery, I nodded. I always kept shopping bags in the boot,
so I was happy with the change of plan. I thought I'd provoke
him a little first, however. 'What about the lunch Griff has
prepared for us? Shall I just go and pop it in the fridge so you
can eat it later?'

'You've got to turn this splendid new car round,' Pa said,
grabbing the bag of food. 'Let me deal with this.'

It was hard not to laugh out loud. Poor Pa. He really didn't
like expeditions to the outside world, but he was equally keen
for me not to know officially about his work for Titus.
Strangely, he was happy to talk about it with Griff, but it was
absolutely taboo between us. I think it was my fault, actually
– I didn't want to know about his forgeries, since I was so
horribly above board myself.

I took him, raving about the Fiesta's features, to Waitrose
in Hythe, Griff's favourite supermarket, where he shopped
far more briskly than Griff until he reached the booze section.
Then he became a good deal more selective. Finally, he
shouted me a sandwich lunch in their little café – less
healthy than what Griff had prepared, but infinitely more
nutritious than his former diet of endless Pot Noodles. And
I do mean endless.

He even suggested a stroll along the front. Clearly, he was
giving Titus as much time as he could to finish whatever he
was up to.

'How's that Morris of yours getting on?' he asked as he
settled on a bench facing the sea.

'Frantically busy. He's investigating some Euroscam, I think.
But he can't tell me about it at this stage.'

'Do you tell him when you're worried about things? Because
I tell you straight, you've hardly smiled today. Old Griff OK?
Because I thought he seemed a bit short of puff last time I

saw him, and at his age you've got to think about angina and other cardiac diseases.'

Since I knew Pa spent all his non-forging hours watching TV, I didn't blink.

'He's actually having a few tests at the moment – says he's part of some medic's research programme.'

Pa snorted. 'What do they call it? On that programme with a shrink? Denial. That's it. You need to keep an eye on him, Lina.'

'I've got to do more than that, Pa – I've got to go and pick him up from the Granville.' I held up the phone to show him the text that had just come through. I texted back that I'd be about half an hour and to have an extra cup of coffee. All the same, I'd collect him before I took Pa home: they rubbed along quite well these days, now Pa saw me pretty often and Griff didn't suspect I was going to abandon him to live with Pa.

Although he looked exhausted, Griff was full of the delights of his lunch at the Granville – the food at least. How much illicit cholesterol, how much unrefined sugar he'd shovelled down I didn't dare ask. He did confess to having shared a bottle of Rioja, and he wondered complacently how Andrew Barnes had dared to drive when he was so over the limit.

'An old acquaintance,' he told Pa blithely. 'Sadly run to seed.'

This from a man with angina and potential diabetes. Still, Andrew Barnes might have actual diabetes and have worse heart problems. As for Pa – who knew what damage he'd done to himself? Being an alcoholic was one thing; being a Pot Noodling alcoholic might be worse. Sometimes I felt very scared.

Griff was wittering on about his previous relationship with Barnes. 'Like me, an ex-thesp. Like me, he's had to supple-ment meagre savings with a day job. His was design: interior and exterior. Lina always says my mauve cords are OTT, but you should have seen his outfit today. Floral shirt – so very sixties, maybe seventies – and apple-green chinos.'

Pa, on the surface every inch the English country gentleman

with his addiction to wearing cords or cavalry twill with a
leather-elbowed sports jacket, managed not to shudder, though
this was possibly because he'd simply no idea what Griff was
talking about. We drove slowly up the dreadful track to
Bossingham Hall, and Pa duly invited us in. Griff accepted
immediately, as I knew he would, and headed, predictably, to
the loo. I found a couple of boxes of assorted china to sell
– bottom of the range, I warned Pa, but a good way of making
a little space, even if not making much cash. Pa reached out
champagne, frowned at it, and put the kettle on. Green tea all
round, then, and a little polite chat before Pa made it clear
there was a TV programme he had to watch. I was happy to
indulge him, because Griff was obviously rattled by something
he couldn't talk about in front of anyone else.

Instead of heading straight back home, I drove through
Bossingham towards Stelling Minnis, parking on a bit of the
Minnis where easy walking was available. At first protesting,
Griff eventually nodded.

'No hidden ears,' he observed. 'Do you truly believe that
someone's already bugged this splendid new vehicle?'

'Who knows? But it's a nice day, and I don't think either
of us has had as much fresh air as we ought recently.'

'For *fresh air* read *exercise*,' he grunted, patting the pocket
he kept his spray in.

'You said it. You were supposed to be exercising to keep
your blood pressure down. Or was it blood sugar?'

He stomped off, mumbling about nannying. At last he had
to slow down, of course.

I stopped by a huge hole. Several other holes nearby, and
a lot of digging, made the patch look like something out of a
kids' sci-fi book.

'A badger sett,' he explained. 'It's years since I saw a badger
in the flesh – a live one, I mean, not a poor dead huddle in
the road.' He embarked on a long, meaningless ramble about
cattle and bovine TB and culling.

Finding a convenient fallen tree, I sat down.

Looking incredibly furtive and guilty, he sat too. 'Very well.
Andrew was scared off.' He raised a finger. 'It's quite a long
story. Andrew was – maybe still is – a promiscuous creature.

He's also extremely loquacious and can be relied on to spread quite confidential information to any handy pair of ears. Oh dear, I think I mixed a metaphor there. He's also much given to boasting. Reading between a lot of lines, all crossed like a Jane Austen letter, I suspect he told a casual . . . "acquaintance" . . . that he was the star of a new production, that he was central to it, that without him it would immediately collapse. His interlocutor was visibly impressed – possibly all his interlocutors were equally impressed. No one expressed anything except fervent admiration. And then a complete stranger – we will not ask in what circumstances they met, loved one – told him to pull out of the play, or else.' At last he paused – it could have been for dramatic effect or simply to breathe.

I jumped in. 'What sort of else?'

'Very precise physical consequences. That sort of else. To do him justice, he insisted that the play was the thing. But then his car was damaged, paint and other things thrown at his house, and the message came through that the original threats – though not so far carried out – would follow. He must withdraw from the play – and thus bring about the collapse of the whole enterprise.'

'But the play didn't collapse. And – to be honest – the things that have happened to the cars, even our van being trapped overnight, have been pretty mild. Stupid jokes at one level. That fish was quite a good one, if you have that sense of humour.'

'I suppose so. Yes, actually, I think it was! Dear me, Emilia's reaction. Overreaction. And the way you stood up to her . . .' He chuckled at the memory.

'So why have the life threats been reduced to irritations – assuming his life really was threatened?'

'He always did overact. But I think he was truly fearful. As you were, when the so-called Charles Montaigne spoke to you,' he said, taking my hand. 'And yet you weren't so scared when that beautiful young man accosted you.'

'Hmm. I'd already quite taken to him, on a personal level. And basically he just told me not to be nosy. Me! Nosy! As if I ever was!' All the same, I had the tiniest tweak of an idea at the back of my brain. 'But Montaigne was much more threatening. Without actually saying anything.' Except about breaking fingers, of course. 'Actually, I am nosy about one thing. Those planks. Did you ask—?'

'I did. When I got a word in edgeways. I tried to introduce the topic obliquely, but in the end I had to ask point-blank. All I got was that they came from some skip, which he implied was near his house, though that could simply have been because his narrative was so jumbled.'

In other words, they could equally have come from a skip on the estate.

A little silence grew, while we looked about us. There wasn't a soul in sight. The sky was the sort of blue that makes you wish September would never end, and all the trees and bushes glowed as if they'd never even had the idea of shedding their leaves one day soon.

Maybe it wasn't so warm, though – or why was I shivering?

Griff took my hand. 'It occurs to me, sweet one, that we are very close to the rectory. As a friend, you might well pop in to see dear Robin, and to ask how things are. And, lest you feel any embarrassment, I could always ask to use the loo.'

I hoped he didn't really need it, as the rectory was firmly locked and there was no sign of Robin's car or anyone else's. I scribbled a note saying hello, then we made way home.

There was still no response from Freya the following evening, thirty-six hours after I'd tried to contact her, and now I was worried enough to try phoning again, although I knew she hated to be hassled. The scenarios I played in my head ranged from her being attacked by Charles Montaigne to lying distraught in a hospital bed having lost the baby. I left a couple more messages, an hour apart, and then gritted my teeth to phone Robin. No, I couldn't quite manage it.

Eventually, I passed the phone to Griff, who'd always had a soft spot for him and could be relied on to sound just right in any tricky conversation.

'They're really both *your* friends, loved one,' he said doubtfully.

'Always dodgy for an ex – even as ex as I am – to call a bloke who has a new woman,' I said.

'I suppose so. But you're such very good friends. But for you there might not be a baby, might there? And Robin might now be an altogether different sort of father if you hadn't talked him out of becoming a Roman Catholic.'

I shook my head. 'I don't think I can claim responsibility for that. More a matter for him and God, surely.'

Griff kissed my forehead. 'Go on: call him.' Or it might have been, 'Call Him.'

I did both. And – guess what – while One might have answered, the other certainly didn't. I left a message that he might have been able to work out, given time and patience. And was more worried than ever.

SEVENTEEN

'Try again,' I told Griff. 'I can see what you're doing. More unobtrusively. Go on!'

We kept on and on until he could take a photo on my mobile while apparently just using it to make a call.

Eventually, he put the phone on the garden table and flopped on the bench beside it. The weather was still wonderful, and the garden was loud with the sound of next door's bees. With luck, we'd get a pot of their honey. 'Exactly why do I need to do this?'

'Because I can't. I'm going to be talking to the guy. I'd bet my teeth he's OK, but even if he is – especially if he is! – I can't go round taking photos of him and telling him I'm going to show them to the police just to make sure.'

'But why now? It's only Wednesday!'

'Because I want your brain to transfer it from the short term memory to the long term, so you don't panic. We'll try again this afternoon and then tomorrow. OK?'

'Not quite. Why take Gorgeous Eyes' photo, not one of the Big Bad Wolf that you consider Charles Montaigne to be?'

'See *him* and I scarper,' I said.

'Very succinct. Just as I had to hide in the car?'

'Exactly. Oh, Griff – still nothing from Freya. I'm beginning to feel – unprotected.'

'Surely, she has a team you could contact.'

'Since the reorganization I don't know any of them.'

He shook his head sadly. 'That nice young man Will – the one I always hoped you'd get together with – working for an auctioneer. Such a waste.'

I nodded, though I had a distinct idea that Will might not actually have left the police at all. Morris had dropped out that he'd had a conversation with him. Morris very rarely dropped things out, so I'd squirrelled that away – and told no one, not even Griff. But it was certainly something to mention to Morris when we spoke tonight. Will – and Charles Montaigne, of course.

Although it was tempting to sit and bask, we drifted back to the kitchen for our tea – always green these days. As the kettle boiled, the phone went.

Before I could even say hello, Freya spoke. Harangued, more like. Very loudly and clearly.

'Look, Lina, I'm really not answerable to you, you know, for my every single action. If I choose not to answer my phone, if I choose not to reply to your cascade of emails, it might just be that I choose to do something of more pressing importance. And as for badgering Robin – I simply won't have it. Understand?' Freya cut the call.

So that was what you got for honest concern. OK, I was worried for myself too. Perhaps that was why what she said hurt so much. I didn't know whether to hurl the handset across the room or cry. Fortunately, Griff relieved me of the phone and provided a shoulder.

'My, my, how the poor lady's hormones are raging,' he said. 'But how very ill-mannered of her to let you be the object of her rage. I should imagine her team tiptoe around her like mice – and then get screamed at for not being assertive. At least you have Morris to fall back on. Not that he and Freya are the best of friends, as I recall.'

'I'm sure he only took this job in Interpol to get back at her for pulling rank on him so often and so publicly. But when we talk, Morris and I, we don't necessarily want to talk what he calls shop.'

He passed me my mug of tea, looking over the rim of his own as he sipped. At last he said, 'Without wishing in any way to pry, I do wonder what long-distance lovers talk about. Even dear Aidan and I, with so many friends and so much experience in common, occasionally dry up.'

'Have you told him about the cat on the roof yet?' I shot at him.

'Tonight. Our regular Skype time. I promise. But it was of you that we were speaking. Have you – as lovers very new to your relationship, and with so many difficult areas to tiptoe round – ever discussed your future, for instance?'

My turn to sip tea. At last I said, as honestly as I could, 'I don't really know if we have a future. He was supposed to be dealing with one specific problem in Interpol's internal organization, but now he's obviously been moved on to doing something else. Something big. And I've a nasty idea that when this big thing is over, there'll be another, and then another. And even if he comes back to England, he'll be in London and shooting over to France every other week to see Leda, which I know he really has to do.'

'Even though she might not be his biological daughter?'

I put my mug down and folded my arms. 'Like you'd turn me out into the cold because I'm not your biological grand-daughter!' As our laughter died down, I added, 'He simply adores her. She adores him. But I've a terrible suspicion that if her "real" parents didn't find him dead useful looking after her when they were working and weren't too mean to hire a full-time nanny, they'd ruthlessly cut him out of her life.' I'd been with him when he'd returned Leda to Penny and her horn-player, and I'd seen the expression on their faces. And to think I'd really liked Penny when I'd first met her.

'And how would he deal with that?'

The words that came out surprised me as much as they clearly shocked him. 'I wouldn't be surprised if he went to work for Farfrac in New York.'

'And would you go to New York too?' I'd never heard his voice so flat and neutral.

'Why should I go there? What on earth would I do in New York?'

'I fancy you wouldn't have *to do* anything, though someone with your skills would be snapped up immediately, green card permitting. I fancy the partner of an antiques expert might just have *to be* – to exist, in other words, as a highly decorative wife.'

I was gobsmacked. 'But my place is here. Here, as in with you and with Pa. I can't go swanning off halfway across the world and leave you two alone. Well, you've got Aidan,' I conceded. 'But Pa – all Pa's got is Titus!'

'And that indeed is an appalling thought,' he agreed.

EIGHTEEN

The very evening I really wanted to talk to Morris, he was working. He took my call while he was in the lobby of a building which tourists took photos of and was about to meet the sort of people I only read about in newspapers – and then only if Griff reminds me I ought to be keeping abreast of current affairs. Since I hadn't mentioned my particular version of the cat climbing on to the roof, I didn't want to worry him by jumping straight in and asking for help – he clearly needed his mind on the job in hand since he told me the meeting was going to be conducted in French. But I asked him to phone the moment he had a chance and made him promise he would – something I didn't ever like doing because it made me sound needy. Actually, I *felt* needy, since Freya still hadn't got back to me about my sighting of Montaigne or the warning from Gorgeous Eyes – or even got one of her minions to do it, which, given our last phone call, sounded more likely and was even preferable, to be honest. If I'd really messed up I would take criticism on the chin, but this time I thought she was so in the wrong that it'd be hard not to tell her so, despite her Condition and her Raging Hormones.

I hadn't quite expected a call at six thirty the next morning, but Morris had forgotten that French time was an hour ahead of ours. It took me longer than I liked to gather my thoughts, but we filled the interval quite satisfactorily.

At last he said, 'Last night you sounded quite unlike yourself, Lina. Desperate. You're not – not . . . Are you?'

It took me a while to fill in his dots. 'Pregnant, you mean? Absolutely not. I leave that to Freya – which is why I wanted . . . needed . . . to speak to someone who . . .'

'So I'm a pale substitute for Freya, am I? Seriously, what's troubling you?' he added, in his sort-of-official, sort-of-tender voice.

'Someone called Charles Montaigne.' Hell, I'd forgotten about warning him the cat was on the roof.

'Charles who?' he asked sharply, not as if he hadn't heard but as if he wanted to make sure he'd heard right.

'Charles Montaigne,' I repeated, ready to bristle if he criticized my pronunciation.

There was a pause, as if he was jotting something. 'OK. Go on.'

'Originally, he just wanted me to work for him. When I said no he got a bit unpleasant. Mentioned breaking bones and things. He's done nothing yet, but that doesn't mean he won't, does it?'

'Indeed it does not.' He sounded very official.

'What with the new antiques centre and the hassle over Griff's play – my play, now, of course – I feel as if I'm in a forest with nasty grey things inching closer by the minute.'

His voice changed to completely tender. 'I'm not surprised. My poor—'

I dived into the next sentence; he should have had this information earlier. Would have done, but for our lack of communication recently. 'There is something else you need to know. Last time he spoke to me it was clear he knew a lot about me. And he knows about my clothes.'

'Clothes?'

'There was a dress designer called Charles Montaigne. Fifties, sixties. I thought I recognized the name, but it wasn't until I came across some vintage dress patterns recently that I remembered where from. So I think he's invented the name to unnerve me. To show how much he knows. He also knows about Griff. About Pa. And also about you.' If he asked I'd have to give him chapter and verse, but I hoped he wouldn't. Because it was too early in the day to talk about such things, which ought to be discussed face-to-face, anyway.

There was a long pause. 'How would you feel about coming over here for a bit?'

My heart leapt. Yes, please. But my head said, 'And leave Griff? I have a nasty feeling that this Montaigne guy might turn his attentions to him if I jumped ship.'

'He could always come too.'

Which meant that Morris didn't have a romantic interlude in mind. 'Oh,' was all I could manage.

'I didn't put that very well, did I?' He laughed. 'I meant, I wanted you here, very much, but could quite see that you wouldn't want to expose Griff to any danger – any more than I would. I like the old guy. Now, I need to think this all through, darling, but – hell, I'm being summoned already. Talk very soon – OK? And for God's sake, take care. I mean that.'

'I will. Morris, before you go, I've been meaning to thank you for the lovely postcards – very sweet of you.'

'Postcards? What postcards?'

'Those of those places in France we've been together.'

There was a very long silence. 'We'll talk later – OK?

End of call. Now what was all that about?

It hadn't been the best conversation I'd ever had. It was too one-sided – too much me, not enough him. And no chance to ask for further details about going to France. Not that Griff would go – not if it meant sacrificing the play.

I was so excited by the chance of reading a few of someone else's lines while she was away that I almost forgot the important business of the evening, which was to talk to Gorgeous Eyes and get Griff to take his photo. We'd had a couple more practice sessions, and Griff really was pretty nifty now. The light was pretty poor, since Emilia had worked us far longer than usual before grudgingly permitting a break. This turned out to be lucky – there was a positive flood of people emerging to make calls. I managed to drift away from them, pretending that I was using Griff's phone – one without the photo facility – and needed to find coverage. Griff tailed me at a discreet distance. All very cloak and dagger. All to no avail. Gorgeous Eyes had evidently given up on me, and who could blame him?

Emilia summoned us all back in, her voice carrying like an old-fashioned train whistle, even though we'd only had ten minutes. I felt like kicking gravel. As it was, I mooched past our car, like the others still safe and sound. So far.

But not untouched – ours, at least. Someone had tucked something under our wiper. He must have done it carefully or he'd have irritated the extra-sensitive alarm we had on all our vehicles.

8.56. Can't hang around any longer. Phone for drink sometime?

He'd added a mobile number and a scrawled signature that might have been Paul.

Now what? I didn't want to drink with the guy, just to identify him. A drink implied all sorts of things, which, with Morris suddenly putting the idea of me and Paris in the same sentence, weren't welcome at all. Unless I could view it as an undercover operation, with no emotions involved at all . . . I was still pondering as I headed back to the oast, where I was greeted by an almighty scream. Not a scripted one. The play didn't have a single shriek. Actually, it could have done with one. If I'd been the author I'd have been sitting in the back for every rehearsal. The actors might have been mangling his lines, but at least he'd have realized that while some were too long, others had breaks in the wrong place. He could have changed them. And he'd have realized how dull much of it was. A scream would have been a welcome addition. But an acted one, not a real one. I was inside that oast before I knew I was moving.

One look told me it wasn't so much a scream as hysteria. Emilia did hysteria remarkably well – all the more reason for the playwright to include a scene involving it. Everyone knew someone should slap her, but no one wanted to be accused of assault. I did the obvious thing: I grabbed an open bottle of water and slung it over her. Good news, bad news. The good was that it turned down the uncontrolled noise, the bad was that her top was silk. At least the water was cold. The colour shouldn't run.

Griff cast his eyes heavenward: he might have been exasperated with me, but equally he could have been getting tired of what he regarded as an interruption to an evening's work.

As before, and with slightly more justification, she turned on me. But she wasn't accusing me of wrecking her top. She was accusing me of theft.

'Of what?' I asked, trying to stay cool.

But my voice was drowned out by the solicitor with the four by four and a sense of humour. Gerald.

'Emilia, I really cannot permit you to make such accusations. All we know so far is that you can't find a ring you're sure you were wearing when you washed your hands. You say you may have taken it off and put it down while you were washing them. Or it might have been after, in the dressing room. Let us conduct a quiet and rational search and hope it's just fallen down somewhere and rolled away.' He gave me a smile I couldn't quite interpret. 'For the sake of everyone's reputation I suggest we hunt in pairs.'

'You mean, so that she can't slip it back and play the innocent,' Emilia said waspishly, pointing at me.

'What a good idea,' I said, so that everyone heard. 'OK, let's find rings, folks.'

It did seem a good idea, until I found myself partnered with one of the less exciting actors – Nose-Picker, no less – who, as soon as he found himself alone with me in the dressing room, tried to kiss me. It was the work of a minute to make it clear he should take himself off, by which time Gerald had wandered in and grasped the situation at a glance. I was so busy being grateful for his company that I forgot to wonder, until we were all back in the oast, where his search partner, Wine-Box Lady, might be.

Griff, perhaps thinking he should restore his family's reputation, stepped forward into the middle of the returning searchers. 'Does anyone have anything to report? Anything at all?' he added sternly. It took me a moment to realize he was in role as an old-fashioned stage policeman. 'No? Any open windows? Unlocked doors? You see,' he added, 'we shall clearly have to involve the police. Investigating the theft of a valuable item isn't a job for enthusiastic amateurs.'

He might have slung a firework into a hen run. Amidst all the fluttering women, Emilia flapped the most. With a most realistic shudder, and without quite elbowing him aside, she neatly upstaged Griff.

'Enough time has been wasted on my poor trinket. It will just be a lesson to me to be less careless in future – and to trust less those whom I thought were my friends.'

Wow and double wow. It was really hard to hate a woman who could come out with lines like that on the spur of the moment.

'But you've made a very serious allegation, Emilia,' Gerald said. 'Two, in fact. First, without any apparent reason, you point the finger at Lina. Now you include the rest of us. Griff is right. We call the police. After all,' he added, with a cynical smile, 'you have to notify them of the so-called theft if you wish to make an insurance claim, which I'm sure you will.'

The police must have been having a boring evening, because within five minutes there were half a dozen officers milling round. They did what I always find irritating – they left their blue lights flashing, as if warning Jo Public not to mess them around because at the drop of a handcuff they could leap into their cars and start fighting crime ten miles away. What would the rest of the industrial estate make of it all? In particular, Gorgeous Eyes and his unpleasant mate. If you were doing anything dodgy all this illumination must have been dead irritating at the very least. Not a single light shone from any of the units, but I had a sense of watchfulness and of fingers being crossed that any police activities didn't extend to checking their premises – or even their vehicles. Not to mention the odd skip.

Having come mob-handed, the police couldn't then lose face in front of each other by saying the whole thing was a waste of time and that the old bat had probably left it at home. So we were questioned just like in an Agatha Christie play, and there was talk of SOCOs and goodness knows what else. Griff's face got greyer and greyer, but I think he was simply worn out, not in any pain – he didn't use his spray, at least when I had my eye on him.

At last, the final statement given, we were allowed to head home. But not before I heard words I really didn't want to hear from one of the officers.

'Tomorrow we'll ask around the estate – someone working late might have seen something suspicious.'

'Emilia really gets up my nose,' I said as I started the car, stating the obvious, I suppose. 'Why do you all let her get away with her bullying? You're all grown-ups!'

'I suppose it is bullying – but that's what actors do: we accept instructions from the director. If we start arguing every point, where would we be?' Griff said.

'It's not the acting part – it's her general attitude, not just to me but to people like that nice woman who brought in the wine box. It's almost as if she's trying to provoke a walkout. But you're all so nice and polite you just take it.'

'I think we're all trying to be mature and professional.'

Forgetting the need for kid gloves, I flared, 'And I'm not? Maybe it's something to do with the fact that she seems to have picked on me as the person she most likes to hate.'

'That was why I suggested the police should be involved,' Griff said, hardly answering my point. 'I know that you're as honest as the day: it needed to be proved to the others.'

'It hasn't really proved anything, though – I bet she told the fuzz I'd swallowed the damn thing. In any case, it's only paste, isn't it?'

'Is it?' Griff sounded genuinely shocked.

'Yes. Like those ear studs of hers.'

'How do you know – ah, of course you know. But so wise of you not to tell the police.'

'Quite. They'd want to know if I'd tried writing on glass with them or whatever you're supposed to do to test diamonds. Actually, I might have kept my mouth shut for Emilia's sake.'

'Really?'

'You said the old bat's not as beautiful as she was. Maybe she's not so well off, either – and it'd be a bit mean of me to broadcast that to the world.'

'I think it's uncommonly generous of you not to. On the other hand, the police will be going to a great deal of trouble for nothing.'

Yes, and maybe ruffling feathers I'd rather have kept smooth.

I dabbed a finger on the radio. Classic FM. Soon Griff was snoring gently. So I was left to wonder what I should do about the note Paul – if that was his name – had left for me. It would feel like betraying Morris if I phoned him. Wouldn't it? Or would Morris want me to, in the interests of digging up a few more facts? Suddenly, I felt more cheerful – what a good excuse to contact him. I found myself humming along.

'Cocoa with skimmed milk doesn't really press any buttons, you know, angel heart.' Griff sighed, peering into his mug.

'I know, but I read somewhere that cocoa – or is it chocolate? – is actually very good for you, and I know full-fat milk isn't, so you'll just have to put up with it,' I said firmly. 'And keep your hands off that biscuit barrel too.' Just to make sure, I grabbed it and shoved it on the top of one of the kitchen cupboards. 'Now you're awake again, I want some advice.'

'Awake again? When was I asleep?'

'For pretty well all of that nice piece on Classic FM. The Brahms. You'd dropped off during the Fauré.' I suppressed a sigh. It was all very well my having a wonderful education in classical music – thanks to Griff, of course – but I hardly ever heard so much as a note of what people of my age ought to be listening to. No wonder my boyfriend was twice my age.

Perhaps, I wondered sourly, he'd already been tucked up in bed and fast asleep when I'd tried to phone him when we'd got in. Tried in vain. And somehow asking his permission to phone another guy was not something I could do on voicemail. Which was why I needed Griff's help, after all.

I stirred my own cocoa grimly. For God's sake, Brahms was one thing, but what was a girl my age doing drinking cocoa? I pushed it aside, almost slopping it over Griff's nice clean linen tablecloth.

I spread the scrawled note in front of me, then turned it round so Griff could read it. For good measure I even hunted for and found his reading glasses. 'There. What shall I do?'

'Why don't you wish to do exactly what he suggests? Because you're attracted to him and fear that you're being disloyal to Morris? My dear child, he's talking about a drink, not a full-blown affair. Go for it, say I. No?'

The cocoa had skinned over. The more I stared at it, the more I felt sick. And then some words came out that scared me. 'What if it wasn't that guy who wrote the note? What if it was Charles Montaigne?'

NINETEEN

Which was why, the following morning, despite everything, I tried phoning Freya again. Still voice-mail. I cut the call without saying anything.

'My advice is to talk to Morris,' Griff said over *The Times*, where he'd just started the easy sudoku. 'Oh, just do it, Lina – there shouldn't be room for shyness like this in a relation-ship, surely.' Obviously, he was struggling. I hadn't the heart to tell him that Pa could shoot through even Super Fiendish ones in a matter of minutes.

Nodding, I headed back to the office to make the call. Even I could work out that I wanted to make it businesslike, as if lust for Possibly Paul had never reared its tempting head. So I spent a couple of minutes jotting things I wanted to say in the order that I ought to say them. It was a complete waste of time, of course, because Morris was up to his ears in what sounded a very lively meeting in French and simply muttered that he'd ring me back before cutting the call.

I headed upstairs for the workroom past my open bedroom door. Tim the Bear looked very sympathetic, and I found myself in a ball on the bed being hugged. Then he sat up and gave me the benefit of his advice. Phone Possibly Paul, he said, and make sure you arrange a meeting in a public place, just as if you were meeting for a blind date. If it turns out to be Charles Montaigne, scarper.

It was hard to argue, and since there was no other advice available, I sniffed, wiped my eyes and took it.

I'd never have thought of a garden centre as a meeting place, but that was what Paul – definitely, now, not just possibly – suggested. To look like a genuine customer, I grabbed one of those low awkward trolleys with fat, unsteerable wheels and managed to push it inside. And there he was, watching the antics of a large bird in the pets area. His smile, as he turned to face me, lit his face and certainly reached his eyes, a good sign, I decided, especially as they were just as attractive as I remembered them. But he said only, 'I need some bulbs,' before heading off to another part of the centre, away from the nosy CCTV camera, presumably.

Lurching from one aisle to another, I trailed after him, suddenly not best pleased to have come all the way to Ashford when I could have been fixing a vase. And certainly not wrestling with the trolley, which insisted on going its own sweet way. I spotted an offer on large ceramic pots, supposedly frost-proof, which I knew Griff wouldn't have wanted me to resist, but which the trolley wanted to bypass. As I dragged the wretched thing to a halt and reached for the pots and a couple of bags of tulip bulbs and some fibre to fill them, a thought struck me like a blow on the chest: what if Griff wasn't alive to see them come up? I think I gasped out loud as I pressed my hands to my mouth.

Paul came back. 'Are you all right?'

Shrugging, I said as lightly as I could, 'Someone walking on my grave.' Which wasn't at all what I wanted to say or, by the look of it, what he wanted to hear.

'Be careful what you wish for, and be careful what you joke about,' he said, cramming daffodil bulbs in a paper bag – only two pounds for a bagful, no matter how many. Clearly, he meant to get his money's worth, even if this whole trip was a smokescreen.

'I certainly wasn't wishing for it. And not necessarily joking. Why am I here?' I passed him another bulb.

'Because you've annoyed the guy I work for and my mum needed some daffs.'

'Is it me or all the actors? You're going to tear that if you pack in any more.'

'They just park and go in. You sniff round. What part are you playing? Miss bloody Marple?'

'I'm not acting at all.'

'Give up, then. And stay away from the estate.'

'Can't. I'm prompt and props, remember. Essential.'

'Well, do as I just said. Park, eyes down, inside. Changing the car for the van was a good move.' He reached for another bag and stuffed it with just as much care.

'What am I not supposed to be looking at?'

'Bloody hell! Just give it up or do as I tell you. I'm putting my . . . job on the line telling you.'

What had he meant to say instead of job? Not *life*, surely!

'It's something to do with that skip I found full of offcuts of good wood, isn't it? Now empty, I'd imagine. And maybe the planks that shouldn't be where they are? Not to mention a certain antiques dealer.'

'Just piss off and do as I told you.' His bag split, and daffodil bulbs rolled everywhere.

It seemed a good moment to obey. And since he was scrabbling around taking no notice of anything except the hyperactive bulbs, I managed to fish out my phone and snap him. It was back in my pocket and I was stalking off, with as much dignity and haste as the trolley would allow, before he was off his knees. He must think a lot of his mother to go to so much effort for her. On the other hand, he must have liked the look of me to go to such lengths to warn me off.

There were only a couple of security cameras, and I worked out how much of the area they covered so I could move the car well out of their range. Then I took forever to stow the things I'd bought into the boot. At last Paul emerged. Funnily enough, he'd parked not far away – he must be a fellow camera-watcher.

Catching his eye, I smiled, and he sidled over, spreading his hands in helpless exasperation. 'Now what?'

'I take it you've not been to work this morning? You're not going to be very happy when you get in.' I explained about the ring and the chance of a visit from the police.

He swore fluently.

When he'd finished, I said, 'I think you're risking more than your job to talk to me. I think you're taking a real risk. Why?'

For answer he grabbed me, kissed me very hard on the lips, and stomped back to his car. I took the number and – feeling a louse – its photo as well.

I had something like evidence. Now all I needed was a bit of concern, a bit of interest, from Freya or Morris. Though perhaps neither of them need know about that kiss.

Or my heart-hopping reaction to it.

Texting both of them seemed better than trying yet another voicemail message. I did it back in the garden centre, safe in the little café, where for some reason the rim of the coffee cup kept rattling against my front teeth. My thumbs kept finding the wrong letters too.

At last I managed, then I sent the photos to Freya. I thought about it for a bit and eventually sent them to Morris too.

I sat and waited – but there was no reply from either, so I trudged back to the car and headed dismally for home, where I found Griff staring without enthusiasm at the pile of mail Mike the Postie had just put into his hand. One of those white envelopes with another card from Morris. I took it without saying anything, looking at the one that had attracted Griff's attention. A brown window envelope – the appointment for the fasting tests he'd mentioned, perhaps. I knew he wouldn't be keen on anything involving going without food, but now wasn't the moment to joke him out of it. Instead, I tucked my hand into the crook of his arm and walked him through into the kitchen.

'I said I'd take you, remember,' I said, putting the kettle on.

He shaped his face into something approaching a smile. 'Of course you did, dear child. The trouble is, it's rather sooner than I expected. Monday. I have to be there for eight thirty.'

The NHS wasn't hanging about, was it? The medics must think that whatever was wrong was more serious than Griff was letting on.

'They must have had a cancellation,' I said lightly. 'When can you have your last nibble? We must make sure it's a nice one.'

Before he could reply, someone rang the front doorbell, knocking hard at the same time. A glance at the security camera trained on the door told us it was Wayne, my fake fiancé.

'I'm supposed to be writing some damned report,' he moaned, as a greeting, eyes rounding as he sat down and took notice of the contents of our cottage. 'Is that clock new? I mean, I know it's old, but—'

'I think you were too busy sorting out disguises and your backstory to notice anything last time we met,' Griff said, bustling off to bring tea.

'Someone said something about a new development. I've not seen the DCI for a couple of days. Meetings or something. That's all the senior officers seem to do these days, run off to meetings. Leave us holding all the babies.'

Perhaps that was why Freya hadn't been in touch and also why she was so ratty.

He added, 'Not literally, of course – except in her case.'

I grinned as Griff brought in a plate of his finest cakes and another of biscuits. He withdrew as if he was playing the part of a well-trained butler. 'Is there any news from Trading Standards or the Met Fine Art Squad?'

'Not that I know of. But these things take time, Lina. Things can be high on your priority list, or even on mine, but they may be at the bottom of the in-tray for management. It depends what the media are likely to be interested in too, if you ask me,' he added. 'Hey, where did you get these biscuits?'

'Griff made them. So if you wanted to get an investigation going fast, you'd tie it in with someone in the headlines?'

He stared at the biscuit as if it might have an answer. 'I didn't quite say that. But I suppose so.'

'So if you could find some Kentish celeb who'd bought a fake at the Centre, things would move along.'

'I suppose . . . Hey, do you know any?'

'I wish. But it's something you might think about. I can't, obviously.'

'You're very keen on pursuing this. Why?'

'I believe there's a big scam going on,' I said. '*Very* big. And I think I may have stirred something up on the industrial estate where Griff's part of a theatre company.' I explained. 'In fact,' I continued, 'that's why you're here. One of the guys working on the estate met up with me this morning to warn me off. And I think he took a big risk to do it.'

'The guy whose photo you sent through?'

'I felt a total heel doing it. He's a good guy.'

'Working for a dodgy organization?' Wayne sneered, reminding me sharply of Freya on a bad day.

'Perhaps he's a decent guy who's had to take a crap job,' I hazarded, 'to pay off his student loan or something.' I wasn't just winding Wayne up. It seemed as good a theory as any.

Until Wayne explained how the loan system worked. Five minutes later he was still holding forth.

Griff must have been more than hovering: suddenly, he was not just in the room but also ready with a couple of questions. 'Did any of your colleagues recognize this young man? Or did the clever facial recognition programs do their work? Not to mention your computer finding his car registration, of course?'

'We're on to it, sir.'

Possibly. His voice said it was on the furthest of back burners. I watched him carefully while Griff continued his attack.

'Wasn't it rather a waste of your time to come out without some hard information?' Griff's smile was full of tender concern. Until he added, 'And Lina's time, of course. She doesn't want talking therapy, Wayne, she needs to know how the case is going and how the police propose to act – and, I would add, how they will take care of her. It seems this criminal is more concerned for her safety than you are – not you personally, of course, but your colleagues in general.'

'There's no need to take that tone, sir.'

'I'm not taking any tone. Just requesting action. Every time we venture to the oast theatre, I fear an ambush. Every moment we spend there, there is some new practical joke. Every journey back, there are the same fears, made all the worse by the darkness.'

'We've even been warned off the public meetings about the new antiques centre,' I threw in. 'Griff was one of the working party.'

'And will you heed the warning, sir? I would advise you to.'

'I don't like threats. I'd rather be there. But some games aren't worth the candle. Unless someone else can be there to watch the play?'

Wayne was visibly puzzled by what I picked up as a suggestion that Wayne or a colleague might want to be there to see who else was at the meeting. 'This is the play at the oast house, sir?'

Griff turned away; I heard his spray in action. He faced Wayne again. 'I actually meant the action at the village hall tonight. But surely the addition of a police officer to the cast of our humble production could be a good idea? The latest merry jape has been to steal a cast member's ring.'

'And did the person report the theft?'

'I couldn't tell you. I'm sure you could ask your colleagues in the Sussex police.'

'Sussex?' A strange expression took over Wayne's face. 'All this is going on in Sussex?'

'Only the events surrounding our play,' Griff said, looking and sounding confused.

Wayne got to his feet, closing his notebook. 'In that case it's nothing to do with me, sir. If the alleged crime's being committed across the county border, it's up to the Sussex police service to deal with it.'

Some words came out of my mouth that quite surprised me. 'So now crime has to respect county boundaries! Hell's bells! Why, Paul came into Kent to warn me – isn't that enough to interest you? Wayne, this is all tied together, I'm sure of it!'

'I'll report your concerns to DCI Webb when I see her. I'm sure she'll be back in touch with you.' He nodded to us and let himself out of the front door.

Griff sat down and leant back with a sigh. 'Do you remember the dear dead days when the police used to hunt in pairs, the idea being, I suppose, that one officer would keep an eye on the other and vice versa? All gone with the cuts, no doubt . . . Thank goodness I didn't invite him to lunch. George the fish-monger has managed to produce not just some lovely salmon, but also what really must be the last samphire of the year. I've had to blanch it, of course, since it's getting tough now . . .'

TWENTY

I t was only the sudden recollection that we had a one-day fair the following day that stopped Griff picking up the phone and demanding police protection when he went to the meeting at the village hall that evening. I'd remembered the gig a couple of hours before he did, when I'd have had plenty of time to prepare, but had kept quiet: it was better for him to have a genuine reason not to turn up – packing the van – than an excuse.

But he refused to give up the rehearsal on Sunday. I made sure we arrived just on time and bundled us both inside without so much as looking round. Amazingly, we got straight to work, with no mention of Emilia's ring, though I can imagine most of us would have liked to ask her if it had turned up. Perhaps we'd all had enough tantrums. A sudden burst of rain during the mid-afternoon break kept all but the most desperate smokers inside. No one seemed to want to talk to Emilia – I almost felt sorry for her. I'm sure she'd have liked to tell us all about whatever accident had caused her to come in with one hand swathed in bandages.

But then I found a very good reason to dislike her. This was the afternoon I should have been reading the part of the actress who was away. Read? I knew it by heart!

'Now, I know we thought of tackling Act Two, Scene Two. But one or two of us were very shaky with our lines earlier this afternoon, so we will run through Scene One again. Places, please.'

Now, Act Two, Scene Two, was where I would have come on. My head told me she'd made the right decision, since the woman for whom I'd been going to understudy would be back next week. But my heart thudded with unpleasant thoughts of possible revenge – really adult things like spray-painting her car for her – as I trudged back to the corner where I lurked as prompt.

Horribly, I battled with tears. The only way I could overcome them was weird. I found myself prompting each actor not just with the right word, but with the right intonation, and in pretty nearly the right voice. There were blushes and some very strange looks. What I'd done was take revenge on the wrong ones. I'd humiliated people who had suffered the lash of Emilia's tongue almost as much as I had. I hung my head in shame as I gathered the props afterwards.

Rather than face the cast, I dawdled in the dressing room area where we stored the larger items till almost everyone had gone home, no doubt puzzling and annoying Griff as well. The windows had a fine view of the rest of the industrial estate, including the unit where Paul worked. Two or three white vans drove up in rapid succession and parked at such an angle I could no longer see the unit, or, drat it, what the drivers were loading or unloading. A figure wandered round my side of the second van. Paul. Someone followed him; even from this distance I could see that Paul was taking a bollocking. A second man joined the first: all three disappeared behind the van. I'd have done anything to hurtle after them and explain that the police presence had been all Emilia's fault, and that they should settle any problems with her.

But even as I stood there, Emilia got into her car and drove off. And Griff was calling me, and I had to go.

We left without saying anything. I didn't say how disappointed I was not to have read the part, any more than Griff spoke of his fears for the next day. Thank goodness for Classic FM to drown the silence. But even that couldn't stop me feeling as if someone had been sitting on my shoulders pressing my head down all weekend.

It was a nice argumentative Radio Four *Today* programme which got us through the drive to Ashford's William Harvey hospital the following morning. Despite his fears of not finding the right department, Griff wouldn't hear of my going into the hospital with him. Reluctantly, I obeyed his orders to go to the Outlet to hunt for bargains – last season's clothes, of course, at reduced prices. But there was nothing in my size except stuff which made me wonder why anyone had ever even thought that clothes that colour and that cut would ever sell in the first place. I wasn't even tempted by the underwear shop.

While I sat in the Outlet car park – much cheaper than the hospital one – I got a text from Paul. *What was all that about the fucking filth? Not good news, Lina.*

I texted back that it was nothing to do with me. Easier than a long explanation. Then I texted again, on impulse. *What if I left the planks we used as a desk outside? Would that help?*

No response.

At long last I was summoned back, to find Griff acting perky, although it wasn't long before I winkled out of him the news that he had to have yet another test the following week.

'Monday or Tuesday: they'll let me know. Nothing to worry about,' he insisted. 'Though they say it will be a bit more intrusive and will take at least half a day.'

'So the cat's still on the roof, but someone's getting a ladder,' I joked, ready to weep with terror. If only there was someone I could share all this with. 'What will you tell Aidan?'

'Do you really think he needs to know?'

'Absolutely. Especially about the ladder.' I squeezed his hand. 'Now, have you had anything to eat? You know you have to think about your blood sugar levels. No? Here, have this banana. Then we might have a browse round TK Maxx – you always nose out something good for me . . .'

I thought about texting Morris, or even phoning him, but pride clicked in. If he wouldn't contact me, why should I bother to contact him? My pride took me through the rest of the day, but by Tuesday morning I was getting really desolate. Just as I was thinking that Morris had forgotten all about me, and my afternoon with the glue and paint was getting longer and longer, the phone went.

'I'm sorry – I've been trying to find time to get in touch all weekend.' So that was all the explanation I was going to get for a silence I found quite weird, given the fact I'd sent him that photo of Paul. And what had happened to yesterday? I was ready to scream and shout and cut the call. Instead, I took a deep breath.

'Well, you've got me now,' I said reasonably. 'How's things?'

'Manic. At the highest level. Now, this man who warned you off the play and the estate: the face is familiar. What does Freya have to say?'

'Fuck all. She sent a minion – Wayne, the man I'd checked out the dodgy antiques centre with – but clearly he was under orders to give nothing away.'

'Maybe he didn't know anything?'

'So why did he bother driving over? No, he was holding something back. Griff and I kept our heads down all weekend, just as he told us to, and the only excitement has been taking Griff for more tests – something to do with Nuclear Medicine, whatever that means. And he's got to go back again next week. Morris, I'm so scared!'

'About Griff or this Paul guy?'

'Do I have to choose? It can't be both?' What I wanted was for him to come back to England now – yesterday, for prefer-ence – and provide strength and comfort.

'I'm surprised Freya Webb isn't being more forthcoming, I must say. I'd offer to have a word with her, but I think it might be counterproductive, don't you?'

We shared a brief laugh.

'Look, this idea of you and Griff coming over here for a bit.'

'I told you, he's got another test next week. If they're coming this thick and fast there must be something really wrong with him.' I swallowed a sob. 'And don't ask me to leave him here, because you know I can't.'

'Of course you can't. But actually I could really do with your advice – professional advice.'

I said cautiously, 'You're the expert. I'm just a restorer.'

'I just want you to do what you did with – what's his name? Wayne? – only for me. In rather grander surroundings. Fancy a trip to Paris?' Wouldn't I just! 'With Griff too, if he's up to the journey? Staying over till Saturday or Sunday, all expenses paid by Europe? – and I can't imagine him saying no to a taxi to Ashford International station, first-class travel and accom-modation, the room just across the corridor from ours at a rather nice hotel . . .'

'Oh, Morris: he's got this damned play. And there's another rehearsal on Thursday. He won't miss that.'

'And you won't leave him at the moment. OK.'

It seemed the conversation was over.

Griff came bustling up as I stared at the dead phone. 'My dear one, don't forget this evening.'

'Eh?'

'This evening. The rehearsal.'

'But today's Tuesday, Griff.'

He sighed, clearly trying not to speak to me as if I was an idiot. 'Emilia changed the day, dear one. Don't you recall? Right at the last minute?'

'Maybe I was collecting props and stuff and didn't hear her,' I mumbled, still ashamed.

'Ah – you were putting those things in the dressing room, no doubt. I'm sorry – I should have told you. But what with one thing and another . . . So can you break off soon? I'll make some sandwiches so you can eat while I drive.'

'I can break off now. But I have to make a phone call – dead urgent.' As he left the workroom, I was already reaching for the phone. 'Assuming I could come over to Paris,' I began, as if there'd been no interruption, 'what's the deal?'

Morris took his tone from me. 'I can probably put everything into place for tomorrow morning. I'll text you the details. And I'd better make sure you get back in time for Sunday's rehearsal, right?'

'Forget the travel for a moment. I'm to do what I did with Wayne, in grander surroundings. Does that mean what I think it means?'

'Consultant antiques expert.'

'But I'm not . . . I mean, you are, with your degrees and such, but I—'

'You've got gifts a lifetime of study wouldn't provide.'

I said sharply, 'You know I can't turn my divvying on and off like a tap.' But at least I'd done all that reading before the jaunt with Wayne.

'I know that. And I also know you observe things I don't even know are there. OK? Ask Griff if you're not the best.'

'He's biased.'

'So am I. Listen, this could make your career. Yes, and mine, to be honest. It won't work if you slide in looking miserable and scared. Think confident. Posh clothes, day and evening, both of you, because I can't imagine Griff wanting to miss out on where you're going to operate. Borrow your father's title for good measure if you want and if it'll make you feel more at home. Oh, Lina,' he added in a totally non-professional voice, adding a few suggestions about how we might pass the hours when I wasn't being consulted, 'just say yes.'

'You did say yes, of course?' was Griff's response. This was the first time Griff had driven our new car, and he made sure we were safely on to the main road before he started asking questions.

'Provided you're well enough.'

'With my pills and trusty spray I'm up to anything, my child. Abseiling down the Eiffel Tower apart. Best bibs and tuckers, eh? And you're to be Lady Elham? My, my.'

My lower lip came out. 'I don't know about that.'

'Maybe a subtle hint – "Of course, this is Ms Townend's professional name: really, she's a member of one of Britain's leading families . . ."'

'I'd like that better. After all, it's true – I'm part of *your* family. And with sarnies as good as these, very glad I am too.'

This evening Emilia was all charming smiles and pretty compliments. She made a particular point of thanking me for all my discreet contributions. She thanked the cast for the special effort they'd made to get here tonight instead of Thursday. Her hand was still bandaged, but very lightly. No ring was visible.

Off we went. Without her marked script.

'Of course we won't need it, will we? Everyone's so good, you could manage without it? Without little me, indeed.' There were lots of cues for obedient bursts of laughter. 'But – oh, Lina, would you be an angel? Just in case?' She slung a huge bunch of keys at me.

Thanks to all that practice on French beaches with Morris and Leda, my catching was good, and I took them in mid-air, without so much as a fumble. Gerald remarked they could use me in the England cricket team.

As I went through the door, she called, 'And darling, the central locking's on the blink – use the passenger door.' I turned to see her making a turning gesture: I had to use the key manually.

Her elderly but still gleaming Mercedes was parked slightly apart from the rest of the cars as if to make a point.

Front passenger door. Keys in lock. And the most amazing racket. I thought our car alarms were loud, but this would have wakened the dead. Or at least brought the occupants of every single unit on the estate to their windows. For some reason, it didn't have any apparent effect on the people in the oast.

It didn't take me long to go and fetch Emilia. Just to make sure there was no argument, I left the theatre door wide open. No one could miss that din.

'Dear God, what have you done this time?' she demanded with a huge heave of a sigh.

I responded with an even bigger shrug. 'Front passenger door.' I slung the keys back.

Gerald, guessing, probably correctly, that she wouldn't be able to catch them, intercepted deftly.

'For God's sake! I said on no account to touch the passenger door!' From a safe distance she zapped, and the alarm subsided.

It was so quiet that you could almost hear the plop of heads being pulled back through windows in the other units as people realized the show was over. Despite myself I looked around, trying to make it a general scan, but actually eager to see if I'd attracted unwelcome attention from Paul's boss. Or bosses. Or even Paul himself. If I could have run up a flag saying sorry I would have done. As it was, I gave a huge shrug as I headed back inside. Only to have to head straight back out again to get the missing script.

As I sat trying to look a cool efficient prompt, but actually smouldering and ready to puff into flames if anyone crossed me, I kept letting my attention slip – once so badly that I did the unforgivable and lost my place in the text. This time, although she'd have been justified, she didn't scream at me. Perhaps she could see the heat shimmering over my head, which was ready to erupt if I was provoked. But why did she have it in for me? From past experience I knew I didn't bring out the best in women, just as I brought out the lech in older men. But surely this wasn't a sexual jealousy thing? Not unless she fancied Griff, in which case she was in for a sad disappointment. In any case, he hadn't been her first choice for leading man – she'd only thought of him when Andrew Barnes had thrown in the towel. And she must have known he was gay.

He was far from gay at the moment: she was lashing into his handling of two vital speeches as if he was an infant learning to read. We all pretended not to hear. As for Griff, he looked iceberg cool, but then, he was a wonderful actor. He ran through the speeches as she demanded; far from being appeased, she wanted them changed again and again. At last she deemed them acceptable – probably because he'd gone right back to his original interpretation and she was too ratty to notice.

The rehearsal continued. The action moving up to the balcony, everyone's attention was off Griff. Only then did he pop a pill and puff his spray.

Eventually, I had to chip in with a missing word for Emilia herself. *Just the word, Lina, nothing clever.* Really professionally, she continued without missing a single beat. But she looked at me with something like loathing.

As I waited for the next slip, I continued to ponder. Was someone putting pressure on her to get rid of me? That didn't make sense – not just me, anyway; everyone here had had some problem with her acid temper since they joined the cast. They'd dealt with it by becoming anonymous, just as Griff had suggested Freya Webb's colleagues would have. I didn't really do anonymity, even when I was trying to creep round under radar. And when I did, blow me if I didn't activate some car alarm. I'd been the one to tip water over her, of course, and point out that the smoked fish was inside the oast, not outside. But she'd been edgy before that.

As for Griff, he'd never explained why people didn't stand up to her bullying – maybe I'd press him again tonight.

Or maybe I wouldn't. I'd had a text come through:

Get the fuck out of here. Go by a new route.

If only I had a guardian angel – or perhaps I did. Wine-Box Lady had a nosebleed, the sort that wasn't going to stop soon. Any other time I'd have grabbed the chance to read her part. As it was, I caught Griff's eye and tapped my watch.

'Early start tomorrow,' I mouthed.

He was on his feet packing away his gear before you could say police raid. I'd never bundled the other props so quickly or so carelessly; in fact, I just dumped everything in the oast roundel and, pretty well scooping Griff up, legged it to the car. We needed to go north-east, of course, so I headed south-west.

Fortunately, he was too full of what he referred to as 'sound and fury' to notice that we were on the wrong road. Only as he saw a sign to Bexhill did he twig.

'Bloody satnav,' I muttered, glad to find a lay-by to pull into to tell it to take us home. For once I blessed the wretched thing's habit of choosing weird routes: no one would predict some of its odd choices. Surely.

And no one did. At last – I shoved a bone-weary Griff into the house, locked everything in sight, and thanked heaven for the next morning's early start.

TWENTY-ONE

D riven by a calm, smart but tough-looking woman in her forties, our car arrived outside the front door bang on six fifteen. It was not, I'd guess from the amount of dials and things on the dashboard, your standard taxi. It swept us up to the main international station entrance, and despite the no-waiting signs the chauffeuse made sure our cases found their way to the top of the escalator without any help from us. She was so solicitous that I believe she'd have popped Griff into a wheelchair at the merest sign of a gasp.

Once on the train, again with the minimum of effort, I couldn't argue with the idea of a champagne breakfast, not just this once, since Griff hadn't been so full of life since the chest pains had begun. If he had any difficulties he gave not the slightest indication: in fact, he was so full of fun, the journey passed in moments, even the bit deep in the Chunnel which had me reaching for his hand.

It would have been nice if the fairy tale had continued with Morris greeting me in Paris with flowers and wide open arms (quite a tricky manoeuvre, now I come to think of it). But at least a man with a discreet sign for 'Monsieur Tripp and party' greeted us and swung us off in another upmarket car into the city that always made me squeak with excitement and disbelief.

The hotel we drew up to nearly made me squeak again, but I decided that the daughter of an English nobleman would treat even somewhere as grand as this as her birthright. Several quirks of fate separated me from ownership of Bossingham Hall, of course, but who was to know?

My lower-class origins gave themselves away when I wondered dourly – but not aloud – who was footing the bill for all this sumptuous modern elegance, not just for me, of course, but for Griff too. His room was indeed just across the corridor from Morris's and mine, and it didn't take him long to tap my door and exclaim at the view, not to mention all the other wonderful things. He gripped my shoulders, shaking them slightly. 'Promise me you'll never doubt that you've earned this, Lina.'

Doubt? I *knew* I didn't deserve it. 'But I've suddenly been upgraded to an international expert. What happened to the foster child from Folkestone?' When he still shook my shoulders, I managed, 'Actually, I know what happened – you did.' I fell into his hug. What if anything happened to him? Could I face any future without him?

He pushed me away. 'My child, I have to tell you there's a bottle of champagne on ice in my room. Let us celebrate being a family. A leading family.'

He lifted my hand high as if leading me in a procession and together we minced through the door. Only to have our silly drama cut short by my mobile phone. We stopped, halfway across the thickly-carpeted corridor.

'Don't turn it off, loved one. The fizz can wait. But not the fuzz; not in the form of Morris, at least.'

Without thinking, I opened the text. But it wasn't from Morris. It was from Paul.

'Go on, read it,' Morris's voice rang out. He was only twenty yards away, and I should have been running into his arms.

If I began to scream, I stifled any sound before it came out. Because of Griff, of course. If I started doing what I wanted, which was collapsing in noisy hysterics, what would it do to his heart? I didn't dare risk giving him a full-blown heart attack. So I took the deepest of shuddering breaths.

'Griff, I need to deal with this. Why don't you go and put the kettle on? There's green tea in the top of your case.'

'For God's sake, there's room service,' Morris snapped. He muttered in French to a passing young man, pointing at Griff's room. Heaven knows what he said. But the minion scuttled off. Then Morris gently pushed Griff out of the corridor through the heavy door.

Griff wouldn't be pushed. 'Lina, my child, who is it?'

I took a deep breath. 'Charles Montaigne. Off you go.'

The moment he closed his door, I handed the phone to

Morris so he could see the message. Instead of a text, we stared at what was left of Paul's face.

'Is this the price he paid for trying to help me?' I asked. 'More to the point, was he – is he – alive or dead?' I tapped the screen.

'Go and share the green tea with Griff. I'll get on to this.' As a lover's greeting, it didn't begin to score on the romantic scale, but I'd never heard more welcome words. 'Thank God you're safe over here,' he added. Perhaps these came a close second. He kissed me swiftly before he hunched over his phone, turning away from me and giving my bum a helpful shove.

'But—'

'Look after Griff!' he hissed.

Since a young man was already scurrying along bearing a silver tray over his shoulder, I obeyed.

I could smell the spray on Griff's breath, but we both pretended we wanted nothing more than a healthful infusion, accompanied by some highly illicit pastries. Unable to pretend any longer, I let him take my hand.

'Has he threatened you, my love? Overtly, rather than implicitly, I mean?'

'Trust you to give me a vocabulary lesson at a moment like this,' I muttered. 'Actually, I think it's an implicit threat.' It wasn't my face, after all. 'But he's not a nice man, Griff, and I'm glad we're safe over here,' I added, echoing Morris, who had still not reappeared. I couldn't hear his voice, but that might have been because of the thickness of the door and the general soundproofing that enveloped us like a giant comfort blanket.

The green tea was very good, as were the pastries. They occupied several minutes, with a few light comments thrown in. But I wasn't the only one constantly eyeing the door, all the time pretending to be interested in the decor or the bloody view.

At long last there was a tap on the door. A peep through the spyhole showed a grim-looking Morris, though by the time I'd unlocked the door he'd rearranged his face into a calming smile.

'That's all that sorted out,' he said, though I noticed he didn't return my phone. 'Well, nearly all. I'll be able to join you for lunch, which will be with the gentleman who asked for your expertise.'

'Old money?' Griff asked quaintly.

'Old as the Conqueror, probably. Don't know how he dodged the guillotine.'

'In that case, with your consent, I will take Lina shopping first.'

Morris gaped. 'She looks pretty good to me.'

'Very good, but not Paris chic. How long do we have?'

'An hour?'

'That's longer than a fairy godmother would have. Come, Lina – what are you waiting for?'

Cunning old Griff had spotted a boutique almost literally across the road from the hotel's main entrance, and he propelled me inside, addressing the stern-looking assistant with a flurry of French. Within minutes, however, I was wearing a suit that fitted as if it had been made for me and was clutching bags containing a further suit, what Griff called afternoon dresses, a cocktail outfit and a full-blown evening dress. I hadn't seen the bill, just the flash of Griff's plastic. When I'd opened my mouth, he'd put his finger to his lips. OK, we'd argue later.

'Thank goodness you have neat feet,' he said, heading for a shoe shop so posh that there were only three pairs, all ominously unpriced, in the window. More carrier bags. One to hold a bag he insisted would be better than mine. That left five minutes for him to deal with my slap and tweak my hair.

I was ready for anything. At least as far as he and Morris were concerned. But every time I looked in the mirror, overlaid on the image of a vaguely familiar Frenchwoman, the battered face of Paul appeared.

TWENTY-TWO

I f our hotel was modern chic, the huge house we were
bidden to – for some reason also called a hotel, though
Morris insisted it was occupied by just one couple and their
staff – was early nineteenth century chic, involving a lot of
Egyptian-style furniture, gilt wherever you looked, pictures
the like of which I'd only seen in galleries, and the richest of
fabrics. We were shown up to a first floor *salon* by a manservant,
no less, who bowed as he opened double doors. Time to be
– well, not exactly my father's daughter, because I never could
work out his take on social class, but perhaps my ancestors'
descendant.

As we were received (there's no other word for it) by our
host and hostess, I thanked heaven for Griff's foray to the
shops. Mme le Fèvre was dressed in a suit as finely tailored
as my own; her hair was trimmed to within a millimetre of
perfection; and she was Victoria Beckham slim, although she
must have been in her fifties, judging by the silver-framed
family photos displayed artlessly on a grand piano, which I
was sure she could play. Occasionally, she showed she was
human by fingering (oh yes, the manicure was perfect and
understated, just like her make-up) with what seemed like
nervousness the sort of brooch you see the queen wearing
when she does a walkabout: elegant but with a lot of serious
stones, with not a whiff of paste about them. Griff hadn't been
able to do much with my nails, but then, I was an Expert, not
a mannequin.

Whatever its state, Monsieur kissed my hand, just as they
do on the movies. I managed to stand still and look gracious.
I think. We had canapés, on which I was quite heavy, and
champagne, on which I was deliberately very light. The stilted
conversation was conducted in charmingly accented English.
Then there was lunch, in a fully-fledged dining room, complete
with original fireplaces (one at each end), ceilings with

wonderful plasterwork, mirrors, matched console tables and everything the heart could desire. It competed with, but didn't quite outshine, the formal dining room at Bossingham Hall.

Lunch was the sort of occasion at which Aidan, with those long conversational manoeuvres of his, would have excelled. I just tried to look alert and not let my mind wander: what was I doing here, when a man who'd kissed me had been beaten so viciously he might not be alive?

There was also another problem. One of my antennae was twitching. Not the one that hunts for cheap goodies to sell dear. The one that tells me I'm handling a wrong 'un.

I was sitting at a table set with the finest crystal (I was sure it was from Stourbridge, for some reason) and eating off Limoges porcelain – and all I could do was smell a dud!

I could hardly check the china – imagine picking up a plate and having a quick peep. In any case, it was all modern, not my period at all. So I applied myself to trying to look both charming and efficient – not necessarily possible, come to think of it – while ignoring the throb somewhere deep in my brain.

Gradually, the problem emerged. Monsieur and some of his friends had once fallen on hard times, and although they had managed to cling (he implied it was a huge physical effort) to their homes, on occasion they had had to put on the market certain items. At no point did the words *buy* and *sell* foul the air. However, eventually they had been in a position to obtain similar items, very choice, very fine. But a rumour was spreading that someone was managing to pass off what could only be described as fakes.

Ah, ha! So this was how I was to sing for my lunch. Actually, I was relieved: it wasn't often my antennae misled me, and I'd have hated them to start now.

I gave them to understand that my father had been forced to retrench too. That seemed to go down well. I didn't spoil the atmosphere by saying I sometimes flogged a dozen or so of his plates in draughty church halls. I certainly didn't mention Pa's connection with Titus and his part in producing fakes. Eventually, we adjourned for coffee to a different salon from the first. The time the porcelain was Sèvres. Hunky-dory Sevres.

At last I was aware that they were all looking at me, as if I were a performing seal that wasn't balancing a ball on its nose despite all its free fish.

Perhaps to jolly me along, Madame took me to powder my nose. En route we passed a huge gilt-bronze porcelain urn – actually, a sort of giant air-freshener – with delicate Chinese-derived pink carp floating around a wonderful mottled blue background. I'd seen an occasional one in a catalogue. Now I saw one for real, I think I yelped; certainly, I had to clasp my hands behind my back to stop reaching out to stroke it.

'If only it wasn't damaged.' Madame sighed, pointing to the lid, which was missing a chunk. 'A maid. Only last week.'

'Damaged?' This time I did reach out. 'Oh dear. Did you save the piece that broke off?-'

'Of course. It is safe inside. But—'

Oh, I did like Gallic shrugs. I wished I could do them myself.

'May I look?' I don't think I gave her time to say no.

'You hold it like a doctor examining a sick child,' she said, peering over my shoulder.

What I needed, then, was a consultant paediatrician. I think that was the right word, but I didn't fancy risking it on her.

'Children can heal without scars,' I said slowly as I replaced the urn on its stand. 'This – well, I do know someone who might be able to help.' Why was I being so tentative? I'd repaired even more valuable items for private owners and for museums. Perhaps I didn't want to muddy the waters of my so-called expertise for sniffing out fakes by telling her I was nifty with the glue pot. 'But there must be experts at hand in Paris,' I added truthfully. 'People who are experienced in this sort of thing.'

'Monsieur Morris mentioned you,' she said firmly. 'He said you were modest about your skills and that I must not take no for an answer.'

'Did he?' Somehow the first part of her sentence sounded right, but not the second. But if my father was anything to go by, putting convenient things into other people's mouths was how people accustomed to rule got their own way. 'Well, since I've never worked on anything by Samson before, it'll have to be a maybe,' I said with a smile.

Her own smile, genuinely warm, I thought, outshone mine. 'But you recognized it as being by Samson. That is expertise indeed.'

By now, thank goodness, we had reached the loo.

Those in my father's wing were designed for use by servants – yes, even the steward whose room Pa occupied was a hired hand, after all. And those on display to the public in the main part of the hall were kept in period and were rather Spartan curiosities. So nothing had prepared me for this palace of sanitation.

But even as I marvelled at all the gilt and the porcelain, even as I choked back laughs, the image of Paul kept floating in front of my eyes.

'I'd like to start in the dining room,' I said firmly, donning my I-am-an-Expert hat so clearly, it might almost have been visible. For some obscure reason I also produced from the new bag a notepad and pencil. My antennae had given me a good start there. With luck, I'd find out what had alerted them. And I always had that preparatory reading to help if necessary. I could do it. I must do it.

Actually, perhaps M le Fèvre had given me a pretty good clue, so I relaxed just a little. They'd had to get rid of some items and had only recently replaced them. So I needn't worry about the table or chairs, nor, as I passed them, the pier tables. But the carved giltwood mirrors – matching, over the fireplaces at either end . . . The silvering was as patchy as you'd expect. But that didn't mean a thing.

'Italian, eighteenth century,' M le Fèvre declared. 'I'm sure they are authentic. They came via a very reliable intermediary.'

And that didn't mean a thing either. I peered at the bevelling, which in old glass is pretty shallow and often unevenly cut. This looked horribly regular to me.

'Let's try the coin test,' I muttered to Griff, who was hovering close, as if aware that I was scared my instinct might wilt in such overheated surroundings.

He produced one with an approving smile. It was a long time since he'd taught me this trick, and since we never needed it in our line of work he must have been afraid I'd forgotten it.

I put the pound coin up against the glass. Old glass is thinner than Victorian, say, so the reflection should appear quite close. But not this close. Only modern glass was this thin. And now I came to look through my magnifying glass (shades of Sherlock Holmes!) I could see all the impurities were industri-ally regular. I passed the magnifying glass to Griff, who responded with a tiny nod. 'I'm afraid you're right,' he said out loud, thus forcing me to give the bad news.

'I'm sorry. The frame is lovely, but the glass . . .'

A bit of science helped all my other divvying, as did the information that M le Fèvre pretty well spat out about which pieces his trusted intermediary had sourced. A pair of commodes might have been antique in that they were made of old wood, and even the screws and nails looked original, but there was something about those dovetail joints . . . They looked so old that they suggested that someone had set out to age them.

Suddenly, I was back in Kent, at a bottom-end sale, looking at dressing cases. Big Dave was talking about modern varnish and modern glue. And then I was staring at a skip full of odds and ends of wood.

'My instinct,' I said carefully, 'is that these pieces have been put together from other items.'

'They've been cannibalized?' Morris, who'd been surpris-ingly silent, prompted me, as if in disbelief.

'It wouldn't hurt to use that word,' I said, hoping to sound wise. As I did when I worried about a table and, worst of all, a beautiful Regency desk. I was sure some of the elegant brass decoration was original. Some. But the sheer number of swags and rosettes worried me. There were simply too many mould-ings, as if someone had seized on a good idea and let it run wild. If I could strip them away, mentally if not physically, and imagine the very new-looking veneer was a loveable battered mahogany, I could see a gentleman's desk. If I put everything back again, I saw . . .

'I'm afraid this is the worst of all,' I heard myself say. 'I'd need to take it apart to show you how wrong it is. But

I'd suggest the person who negotiated the sale is the one to do that. You see, if you could restore it to the original, it would be worth – on the international market – tens of thousands of pounds.'

'One went at auction the other day for ninety thousand,' Morris agreed.

From the silence that followed I gathered that they'd paid a good deal more than that. At last, Madame broke it with a tiny cough and the sort of polite smile that takes a lot of effort when you'd rather be spitting with rage.

It seemed that afternoon tea was in order, English-style. Query: how did Madame stay so thin if she ate so many meals? She didn't look like a woman who spent hours in the gym.

Morris came and joined me while Griff charmed our hosts with stories, some possibly truthful, of his life in the theatre. 'You had me on the edge of my seat once or twice there,' he said. 'But by God you came up with the goods.'

'Maybe I can dispense with my antennae,' I said lightly, knowing that even if I tried, they wouldn't dispense with me. 'Has this been any use? Apart from upsetting a couple of perfectly nice people with more money than sense. I mean, Morris – have you seen the loo?'

'It has been my pleasure,' he said gravely, as if discussing arrangements for a funeral.

'The last thing I want,' he said, back at our hotel half an hour later as we lay on the monster bed in each other's arms, 'is to keep taking you and Griff out and making you do your act over and over again, as if you were a pair of performing bears, but the victim who's invited you to dine this evening is even bigger than the le Fèvres. You'll recognize him and his pad from TV, even if you are invited to use the unofficial entrance. And you can bet my pension that the phone lines have been trilling all over Paris with the le Fèvres' news, so you may get even more invitations and even more fees.'

'If I do, I'll ask for your guidance about which I can accept and which safely turn down,' I said. 'Because Griff's health is more important than my junketing round the city.' He was safe in his room lying down for a rest at the moment. Safe, because there happened to be a policeman lurking in the corridor.

'On the other hand, he's been like a kid at the zoo, hasn't he?'

'True. And I've not seen him reach for his spray once. But for all I said I could manage without my divvy instinct, I daren't. And I daren't try to force it. If Monsieur le Fèvre hadn't told me which pieces were replacements, I might have had egg all over my face.'

'He didn't tell you the desk was new.'

'He did. By looking at it so anxiously.'

'We'll make a detective out of you yet,' he said.

I sat up sharply. 'What about Paul?'

TWENTY-THREE

'You always want the truth, don't you?' He sighed, grasping my hand. 'Well, here it is so far. The Sussex police are on to it, as you'd expect. They've checked A and E at all the hospitals in the area. Kent, London, Hampshire – I'm sure they've done a thorough job.'

'But they've found nothing.'

'In a sense, that's good news.'

'No body, you mean?' I asked bitterly.

'So far, no. So far, so good, I'd say.'

'The man tried to warn me off. I should have given up on that bloody play as he said. And made sure Griff did too!'

He got up and poured me a glass of mineral water from an elegant and expensive-looking bottle. 'And how would you have done that? Once Griff's set on anything, it'd take a miracle to stop him.'

'I don't know – I could have confiscated his pills or something.' I gulped down the water, which was foul. 'There's something more serious, remember, Morris. Charles Montaigne knows about your daughter. He knows about Pa. He even knows about Mrs Walker and her fiancé.'

'He may know more. Those postcards of France, Lina – it wasn't me that sent them.'

'Not you? But – oh, my God!'

'Another reason I wanted you safe with me. Now, I know this sounds brutal, but I've not got much time. How do you get Charles Montaigne connected to the play? Not a man for am-dram, surely.'

'But a man for revenge. He threatened to break my fingers, for starters.'

'My God! You never told me that!'

'Well, not so much a threat as an implied threat. I told Freya Webb, and at the time she was very interested and promised to investigate further. But, apart from that visit of Wayne's I told you about, I've heard nothing, nothing at all. And she'd already warned me in no uncertain terms to keep out of her hair. Griff said that her hormones were raging. All I can say is, the rest of her was too. I've seen nothing of Robin either, or I could ask him.'

'And your theory is?'

'Overwork?'

'A hell of a lot of that, with all these cuts.'

'Or,' I added more soberly, 'trouble with the pregnancy or between her and Robin?'

'Marry in haste, repent at leisure,' he mused bitterly, speaking from experience.

I didn't want to go down that avenue; I really wanted Freya and Robin's child to be brought up in a Velcro-tight marriage. 'But we weren't talking about Freya. We were talking about people who might be at risk,' I pointed out.

'And the rationale is?'

I could have shaken him for being so dense. 'My theory is this. The unit on the industrial estate which I wasn't supposed to go anywhere near is dealing in something illegal – just what we won't discuss yet. I get warned off because I was nosing round – I wasn't looking for anything, just mooching. I might even have been trying to get a signal to call you. When the police turn up mob-handed because some stupid over-the-hill actress says someone's stolen a priceless ring, the people warning me off think I've got something to do with their arrival – hence I get another text from Paul, saying getting in the fuzz wasn't a good idea. Maybe his employers knew he was trying to get rid of me gently and thought he should have done a better job.' I sipped the horrible metallic water.

'It wasn't just Griff and me they wanted out, by the way,' I added, recounting the whole catalogue of harassment, ranging from Andrew Barnes' fright to the silly business with smoked fish. 'I still reckon they were after the planks that Griff was using as a desk top. Andrew claimed he got them out of a skip near his home; I reckon they came from a skip outside the unit where Paul works. Anyway, he had the fear of God put into him so successfully that he quit altogether. And Emilia, the woman in charge of the whole shebang, is acting dead weird. The other thing I can't work out is why they don't just burgle the place – the locks are pretty simple.'

He held up a hand to stop me and then made little rewinding gestures. 'But how does this relate to Charles Montaigne? And how to the safety of Leda and the rest of them? Montaigne wants you to work for him. You say no. He gets peeved and steps up the pressure, including references to your personal life. But what's he got to do with Paul Whatshisname?'

'I don't know,' I said. 'But I think he might just be his boss. I've seen him on the estate, though I don't think he saw me.'

He was about to say something but thought better of it.

'Meanwhile, in early September, I came across a load of wooden items at a fair – a very mixed bunch, just as if someone had been practising restoration skills . . . or otherwise. Hell, they were a mess. There's a whole lot of dodgy furniture at the antiques centre down the road from Bredeham: I think I told you that Griff's on the action committee to shut them down.'

He gave a sigh laden with exasperation. 'He'd just have be, wouldn't he? So are you saying the unit is somehow connected with the problematic items at the centre?' When I hesitated he continued, 'What was the quality of the china at the centre?'

'I didn't get a close look because we were being well and truly monitored by that time. But what if Montaigne wanted me to do a really good job on badly damaged goods he'd then pass off as genuine and undamaged?'

'I can see that Freya would think there were too many ifs, Lina, and wouldn't want to commit manpower without more to go on – particularly when every officer has to look at each paper clip twice.'

'But you've got a much closer interest in the business than she has if he knows about Leda. Come on, you cared enough to get me over here – or was that just to do my divvying?'

'I cared enough about you and, I have to admit, about my job. I'm still on secondment to Interpol, but my role, as you've gathered, has changed somewhat because the man you're going to dine with tonight has burnt his fingers on some wrong 'uns. When the topmost brass say jump, I just have to ask how high.

Monsieur and Madame le Fèvre were high-class guinea pigs. If you did the business for them, then you could be trusted to do the business for the Prime Minister.'

'The Pri— Hell's bells, I wish you hadn't told me. I can't do Prime Ministers! Not if it involves eating and drinking with them.' I looked at him. 'Your career's on the line? OK. But that doesn't mean I'm not scared shitless.'

He shook his head. 'He's actually more "ordinary" than Monsieur le Fèvre.' He inserted quotation marks with hooked finger. 'You'll be fine.'

'Without you?'

He looked nonplussed. 'Why without me?'

'Because you have to check that Leda's safe. And get Freya to check on Pa – talk to her boss, if Freya acts awkward. And someone must tell Mrs Walker she mustn't dream of opening the shop. I'll call her and Pa myself as well, but you know Mrs Walker's a born martyr and Pa – well, he's Pa.' I managed a smile. 'I don't know how long all that lot will take you, but you have to do it. And Leda's your priority. Look,' I added, urgently shaking his wrist, 'if Charles Montaigne knows so much about me, I'd guess he knows I'm over here. Join the dots.' This time I didn't attempt a smile.

My calls took only a few minutes and had me fizzing with frustration, since neither Pa nor Mrs Walker thought there was any threat to them. Let the police try to persuade them. Morris nodded, but was too involved in his own call – in French – to do more than that. I called Griff on the room phone to say I was taking a shower and I'd be over to his room for him to check my slap and the dress in half an hour.

I was covered in foam when Morris, fully dressed, but not in a DJ, put his head round the bathroom door and tried to yell over the rush of the jets. He'd seen me naked often enough, but not naked and wet with a hotel shower cap drifting over one eye. But I might have been wearing thermals buttoned to the neck for all the notice he took.

'I have to go. A car will take you: don't go down to the foyer till they ring for you. The driver works for – well, you can trust him. Raoul. I won't let you down altogether, but I will be late. I've notified the PM's private secretary.'

My eyes rounded. 'You can just tell a prime minster you'll miss the soup?'

'On this occasion, yes.' He took my steamy face between both hands and kissed me on the lips. And scooted before I could ask what was up, not turning round when I called after him. But, afraid that the situation was as serious as his face suggested, I didn't call again.

The evening was a repeat of the afternoon, only in a posher dress (a slender column of silk – think Pippa Middleton's bridesmaid's outfit) and with slightly less good champagne. The only difference was that I did my divvying act before we dined, since we were waiting for Morris. If the Top People were irritated by his non-appearance, they were far too polite to show it, and I did my best not to reveal my screaming anxiety. Griff repeated his charming anecdotes, and I picked out a really obvious fake escritoire, so bad that the PM's wife said she was ashamed not to have seen the problems herself.

At this point four other couples arrived, all dressed to the nines. More canapés and more champagne. A terribly camp young man materialized and fawned over Griff. Still no Morris; with no more not-exactly-party-tricks to fall back on – and I certainly didn't want publicly to pull modern rabbits out of antique hats – I felt completely at sea. Fingering the Cartier watch Pa had given me, I thought briefly of Pa's mother: presumably, she'd had hours of training to prepare her for occasions like this.

I hadn't.

Just as it was clear our hostess thought the food couldn't be kept warm any longer, Morris appeared, so sexy in his black tie that I was hard put not to grab him by the hand and drag him off to some official bedroom. Or I would have been, if his face, when not stretched in official smiles, hadn't been stressed enough to crack.

Considering it was a very formal meal, we rattled through the courses as if we were in an overbooked restaurant with someone waiting for our table. This suited me, because I could see that, despite his gaiety, Griff was fading. I'd also noticed Morris shooting swift glances at his watch. On the other hand, I couldn't imagine getting a chance to wear a dress like this again, so half of me was disappointed that Morris and I weren't going to go on to somewhere special later. A pretty large half, to be honest.

But it was something that Morris joined us in the car back to our hotel. Something, but not a lot, because all he had time for was to change into jeans and a sweater – he was off out again.

'Leda?' I prompted as he gave up wrestling with his cufflinks and held his arms out for me to deal with them.

'Safe. But under threat, I'm sure. Despite what I said about having a regular, full-time nanny, Penny and her bloody horn player insisted on relying on an agency – some crap about not wanting Leda to get too fond of a stranger. This afternoon the agency phones to say the usual women aren't available, but they've just signed a new recruit – would they like to try her? Wonderful references, blah, blah. They're just off to work when I call – thanks to you. And they panic – thank God – and contact the agency. The agency says they've had a call from Penny to cancel the nanny's booking.'

'My God!'

'But of course Penny is booked for a concert, so whatever her maternal feelings,' he said dryly, 'she's unable to stay behind. Guess what, there's a horn solo scheduled too. So I dashed off to stay with Leda until the real nanny turned up. She took her out – my insistence – to some friends of Penny's, with a plain-clothes officer for company. I also organized a reception committee for the new "nanny" at their apartment. They've picked someone up. I'm not allowed to participate in any way in the interview, of course, but the authorities have cleared it for me to watch.'

'Having dinner with the PM might have helped with that? Oh, hold still just one more second!' At last I released him.

Horribly alone in the huge room, I called Griff to see if he was up for a late-night drinking chocolate. He insisted he was, but I could tell he'd been asleep until the phone had woken him. I think he fell asleep again even while he was claiming to be wide awake.

Somehow I couldn't face trying to sort out enough French to organize room service for myself. It was only as I managed to wriggle out of the dress that I realized they'd probably have understood English, Croatian or even Outer Mongolian in a place like this. By now I couldn't be bothered. Perhaps when Morris got back, though probably a stiff whisky would have been more his thing.

But I didn't find out, because when I woke the next morning I was still the only person in my bed. And not even Tim the Bear for company.

Griff and I were just finishing our highly calorific breakfast in Griff's room when there was a tap at the door. I peeped through the spyhole to see Morris winking back at me.

'It's like trying to unravel spaghetti,' he declared, heading straight for the coffee pot.

I washed out my cup.

Griff poured. 'So you spent the night watching other people ask questions,' he prompted. 'And to judge by your appearance, that must be almost as tiring as doing the interrogation yourself. Did you not sleep at all?'

'Not yet. I shall snatch forty winks when I've finished your breakfast for you and then get back.'

'And the news is?' Griff asked.

'Thanks to the information you've provided about the fake furniture, one way or another there's a lovely big case building against some people I've had on the radar for some time.'

'First things first,' Griff protested. 'The threat to your daughter's safety?'

'The heavies that turned up at Penny's apartment claim they've no idea who employed them – that it was a cash in an envelope on a street corner sort of contract. The person who called the nanny-agency predictably withheld her number. However, given the seriousness of the situation, the police and mobile phone company are using a system called triangulation which establishes at least where the phone was when it was used.'

'But you could shove it in your pocket and nip down into the Metro and travel heaven knows where,' Griff objected.

'Heaven might not have its eye on everything, but there must be CCTV cameras everywhere in a city this size,' I said.

'Actually, not as many as in London, which I read somewhere is the CCTV capital of the world,' Morris said. 'Anyway, some poor minion has the job of checking all available footage for known villains.'

'Assuming it was the said known villain that made the calls,' I said. 'Could be another cash contract job.'

'It could be,' Morris agreed, lifting a silver lid to see what the salver underneath might hold. 'Hmmm. I love pain au chocolat. Shall I order some more?'

Griff laughed. 'If you think Lina will let me eat such delights, you don't know her was well as I think you do. They're yours for the taking.'

'Until the great god Type Two Diabetes gets you too,' I said, not quite joking. At what age should you start worrying about such things? I'd read somewhere when I was checking up on Griff that stress as well as diet might be a factor, and Morris had enough of that for two in his life. Perhaps breakfast wasn't the best time to nag a man who'd not slept.

'I don't suppose you recall the name of the stall selling dodgy wooden boxes, do you? At Hythe?' he prompted.

'We do so many fairs,' Griff murmured.

'And that one was really only memorable for the way Emilia seduced Griff,' I said. My eyes rounding, I added, 'As I was saying yesterday, she's been very weird recently – you don't suppose she's in cahoots with Montaigne and his merry men?'

Morris grimaced. 'Connection?'

I sighed. 'None except the location of the oast, spitting distance from the unit where Paul works.' I used the present tense on purpose. There was nothing on the photo to suggest he was dead, if not a lot to show he was alive.

'If there is one –' he yawned – 'we'll find one. In fact, if you've got her address, Griff, I'll get the police to talk to her. And check the unit, if they've not already done so when they were looking for Paul, of whom there is still no news, as far as I know. If I were him, I'd have gone to earth and would plan to spend a long time with my head down, licking my wounds. Assuming that's physiologically possible,' he added, raising his hand in apology when he realized I didn't appreciate his so-called joke. Quickly changing the subject, he continued, 'As for the *soi-disant* Monsieur Montaigne, the French police are after him as we speak. They should have him in their hands by tomorrow morning.'

'I'm not so sure about that nasty little word *should*. He's over here, is he?'

'We believe so.'

'Oh, stop sounding like a policeman,' I said, suddenly tetchy. 'Is he or isn't he? I don't want him leaping out of the unit the moment Griff and I turn up for Sunday's rehearsal.'

'Neither do I, believe me. In fact, I'll get the Sussex police to check that he isn't. I'm sure I've mentioned it – had them look for blood there – but you can't be too sure. I suppose,' he added casually – or not, 'that you still don't remember the name of the stallholder at Hythe?' He smiled apologetically. 'Coming at it again sometimes works. No?'

I pressed my fingers to my temples. I'd have given my eye teeth to have made his trick work. But at last I had to say, flatly, 'No. But the hotel should have the name of the organizers,' I added. 'As for Montaigne, I gave Freya details of his mobile phone, even his car reg numbers. Why reinvent the wheel? Just talk to Freya. She surely can't tell you to mind your own business.'

'I wouldn't put anything past Freya, especially a pregnant Freya.'

'She was going to get Trading Standards to check out the provenance of the stuff on sale at the antiques centre – they might have thrown up something useful too. Hell, Morris, why do I get the feeling this is a totally fragmented investigation?'

'Because it is. Budget cuts.'

'But a bit of – what do they call it? – joined up thinking would pull everything together.'

'Look, they cut resources, they retire canny old senior officers – and that's just the police. Local government's on its knees, so I dare say our equivalents in Trading Standards are gasping for breath too.' As if to demonstrate, he gave a huge yawn. 'It's no good: I've got to hit the hay.' He literally staggered as he left the room. He held on to the door jamb as he paused to say, 'I've worked out a possible timetable for you today, Lina – with luck I'll touch base with you for lunch.'

By the time I let myself into our room, he was sprawled across the bed, fast asleep, and didn't even stir as I made myself ready for the punishing schedule he'd prepared.

TWENTY-FOUR

The more I saw of the French elite in their wonderful houses, surrounded by antiques to make your mouth water, the more I understood the French Revolution. I've an idea that Griff, normally keen on a bit of aristocracy, at least when it came on TV in the form of Royal Weddings, was beginning to feel a bit republican himself. One consolation was that we were safe from Montaigne while we hurtled from one great house to the next to do our party pieces: the car had been changed for one with serious security, protected for good measure by seriously armed cops.

There was no sign of Morris during these jaunts, and he texted that he had to scrub any thought of lunch. Eventually, he texted me to say he'd meet us for room service dinner at the hotel no matter what.

The no matter what involved Leda. It seemed she was going to have a cot put up in our room. She looked very peaky and had a snotty nose, so I didn't argue. In the event, she refused to eat the baby meal brought up early for her and took ages to settle in the cot the hotel found. The three of us ate our own supper in silence lest we disturb her. Griff tiptoed furtively out, wishing us well in a stage whisper. We retreated swiftly to bed, only to have a call to Morris's mobile wake her. She refused point-blank to return to the cot and eventually spent the night lying between us, only stirring when Morris and I decided to try to take advantage of the huge sofa at the far end of the room. Something – probably to do with the genes Pa had wished on me – told me that parenthood was decidedly overrated. Not, of course, that it was even certain that Morris was a parent: Penny and her new partner were still agitating for a DNA test. In their shoes I'd just have gone ahead and got one – not very hard to do, after all – but perhaps they were afraid that it would confirm that Morris really was Leda's father. As for me, nocturnal activities apart, I quite liked her, but someone had really let her table manners go to pot, and her breakfast, in the form of croissant and apricot conserve, turned out to be a really tricky thing to get out of a designer suit.

Just as I was afraid that Griff, who'd joined us in our room, was going to explode, the regular nanny arrived, accompanied by a really sweet-looking policewoman with a nifty little gun, and Leda was taken off to nursery. If it hadn't been so early, I swear we'd have reached for a bottle.

I waited for the waiters (yes, plural) to finish clearing the debris before turning to Morris. 'Now what? This divvying business is all very well, but surely you and your colleagues have got more than enough evidence by now. It's time to get back to normal – ordinary pots, ordinary clothes, ordinary food.'

'She's worried about the amount of cholesterol I'm packing in,' Griff said.

'Aren't you?' I asked sharply.

'Sweet one, if they're spending all this time hunting round my cardiovascular system, I'm sure two or three days' indulgence in *haute cuisine* isn't going to make much difference.'

Morris took my hand. 'So are you worrying about wearing out your gift?'

'To be honest, I've been doing what any other dealer would do – looking for clues. So I don't feel entirely honest.'

'Nonsense. I didn't mention your divvying at any point, just your expertise.'

'Including my restoration work? Madame le Fèvre said you'd told her not to take no for an answer.'

'And did you believe her?'

I couldn't resist when his eyes twinkled like that. 'I thought she was trying to con me, like Pa does. Seriously, I'd have a shot at repairing her damaged urn, but it'd mean bringing all my gear over here and staying until it was finished. Not as their house guest, either.'

'I'm sure you'd be more than welcome, both of you.'

'People like her would never understand that some days I could only work a couple of hours and would then have to wait while glue hardened or paint dried. Or if she did, she'd keep finding other things that needed my attention, but would expect them done as part of the original deal. So I'd insist on being a free agent.' My smile added, *with you*. But my smile didn't last long. There was Griff's operation to factor in.

Griff's operation? I bit my lip. Was that another bit of divvying or a bit of observation? Whatever it was, I wanted him back home near the hospital, not dancing attendance on the whims of other people. But to reassure myself as much as anything, I added, 'And I can't even consider coming over till after the play. I may not be the star, but Griff is, and I'm not going to do anything to interfere with that. So they've got my time until the train we've got tickets for on Saturday.' Assuming it's safe to go home then, another voice added in my head.

Griff shook his head sadly. 'It seems so sad for my poor angel to come all this way, to the most romantic city in the world, and see nothing of it. It's at its best in the spring, of course, but the quality of the light in the autumn is unsurpassed.'

Morris's face told me all I needed to know. He'd got to work. Which meant I might as well, I reached for the day's work list.

The only interruption to our toil – it had long ceased to be a pleasure – was a text to Griff from the hospital. They'd had a cancellation and wanted to admit him for his next test at seven thirty on Monday morning.

'Say yes,' I said. 'Don't even think of arguing.'

I stood over him while he phoned to reply and take instructions I made him jot down. Empty stomach – check; an overnight case just in case – in case of what? – check; someone to drive him there and collect him – check; bed rest for the remainder of the day.

I also picked up something else – a word I couldn't place. 'Angiogram?' I said, as soon as the call was over.

'It's a look at the heart from the inside,' he said blithely. 'A tiny camera they insert via the groin. Just routine.'

'Just routine my arse,' I said, relying on our host not to speak that sort of English.

'Oh, it is,' Griff insisted. 'They do dozens a week.'

'But not to you,' I said, but not out loud.

Dear Griff pretended to be too exhausted to have supper with Morris and me on our last evening, sending us off together with an instruction to enjoy ourselves and not talk too much shop.

'I still think you'd be safer here,' Morris said as we slipped out of the hotel the unofficial way and walked hand in hand like a pair of ordinary lovers.

'Have there been any problems for Pa or Mrs Walker?' I asked.

'None so far. But local officers will keep an eye on them.'

'Oh, that's reassuring,' I jeered. 'One community support officer on a bike every three days. That'd really scare me if I was going to harm them, I don't think.'

'I didn't ask for the cuts,' he said.

'Of course you didn't,' I agreed, realizing too late I was likely to ruin our precious time together. 'What about protecting Griff and me?'

'That's different. But I'd like you to go back on Sunday, rather than tomorrow – hang the rehearsal. Just hunker down in a hotel in Ashford, next to the hospital, if necessary.'

I squeezed his hand. 'We'll both have to work on Griff,' I said.

He drew us to a halt by a place I'd never have noticed. 'Only locals know about this place – guaranteed no tourists. The only downside is that the waiters will correct my pronunciation.'

My stomach clenched. 'You've eaten here before then?' Perhaps because of Paul's kiss, I had visions of him with an endless chain of glamorous women colleagues. Or with Penny.

'Only with my colleagues to check it out. I didn't want to land us with a turkey, as it were. And the champagne should already be on ice.'

We'd got to the coffee stage before his phone rang. I shrugged and smiled. To my surprise, however, he slipped outside to take the call.

I sipped slowly. Dead slowly. But then I had nothing left to drink, and my French wasn't up to asking for more. Waiters came and went, with bigger shrugs than mine.

Just as I was fishing out my credit card and hoping I could find my way back to the hotel, he reappeared, soaked to the skin.

'It's started to rain,' he said, unnecessarily.

'But?' I asked, prompted by the twitching of his lips and a glow he couldn't quite suppress.

'We've got your old friend.'

For a dreadful moment I thought he meant Titus Oates. I knew Freya was after him, but surely he wasn't on Interpol's radar.

'The *soi-disant* Charles Montaigne.'

'Ah. Wow. But before you say anything else, tell me what you meant by the words you said before "Charles Montaigne". It's the second time you've used them and—'

'I'm sorry. It's the French equivalent of so-called. Now can you cheer?'

I looked around furtively. 'Would it be allowed in here? Actually, if it wasn't so tiny, I could leap in the air and do handsprings! Does this mean we're safe?'

'Let's call for the bill, and I'll tell you all about it on the way back to the hotel.'

'That means you won't be coming into the hotel.'

'Only to pack my bag to go back to England. This is one interview I really do want to be in on, Lina.'

'Isn't it against his human rights to be interviewed in the middle of the night?'

It seemed it wasn't. As we huddled under his umbrella, dodging puddles, he told me that thanks to information received – would I ever get used to his slipping police jargon into our conversations like that? – the so-called Montaigne had been picked up at Folkestone, trying to buy a ticket for France. 'Silly sod didn't realize that his car reg would be checked – and found to be false.'

'Hang on – Freya knew it was. She was going to check it out.' What the hell had she been up to?

'Maybe he'd got more than one. Anyway, he's being held in Kent, on suspicion of all sorts of fraudulent activities.'

'Only fraud? A clever lawyer'll make sure he gets bail.'

'Uttering threats – that's against you, of course. I'd like to pin the assault on your mate Paul on him too. I'm going back on the first Eurostar I can get – so if he's lucky, your poor Monsieur Montaigne will get a night's kip. Even if I don't. That's the downside. The upside is that you and Griff should be able to come back on the train you planned and resume your calm and peaceful lives in the tranquillity of the Kentish countryside,' he added ironically.

'And Griff gets to go to the rehearsal, and I get to take him to hospital on Monday. Phew.'

'I'd have made sure of that, even if he'd gone with a police escort,' he said, squeezing my hand. 'The only thing that surprises me is that his partner didn't cough up for immediate private treatment.'

'Aidan? I'm sure he would have done, and with great pleasure – but Griff's not giving him the whole story, any more than he is me. I can see why. Aidan's in New Zealand, for heaven's sake, waiting for his sister to die.'

'Given a choice between a sister dying and a lover needing support, I know where I'd be.' He kissed me.

But what about the choice between a daughter screaming for attention and his lover needing support? I wasn't at all sure about that. So I changed the subject with a great crunch. 'You'll go easy on Paul Whatshisname when you catch up with him, won't you? He tried to warn me off – even to protect me. And look where that got him.'

I'd pressed a policeman button again. 'I'd really like to run him to earth. I don't like it when people get beaten up and then disappear. Though if I'd been him I'd have scarpered, believe me. Now, are we going to talk shop all night or are we going to make the most of the next hour?'

TWENTY-FIVE

Our cottage was still in one piece, and so were we. We quickly fell into the routine we used every time we'd been away for a fair or sale, to enable us to resume normal life as quickly as possible. There were differences, of course: hanging up the French clothes took longer than shoving T-shirts into the washing machine. Plus, instead of our usual slouch on the sofa with a sandwich, we had Morris staying with us overnight, so Griff was getting in a tizzy about feeding him properly. And tizzies were definitely off Griff's menu.

'There's enough for an army in the freezer, Griff,' I said sharply.

'Of course. I keep forgetting he's practically family.'

It was my job to check our emails and to prepare invoices for all our French clients, with the exception, it seemed, of the prime minister. The amount I was to charge seemed eye-watering, but Morris had assured me that other dealers charged far more. I wasn't exactly bargain basement either, however, and worked out that even in euros I could probably have paid for Griff's treatment without bothering Aidan. What if I'd got anything wrong? What if I'd conned the French Prime Minster? It was his government that had forked out for our travel and accommodation, after all.

Tim the Bear pointed out that someone like Harvey Sanditon wouldn't have turned a hair at demanding such fees, and he wasn't as good as I was. But Tim was as worried as I was by the price of the clothes I'd hardly worn and was tempted to nod when I whispered the words *dress exchange* or *eBay*. I was also worried that Griff had paid for everything on his personal card. I must make sure I paid him back.

Tim the Bear couldn't shake his head, but he gave me a hard stare. Griff would be not just offended but really hurt if I wasn't careful. I'd have to raise the subject very tactfully. And actually, Tim the Bear said, wasn't all this talk of money the sort of middle-class thing my father would deplore? At this point I cuffed him and put him back on the bed while I phoned both Pa and Mrs Walker with the news of Montaigne's arrest.

It was clear from Morris's face and his general behaviour that there was some problem, but he insisted he was just bone tired; given the amount of sleep he'd had over the last few days, I could scarcely argue, but I sensed a much deeper issue than that. However, cross-questioning was the last thing he wanted, and when Griff declared that he for one needed an early night, Morris announced that he wasn't the only one. He did no more than look askance at Tim before rolling over and falling asleep. Tim looked askance back but didn't say anything either. Neither did Tim snore.

If we'd been up in time, we might just have made it to one of the services Robin would be conducting. But both Morris and Griff were sleeping the sleep of the just, so I slipped out on my own to the local church. I always suspected that prayers counted more in a church and I wanted to make sure Griff got all the protection he could over the next few days. He might be making light of everything, and I might be going along with him, but I was as scared as it was possible to be.

Our vicar, peering earnestly into my face as he shook hands afterwards in the porch, asked if he could help: it was only the queue of parishioners behind me that stopped me bursting into tears. I managed to say that Griff wasn't as well as he could be before I gulped to a standstill.

'I'll add him to my prayer list,' the vicar promised quietly.

At least Griff had an expert on his side. I popped into the shop and bought our Sunday papers with a slightly lighter heart.

Griff had a different expert with him when we set out for the oast house and the afternoon's rehearsal. Morris, saying he was sick of the news and entitled to a day off anyway, had decided to come with us. Griff tucked himself into the back, his script on his lap, just in case he'd forgotten anything since Tuesday. Morris managed not to criticize my driving too heavily, though he did remind me that before he'd found his

niche in fine arts, he'd taken police courses in pursuit and
protection driving.

'So if we need to make a quick getaway, I hand over the
keys to you.'

'Exactly. Do you always leave it so late to signal?'

'Only if I'm talking to you.'

We were the first to arrive. There was police tape round
the unit where Paul worked, but no officers around – at least,
none that I could see. Since we had no key, I parked up and
waited. We were soon joined by Emilia, who abandoned rather
than parked her Merc. She got out awkwardly and staggered
to the door, fumbling in her bag for the key, which she had
difficulty in inserting into the lock.

'It's to be hoped, Morris,' Griff said, 'that you don't carry
a breathalysing kit.'

'If she's as pissed as she looked,' he replied grimly as Emilia
disappeared inside, 'I bet I'll know a man who does.'

At this point the scream started. It went on and on. Morris
and I were out of the car, but he turned to point to Griff.
'Stay!' he yelled, as if Griff was a stubborn mongrel. I didn't
have time to register Griff's reaction, but zapped the lock
anyway. Just the once, to lock the door. I didn't want the alarm
joining the still terrifying scream.

I wanted to say, 'Just another practical joke – don't worry.'
But the words stuck in my throat at the sight and sound of
the flies. And the smell.

'Get her away from here,' Morris yelled, grabbing Emilia
and literally hurling her out of his way; as much as anything
else, it stopped me following him.

She staggered and fell into my arms. And then slithered
out of them and started twitching. I'd not seen anyone having
a fit since I was a kid. All I knew was you were supposed to
turn them on their side and stop them choking on their tongue.
I unzapped Griff: he might know what to do. In fact, he was
already busy – he'd got his mobile out and was thrusting it
at me.

'No signal! Run till you find one. Ambulance, of course.'

I ran. And dialled as I ran, even remembering the map
references to get them there more quickly.

There. The ambulance was on its way. Sorted. But it wasn't.
I wasn't the only one on the estate. When the police had picked
up Montaigne, they'd missed some of what I were sure were
his mates, the heavies that had yelled at Paul. And they'd
spotted me. There wasn't time to call Morris. Still clutching
the mobile, and pressing the redial button, I asked for police.
Got them. Told them where I was. Coordinates again. But it'd
take them ages to get here. So I pretended I still thought I
was on my own and crouched down as if I was throwing up
or having a wee – whatever. The mobile – thank God Griff
favoured a sleek dinky little job – went in the place some of
my old mates had used when they needed to smuggle something to their boyfriends in the nick. Since I'd left it switched
on, it would give the police a signal wherever I fetched up.

Now wearing scarves across their faces, the heavies were on
to me. I managed a couple of really good screams, enough to
make Morris and Griff look my way, before a hand clamped
my mouth. It was too big to bite, but smelt amazingly of
lavender soap.

Morris was running towards me but stopped in his tracks.
I felt something cold and hard against my temple, so I gathered
they had a gun and I was the target if anyone did anything
daft. Me included, of course.

The only way I could stay sensible was to think as if I was
Morris. He'd got at least one sick person on his hands. With
his heart, Griff might make Patient Two. And rushing a man
with a firearm from a hundred yards away wasn't a great idea
either. He'd be on the phone. Or – I saw him drop to his knees
– was he doing CPR? If only I could see on whom.

By this time I knew I wasn't going to see anything more.
I was in the back of a predictable white van. At least, as they
duct-taped my hands, feet and mouth, I managed to get in a
couple of serious bites, earning kicks for my pains. I told
myself the bruises would heal. With luck the bites would leave
scars a dental expert could match to my teeth if I was no
longer around to identify my kidnappers.

Strange, I thought as I looked at the things I shared the van
with, that I could think quite coolly about my own death, but
not about Griff's.

But positive thinking would be better all round. I was giving the police all the help I could, after all. And Morris would make sure they pulled out every stop going, so long as such things like violent abduction weren't in the hands of someone as uncommunicative as Freya. So I stared at the ropes and spare tyre and toolboxes, big metal jobs, nothing like the plastic one I stored some of my tools in, as if I was playing a game that Griff used to play: he'd put a load of items on a tray, give me a few moments to memorize them, cover them – and then ask me what I'd seen. So I made myself register them, and then turn my attention to smells – glue and wood.

Evidence, of course. But what if Montaigne told his gorillas to get rid of all the evidence – including me – by driving to some isolated spot and torching the lot? I would in his situation. But I rather thought he was the sort of man to enjoy playing cat and mouse. He'd torture me a bit first – probably break my fingers, as he'd once threatened. If I knew him, he'd do it himself, assuming he was around.

Don't be silly, I told myself. He's in custody, being questioned.

Only fraud. He'll easily get bail.

Not if he's defrauded a prime minister, for goodness' sake.

What if the gorillas are acting on their own initiative? Where does that leave me?

We'd been on the move about ten minutes, I thought. After a dreadful jolting on the industrial estate roads, we were now on something much smoother and going pretty briskly. So which road would that be? Now would have been just the moment for the bloody satnav. Some hope. They weren't going all that fast – I could hear vehicles overtaking us on the right, not the left. Presumably, they didn't want to attract anyone's attention by speeding. Then there was a huge swerve that almost tipped the van. I told myself someone had tried to block their path. The police? Let it be the police, please. But it could easily have been someone on a bike or just a Sunday driver.

Now we were bucketing along. A look at all the loose stuff already battering me told me that a crash at this speed could hurt a lot. There were things that might fall on my head, things I might hurtle into. I tried to get into a hedgehog ball, but it was impossible to stay balanced with my hands behind my back. In any case, that sort of position didn't do much for hedgehog survival on the roads, did it?

The van swung right and ricocheted off something metallic. I dreamed of stingers and proper road blocks, maybe even a helicopter – but then I recalled reading something about airborne crime-fighting being off the menu because of the cuts. Just a rumour, I hoped. If the French thought I deserved a bulletproof car (OK, it was probably just a prime ministerial spare), surely Kent and Sussex between them could manage something.

A huge lurch to the left threw me into one of the metal toolboxes. I bounced; it didn't. A few more bruises, I told myself, that's all. Actually, I wasn't so sure. Knees have a lot of bones near the surface, not to mention nice vulnerable cartilage. What if I had to use a crutch? What use would I be to Griff after his operation?

This road was much bumpier, and there was no sound of traffic. None at all.

Hell, we weren't on some private estate, were we? The South-East's got plenty of those, not all owned by decent upright guys – and I'm not just thinking of Pa and his low-key forging activities.

That was a cattle grid, surely. And then we started to bounce across potholes. I spat out all the rude words Griff wouldn't let me use before seven in the evening. They'd never trace me here – not if coverage was as bad as it was in lots of rural Kent.

This was stupid. I should be planning what to do next. I should be trying to saw through the duct tape on my wrists using the sharp edges of the damned toolbox. I should be—

We must have hit another extra-deep pothole. Because I heard something slithering, sensed movement towards me and all these bright lights came rushing towards me. There must have been one moment of consciousness left, because I wondered if these were the lights that meant I was dying and going to heaven.

TWENTY-SIX

Maybe St Peter didn't like the look of me, or maybe the blow wasn't as hard as it could have been. In any other situation I'd have groaned and stretched a bit, and then quipped about no sense and no feeling. However, since the van had stopped and I heard footsteps approaching the doors, I lay doggo. I'd like to say I planned to leap up and run, but the duct tape stopped any thoughts of that. The more I knew about their activities the better, and if they thought I was spark out then they'd speak more freely. I had an idea that if you were unconscious, your body was floppy, so I concentrated on relaxing as deeply as I could in the circumstances – which were not exactly a yoga mat in a scented room.

'What the hell have you done to her?' I didn't know the voice. If – big if – I'd hoped to confront Montaigne, it wasn't going to be now.

But whoever the guy was, he was talking about what to do with me.

It would have been nice to chip in with one or two suggestions, but I was beaten to it. There was a helicopter overhead. It was hard not to sigh with relief. The police had arrived. Or had they? I couldn't imagine a man like Montaigne, almost certainly with access to the sort of fancy lawyers to get him immediate bail, wouldn't have his own rapid transport, or at least access to someone else's.

By now it was so close that I could hardly think for the noise, funnelled towards me by the open van doors. There was yelling, but I couldn't hear what or from whom.

What I did smell was petrol – felt it too as it sloshed over me. My God, they were going to do what I'd been afraid of; they were about to torch the van and me with it. And I couldn't move – not because it was unwise, but because I was still taped up. I couldn't even yell, of course. Dare I risk a wiggle, to show that I was coming to? Would that make them more or less likely to roast me alive?

The chopper sound got less. And less. The newcomer and the heavies must still be there, but I couldn't hear them. Ah, muttering. I strained my ears.

A mobile rang. Please God it wasn't the one I'd hidden. That was one secret I certainly didn't want given away.

No. It must be one of the heavies'.

'Fuck off,' he said. No, it was the newcomer.

It rang again. 'Just fuck off and tell the boss I'm handling it.' He must have cut the call and turned to talk to the gorillas. I could hear muttering. They sounded less keen on the fire option than he did.

At last I picked out a voice. 'It's one thing killing one of the filth, but she's only a bit of a kid.'

One of the filth? Please don't let it be Morris! Not when he told them to leave me alone. It couldn't be. I'd have heard the shot. Wouldn't I? So who was it? One thing: if a police officer is killed, all the stops are pulled out.

Meanwhile, there was a rumble of what sounded like agreement. So both heavies were more soft-hearted than the newcomer.

Another phone call. Please let him agree to hand me over. Please. But it wasn't the police after all.

'I'm in a bit of a spot. We've got a passenger we don't want. No. Not yet. The boss's lawyer says she could be useful.' He didn't specify how, but useful sounded like a vague promise of a future, after all. And I wanted a future. Someone had to look after Griff. And Pa. But having a future involved getting rid of the petrol. No one would want me anywhere near a spark the way I was. Me especially. Maybe it was time to regain consciousness and persuade him that it'd be better not to kill me, which his heavies would agree with. I could do innocent waif easily enough.

A bit of a twitch, bit of a moan. The moan was genuine – my God, that leg hurt. And my head, come to think of it. I tried to push myself upright, but failed, very convincingly, for the simple reason I couldn't actually manage.

'Now what?' asked a heavy.

I didn't hear an answer, but I was lifted out, fairly gently, and dumped on grass. I saw them backing away. Well, I was pretty much a fire bomb, primed and only needing a careless fag to finish me off. Maybe not too many naked flames in the middle of what seemed to be parkland, however. I closed my eyes as if drifting off again. It was either that or try screaming for non-existent help through a taped mouth.

'Sand? That's what they use for petrol spills at a filling station,' the other heavy muttered.

'And where are we going to find sand? If he hadn't been so fucking gung-ho, we wouldn't be worrying about sand.'

The newcomer – a man with a fashionable shaven head – said, 'Strip her off. It should evaporate off her skin.'

'We need to wash it off, too – remember young Dean. He got a bad rash messing with petrol – couldn't work for months – and that wouldn't please his bloody nibs.'

'The grass is pretty wet – we could roll her on that. And maybe if the rain comes on harder . . . Look, just cut the bloody trousers off. If you cut the tape round her legs she'll scarper.'

Not with this knee, I couldn't. Bugger that, Lina, I told myself – you'll bloody run if you have a chance. On the other hand, what about their guns? Shooting someone in the back might be easier than burning them alive. Less smelly, too.

Time to remind them I was human. A few whiny, grunty noises.

Despite his boss, Heavy One pulled the tape from my mouth. And then my wrists and ankles.

'Strip,' Shaven Head said, encouraging me with a gun.

'But—' Heavy Two began. They weren't very good at this, were they? It was as if their main job was something else, and they'd suddenly found their job-descriptions had been enlarged.

'OK, I'll do it myself,' I gasped. 'But put the gun away. Or we'll all go up.' I liked the way I'd said *we*. I'd read some-where that victims should remind their assailants they were all human. Or was that kidnappers? 'Like a suicide bomber,' I added, trying to stand but failing, with a mixture of dizziness and pain. 'But . . . I mean, would you watch your daughters

do this?' I unbuttoned my jacket, managing to swivel away
on my bum. Over my shoulder I asked, 'Can't I borrow a
sweater or something? Overalls?' Then I remembered two
problems. First, as they said, I wanted to wash off as much
of this as I could, so bugger modesty for a bit. Second, when
they did strip searches at prisons, my mates had told me, they
made you squat, so whatever you'd hidden dropped out. And I
really did not want them to know about that phone.

I was down to my bra and pants. And dithering with cold
and fear, while I used every drop of rain that landed on me
to sluice away the petrol. One of them dug in the van and
produced a couple of Buxton water, half empty. Sheepishly,
and looking anywhere but at me, he handed them over.

Shaven Head's phone rang. 'You're joking,' he told the
caller. 'No, we'd have seen them. I tell you, I'm handling this,'
he added.

Them? Could the cavalry at last have got its act together?
But where on earth were they? Pretending to be trees, like in
what Griff insisted must only be referred to as the Scottish
Play? Or were they relying on clever things like guns with
telescopic sights?

Shaven Head hunched over the phone, turning so none of
us could hear. Us? I had an idea the heavies were as keen as
I was to go home. I turned to Heavy One – he had a knobbly
face, the sort you see in World War I photos of working-class
lads turned soldiers and shoved out into the trenches, and was
holding out his sweatshirt. On me it was long enough to be
an almost decent mini. I pulled it on with a grin of thanks.

'I need a wee,' I called, gesturing to a small bush twenty
yards away the bush.

I limped away, just a few paces. And then a few paces more.
Still Shaven Head talked.

'Could you just—? You know?' I suggested.

As embarrassed as I was, they turned away. I managed a
stiff, awkward squat. Within a second, the phone was out –
yes, it was still on, the call still open – and in the huge sleeve.
And then, since I'd not exactly been lying, I used the bush
anyway.

Given half a chance, I'd have spoken into the phone, but

Shaven Head wasn't pleased at his underlings' kindness. To spare them a further bollocking, I hobbled slowly back towards them. Hell, I wasn't getting that syndrome you got when you became fond of your kidnappers, was I?

Here we were, grouped loosely around the van. No one seemed to know what to do next.

'I don't suppose you've got a first-aid box, have you? I really ought to strap this knee before it seizes up altogether.'

Heavy Two burrowed in the cab.

I turned to Shaven Head, stroking my chin with the hand nearest the mobile. 'There's no need for Montaigne to do this to me, you know.'

'You might tell him that when you see him,' Shaven Head said.

'I will. And I'll tell him I really didn't like it when he tried to kidnap that little girl.'

The heavies emerged, one carrying a first-aid box. 'What's that about a little girl?'

'None of your business.'

'My boyfriend's baby daughter,' I said at the same time. 'Trying to kidnap her really wasn't necessary.'

I shut up. Shaven Head was looking at a point over my shoulder. His eyes rounded. I turned too. Out there, strolling towards us, was none other than Montaigne. What the hell was he doing roaming round Kent when he should surely have been in custody? Bloody clever lawyers! I almost snorted with rage, feeling in my attitude to criminals horribly like Disgusted of Tunbridge Wells. However, I didn't. It'd be nice to know exactly what Montaigne had in mind for me before he inflicted whatever it was. Or maybe it wouldn't. After all, he was carrying a gun. He raised it, aimed and fired at the van.

Talk about making a statement.

We all backed away, the heavies grabbing me, one on either side, seemingly to detain me, but actually helping me move faster.

'Get her to the house,' Montaigne said.

'The house?' I squeaked, still hoping there was someone in the police control room listening. Surely, they couldn't wait

much longer before trying to rescue me? 'I thought we were
in some park.'

'Never stops talking, this one doesn't,' Shaven Head
muttered. 'You heard the boss. Get her moving,' he added
anxiously. When that van went up, it could still take all of us.
I knew nothing about the explosive powers of diesel, but the
petrol they'd sloshed was going nicely, and all those tools
would make neat little missiles.

We moved. And found, just over the brow of the nearest
hill, a couple of what looked like golf buggies. I was to share
with Montaigne and Heavy Two.

'Ooh, I've never played golf,' I told Griff's mobile. Please,
please come soon. Any moment now I'd run out of silly things
to say. Or they'd tape my mouth again.

We all piled in. Given the circumstance, you'd have expected
pace, urgency. But, of course, the little procession was incredibly
sedate, even when the explosion we'd all been waiting for shook
the skies. All the birds that had been quietly minding their own
business rocketed into the air, yelling much as I wanted to yell.
Then, as the house, a pretty Georgian gentleman's residence,
came into sight, I wanted to coo aloud with pleasure. Why not?
Another bit of assistance for the silent listener. I hoped.

'What a gorgeous house. Eighteen hundreds?' I asked.

'You know too damned much,' Montaigne said.

I shut up and looked at the house. At least, unlike the parkland, it would provide plenty of cover for the police, should
they need it. Not the house itself, with its plain, elegant lines,
but the outbuildings.

'So where's the pot you want me to glue?' I asked.

'You'd have saved us all a great deal of trouble if you'd
asked that before,' he said bitterly. 'But then you had to go
poking your nose into matters that didn't concern you.'

'Business.' I shrugged, scratching my ear now. 'I just made
a business decision when you set up that antiques centre on
our turf. You seemed to take it personally.' I wittered on, saying
whatever came into my head. 'Hell's bells, if you'd got planning permission in the usual way, no one would have so much
as squeaked. And if you'd asked me to restore china on my
usual terms, I'd have jumped at the chance. Really bad thinking

on your part. Mind you, I was impressed by your knowledge of the fashion business. A good alias you've chosen.'

'I'm honoured by such praise.'

'You really should have kept me on side. Because now I doubt if I could do anything worthwhile at the moment.' I spread my hands, which were shaking with a life of their own – genuinely. 'I'm very upset. And as you know, a happy worker is a good worker. Or do I mean that the other way round? So though I'll glue your cracks, I don't suppose I'll be up to the museum-quality work I prefer.'

'I think you're beyond bargaining, Lina. After your activities in France.'

'My activities! What about yours, trying to snatch Leda? I told your men what I think of that.'

He whacked my mouth with the back of his hand. My brain supplied the words he probably meant to use: 'That's just a foretaste of what's coming.'

But neither of us said them aloud. Because from nowhere – actually, from the stable block – emerged a mob of black-clad figures, just like you get on TV, all with their guns pointed at us and all yelling at once. Hands up. Lie down. Face on the ground – except the guy waving a gun at me called it the floor, a mistake that always irritated Griff.

Hands up, I lay face down on the ground. Nasty sharp large-sized gravel, just right for a carriage drive, but not much fun for a half-naked human with a vicious knee and bleeding lips.

'You! Down. Face down!'

Only when someone came to handcuff me did I lift my head enough to mutter, 'But I'm the victim here. And you'll find the mobile in this sleeve.'

TWENTY-SEVEN

Victim. It wasn't a word I'd ever liked using of myself. Survivor, yes – that was something to be proud of. But a victim was someone who had things done to them.

And now I was in the hands of the police, swathed in a foil blanket, I felt more of a victim than I had while I was being assaulted. Not that they weren't kind. They were. It was their very kindness that was almost suffocating. Their kindness, and their complete inability to answer my questions. One: where and how was Griff? Two: where and how was Morris? Please God, please, please God, don't let him be the policeman the men had said was dead.

I suppose it was because the police wanted to ask me lots of questions, and they were honour bound not to ask any until I'd been checked over in A and E – in Brighton, of all places – where I swapped the foil for a backless hospital number. Every injury, however minor, was photographed – I supposed grumpily it was for someone's benefit, only realizing eventually that it was for mine, if I ultimately wanted compensation. Once I'd been photographed, each injury was treated in turn, with X-rays and scans on the house, it seemed. My goodness, when the NHS had an emergency on its hands, even if I had nothing seriously wrong with me at all, it pulled out every stop.

In the event, all they decided to do was give me some cream to treat the patches of soreness and itching which were apparently the result of my petrol bath. Thanks to the gorillas and their water, they weren't too extensive. Eventually, after what seemed like hours, I was returned to a waiting constable about my own age, who said that her name was Rach. She pressed a white suit into my hands; I emerged from the nearest loos looking like a polar bear whose pelt had stretched in the wash. The least said the better about the blue overshoes. Kind she might be, but she insisted that she was too low down the food chain to answer any questions. Her job was just to drive me to Police Headquarters.

'I really need to know about my boyfriend and my grandfather. I'm desperate,' I told her, bracing my legs as if she was going to drag me somewhere. I unbraced quickly. Too painful.

She set us in motion. 'I really don't know.'

'You'd know if a policeman was killed this afternoon?' I pressed.

'Oh, yes. Everyone'd know. Now, do you have a bag or anything? Because we should be on our way.'

I shook my head, falling into step beside her. At least now we were off hospital premises I could try phoning. Surely, Griff would have picked up my phone wherever he was going.

His was as dead as a doornail. No charge left at all. Well, what did I expect, leaving it open so they could trace me? At first the guys arresting Montaigne and his merry men wanted to take it into custody too, but eventually, when I'd told them where it had been, had agreed to let me keep it.

'Can I borrow your phone?' I asked as she helped me into the car as if I was a pensioner on Valium. 'This one's out of battery.'

She handed it over with a grin. 'Going to phone your boyfriend?'

I clapped a hand to my face. 'Oh, no! His number's in my own phone. This is someone else's.' Actually, Griff might well have had Morris's number, but I was just too confused to think clearly.

'You mean you've got the wrong phone?'

'Someone lent it to me. And he's got mine.' I hoped. At last, I took a deep breath, just as the therapist had told me, and tried to think. Yes. The obvious thing was to phone Griff and ask, but I couldn't remember my own number. Griff's, yes, but not my own. And of course I couldn't get it off the dead phone.

I hit myself again, harder this time, hard enough to make a mark. You'd think I had enough pain given the state of my knee, but I needed a bit more. All the years I'd been battling with self-harm, and I had to choose now to start again. Sitting on my hands was the only answer. In any case, I told myself, Morris would be waiting for me – I couldn't, to be honest, work out why he'd not been holding my hand during my hospital adventures, but assumed it might be police procedure.

No, I wouldn't fish my hands out, not unless I could do something sensible with them. What I needed was a good idea. And at long last one arrived. 'You don't have a charger handy, do you?' I asked.

'Back on my desk.'

So that was that for a bit. I continued to sit on my hands.

Tea, sympathy, a soft interview room, two gentle interviewers who wanted to be called Julie and Mike, both detective sergeants – what else could a victim of crime want? Oh, and I got congratulations for the cool way I'd left my phone on (Griff's, of course) and tried to update the control room on the way things were going. We all agreed it was a shame the battery had failed when they'd wanted to tell me to hang on till the team could deal with the kidnappers in the least dangerous way.

But I wasn't happy at all. The two people who should have been there to comfort me were nowhere to be seen. I know I'd been making a fuss about calling them, but deep in my heart I'd thought they'd be sitting side by side waiting for me – first in A and E, and failing that in the police foyer.

'Before I give you any more information,' I said, 'I want to know what's happened to Griffith Tripp, my grandfather, and to DCI Morris.' Since the word partner applied to both in different ways, I thought I'd tweak the truth a bit. Only a bit. 'And there was an elderly lady having a fit that triggered the whole event. Emilia Cosworth. How's she? And is she connected with what's been going on?'

Mike held up a hand – amazingly well manicured, far better kept than mine – and said, 'That's a lot of questions. Can we come to them when—'

'The last one's just courtesy,' I said. 'But I need to know about Griff. My grandfather. He's not well – he's having heart tests – and I need to speak to him. Rach, that nice woman who brought me here, promised to find a charger for me, but she hasn't so far.' I poured out all my telecommunication problems again. They were never going to be interested, but the words kept coming, and blow me if I didn't start crying.

'You've had a very difficult afternoon,' Julie said, passing me tissues. 'Go and find a charger, Mike, for goodness' sake. Will DCI Morris's number be on Mr Tripp's phone?'

'I hope so.' I was really letting myself down with all these tears and snuffles. 'It'd be in my diary, too – only, I left my bag in the car when I went walkabout. And – it's a new car – I can't even remember that number.' Rather than hit myself, I literally grabbed my hair and pulled it as hard as I could.

Julie put her arms round me, pulling my hands into a firm grasp. 'Shock,' she said firmly. 'After the trauma. It'll all come back. But this is why we need to talk to you now, before your brain wipes all the nasty details it'd rather forget and lets all this everyday stuff take over again. Just start talking about what happened this afternoon while we wait for Mike.'

The length of time it took Mike to come back you'd think he'd walked all the way to the nearest phone shop only to find it was closed for the night. And then walked back. Meanwhile, Julie had kept my mind off my hands by asking question after question – 'Just for the DPP,' she'd insist, whenever I wondered why.

Eventually, the story of my afternoon was well and truly down on paper.

'Look,' I said at last, 'this just isn't fair. I need – really, really need – to talk to Griff. And to know that he's OK. And Morris. Please, can't someone help me? It doesn't take this long to find a bloody charger, for goodness' sake! And don't start talking about staffing levels and prioritization.'

She had the grace to look embarrassed. 'Mike has been gone a while, hasn't he?'

'Too long. And no, I don't want more tea. I want – if you can't help me – to go home and make calls from there.' Brighton to Bredeham? Another hour and a half of not knowing. 'Look, Griff's booked into the William Harvey Hospital first thing tomorrow. I have to take him. And I still don't know where he is!' Suddenly, pennies started to drop.

Painfully. OK, I'd been stupid not to think of it, but these people were paid *not* to be stupid. Why hadn't one of them simply suggested I call home to see if he was there? Because they knew he wasn't – that must be it. But I needed to know for myself.

'Can I phone home?' I asked, sounding horribly humble. 'I know that number at least.'

She passed over her mobile. But the call only confirmed what I feared.

'One of your officers must have turned up at the oast when I dialled nine nine nine. They'd know what happened to Griff and Morris. Hell's bells, a DCI with Interpol must qualify as being interesting, even if an old man isn't.' When she didn't respond, I added, 'And what was that one of the heavies said about killing a police officer? I worked out from the timescale that it couldn't have been Morris.'

'Why do you call him Morris if that's his surname?' she asked.

If Mike hadn't walked into the room, I truly think I'd have hit her.

He was carrying what was left of a phone in a polythene bag. 'Sorry, Lina, this got damaged back at the oast. There was a bit of a kerfuffle with that old lady having her fit. Your grandad was trying to help DCI Morris and must have dropped it and – well, it looks as if the ambulance . . . Well . . .' He held up a hand to stop me screaming. 'So I've been trying to locate the old gentleman using other means. He's OK. That's the first thing. He's fine. Apparently, he insisted on accompanying Ms Cosworth to hospital, where she was detained. DCI Morris – he'd followed the ambulance in your car, apparently – offered to take Mr Tripp home, which he started to do. But Mr Tripp complained of chest pains, so Mr Morris took him straight to the William Harvey Cardiac Unit where I understand he's due for an angiogram tomorrow?'

'Yes, the tests I told you about.'

'Right. Mr Tripp is still having tests, and Mr Morris is with him. So when you're ready, we can take you there.'

I wish I could say that I'd thanked him properly and thanked God for Morris being so sensible and having the right priorities. But all I managed was to put my head in my hands and cry.

'Post-traumatic stress,' Julie muttered. 'Only to be expected. You'd better call the medics.'

That was enough to make me pull together. 'What? And waste more time here?' I gave a huge sniff. 'There'll be plenty of medics at the William Harvey. Just get me there.'

I expected the lowly Rach to drive me; I got both Julie and Mike. And a police tracksuit and a mysterious anonymous pair of flip-flops.

Julie drove. 'You never told me why you call DCI Morris by his surname,' she observed, over her shoulder.

'All his friends do,' I said, non-committally. As if I was about to tell anyone I was going out with a man called Reg. 'And you never told me why one of the heavies said stuff about killing a policeman.'

Julie made a great fuss about a careful turn at an awkward junction.

Mike replied, 'Oh, there's a lot to come out in the wash yet. I promise that you'll be fully briefed in due course. Fancy some chocolate? I got some while I was trying to locate your grandad. He really is in the best place, you know.'

If they were going to clam up about the dead cop, presumably it was because they were acting on orders. Taking the chocolate as a peace-offering-cum-supper, I treated them to a long explanation of why they should give up this brand and make sure they always bought Fair Trade. Very long. If I thought about the poor devils toiling away for other people's profit, it always made me cross, and what better way to get out of victim mode?

TWENTY-EIGHT

M ike and Julie dropped me by the main entrance of the William Harvey. In a far corner of a largely deserted car park I could see our car: oh, yes, I could remember the number now I saw it. So where was Morris? I checked in all the public spaces but couldn't see any sign of him. Although Mike had promised Griff was all right, I was ready to panic. If I knew hospitals, they only let visitors stay on this late if there was something really wrong with the patient. Really, really wrong.

I headed for the cardiac ward, ready to wring tears from the eyes of any nurse who tried to stop me seeing Griff by declaring I was his granddaughter, just as I had to the police officers, and blow the legalities. Mrs Walker swore that her sister-in-law had been denied information about her husband, in intensive care, because she'd kept her maiden name and the computer only wanted to admit Mrs Thingy, not Ms Somethingelse.

To my amazement no one stopped me, and I found Griff in the first side ward I looked in. He'd been reading the *Observer*, but as I put my head round the door he laid the paper to one side and held out his arms. Neither of us could say anything; head on his chest, I listened to the beating of his heart and wondered how it dared to be ill while it was beating so well.

At last he pushed me away, but we didn't let go each other's hands even as I was pulling a chair to the bed.

'When they wanted to clear the crime scene, I said I'd accompany poor Emilia to whichever hospital they took her to,' he said, 'and Morris drove our car in the ambulance's wake. When they said the tests would take time, Morris insisted I go home – he said I'd only be in the way of the police looking for you, and that at home they'd be able to contact me, with no worrying about poor mobile signals. You know how crabby he is about our rural reception. And then he noticed I was trying to make my puffer work and it didn't seem to be doing any good, so he turned on to the motorway and drove at speeds likely to give me a proper heart attack. Actually, he did very well. Anyway, to cut a long story short, here I am. No machines, no nothing. Just regular observations. So you can see I'm not at death's door. They only kept me in because they said they couldn't trust me to starve without you to keep on eye on me. The angiogram goes ahead as planned tomorrow. But you are to go home and rest. Before you do, however –' he pulled me conspiratorially towards him – 'you are my bona fide granddaughter. Ah – you've already decided that, haven't you?'

'About the same time you decided, I should think.' I gave him a version of the afternoon's events that the American military would call *redacted*: in other words I filleted out all the really terrifying bits and tried to make him laugh with my descriptions of my successive outfits. He loved the idea of where I'd hidden his mobile and made a joke so blue that he surprised me into a shout of laughter, which kept bubbling up.

'There's no sign of Morris,' I observed casually, when I could speak again.

'No. He left the car keys in your bag in this locker – top shelf. And a note,' he added with a kind smile.

'Oh.'

'He was summoned back to France – he waited as long as he dared, but it seems Interpol won't grant compassionate leave for your own grandfather's illness, let alone your girl-friend's not quite grandfather.'

'Oh.'

'Apparently, the French and the English authorities are already bellyaching about who gets to try Montaigne – does kidnap cap diddling a prime minister, that sort of thing.'

'Oh.'

'Actually, I'm not sure he's well. He was sniffing a lot, and his throat was really gravelly. Maybe too much emotion – quite possible, you know – or maybe the start of poor little Leda's cold.'

At this point a nurse registered my presence and strode in

to ask what I was doing. He was built like a fast bowler and moved as if he was starting his run-up.

'I know, I know,' I said, hands up. 'Grandpa will tell you why I came so late.'

'You're the woman that the police were talking about, aren't you?'

'Yes.'

'Well, in other circumstances I'd say you could stop and share your grandpa's cocoa. But since he isn't having any, you'd better scarper and get your own. He'll phone when you can come and collect him – about midday, maybe half an hour later. Make sure you've got him a nice lunch ready – he'll need it.'

It was only when I got home that I remembered about Morris's note. But before I read it, I checked our security, had a shower, slapped on some anti-itch cream and started some supper. Cheese on toast. I hadn't had that since Griff had been told to reduce his cholesterol intake, but there was no reason why I shouldn't rub in the garlic and slosh on the Worcestershire sauce the way he'd shown me – I wasn't going to be kissing anyone for a bit.

Full of cheese and halfway down a glass of Griff's favourite Burgundy, I fished the note from my pocket and spread it out in front of me.

I never mind being grovelled to, especially when the grovel-lings are accompanied with lots of nice endearments. And he'd been right to stay with Griff, I had to admit that, even though he was worried he might have given Griff what felt like the start of flu. And he couldn't have done anything to help the police – might have got in their way. But I did wish, more deeply in my heart than I cared to admit, that he'd stuck up a couple of fingers at his Interpol colleagues and been late for their urgent meeting. It was only about money, after all. Rich people whose pride had been hurt wanted action. Let them wait for it. If they hadn't been so keen on their status symbols, they'd never have been duped in the first place.

I knew I was being unreasonable, denying all the principles Griff and I lived and worked by. But all I'd wanted was the comfort of a hug – ten minutes, tops – and all I got was a piece of paper, now stained with a couple of tears and great big cheesy thumbprint.

'You just mark my words,' Tim the Bear said, when I crawled up to bed, 'he'll try to sweeten you up with another damned limited edition collector's bear.'

Monday morning found me in housekeeping mode. Nothing could have kept me in my workroom. Nothing kept me anywhere for long. But in between my flittings I stripped Griff's bed, made it up with fresh linen and ensured he had fresh towels and a newly vac'd bedroom. As a treat I spring-cleaned the bathroom – truly, I like few things better than to polish taps and baths.

After that I tackled the living room and kitchen. Then the office. And why not deal with my room? All the traipsing up and down stairs might free up the bruised knee. If not, tough.

It was still only eight thirty.

There was nothing to stop me nipping into Maidstone to buy a new phone. Griff wouldn't be phoning till twelve thirty at the earliest – probably much later. But I had to stay within earshot of the landline. I sanitized and recharged his phone. He'd be relying on the hospital payphones to contact me.

What about some cooking? That would pass the time.

I couldn't face it. Griff was the cook, after all.

The phone. Surely, it couldn't be Griff?

It was. Just to say hello and that he was fine.

Back to work. If only there was something to do.

Eventually, I did the obvious thing: I went back to my workroom and started to tackle the backlog of hideous Toby jugs I'd been putting off for days.

They stared at me reproachfully when I opened the cupboard I'd stored them in, just as they had when I'd taken advantage of a stallholder's ignorance to get some cheap Swansea ware. The day I spotted all those dodgy boxes, of course. Were they connected to the goings-on in the unit near the oast? I must ask the police.

Could I really work on one of those ugly faces?

I hadn't checked the day's emails. What was happening to my mind?

When my restoration work built up, the online business was in the hands of Griff. On the other hand, our clients weren't to know that he wouldn't be working today, so I'd better switch on the computer and at least warn them of a delay responding to their enquiries. If I'd hoped for a message from Morris to my personal email I was disappointed, so I switched quickly to our business account.

There were a couple of straightforward questions, both of which I could manage. But then there was a long email which fortunately had all the preceding correspondence attached – in reverse order, of course. Ulysses S. Grant? The guy whose Parian ware bust I'd bought for twenty pounds? What the hell was Griff doing asking twenty grand for it? OK, twenty thousand dollars, not pounds, but all the same. Not just asking, either. The guy he was corresponding with was definitely nibbling. Not enthusiastically, but nibbling – like those little fish they put in foot spas, maybe. He was upping his offer by a few hundred dollars each time Griff declined an offer. What if I upset Griff by accepting too low a figure? What if I put off the buyer by being greedy?

Twenty thousand dollars. It was a big secret for Griff to keep.

After a good deal of lip-chewing, I made a note to ask Griff's advice and sent the guy a reply saying the person dealing with the bust was out of the office today but would contact him tomorrow.

If Griff had been working on a twenty-thousand dollar deal without telling me, what else had he been keeping quiet? If I switched on the computer again I could actually check all his Internet use, not to mention the rest of the business emails.

That wasn't how we worked, was it?

There was a shelf of really lovely china awaiting my attention, but, now I came to look at my hands, I wasn't sure if they were steady enough to deal with anything really delicate. So, praying for a diversion, it was back to the Toby jugs.

I got the ugliest of the bunch nicely taken apart. He'd been badly glued, and the only thing to do was start all over again.

The house phone rang. I nearly dropped the piece I was holding. But it was only Julie, asking how I was.

'You're never working! Not after all you went through yesterday.'

Now wasn't really the moment to explain the difference between full-time salaried workers and freelance self-employed ones. 'Keeps my mind and hands busy,' I said.

'Would you mind if I popped round? You asked various questions yesterday and I'm beginning to get a few answers. I'll be with you in – say – ten minutes.'

She cut the call before I could argue.

She brought Mike. Both looking solemn, they established themselves in the living room, round eyed as they checked out the lovely furniture. I just hoped they wouldn't have the same attitude as Wayne.

Balancing the eighteenth century coffee can on his knee, Mike said, 'Yesterday you were asking about the death of a policeman, and we hadn't the slightest idea what you were talking about, to be honest. Well, we've now established who he was, and why he died. I'm afraid it's not pleasant listening.'

I put my hands to my mouth. 'Was it his body that was in the oast house yesterday – the theatre? DCI Morris made sure I didn't see it – and then I was rather too busy doing other things.'

'Quite,' Julie rushed in, as if she'd rather not be talking about the oast. 'How's that knee of yours, by the way? I should have asked earlier. And any problems after the bang on your head?'

'I'm fine,' I said, because I was – as long as I didn't think too hard about the oast. As if I could blank out the face on my mobile phone, I buried my face in my hands. 'How could I be such an idiot? It was Paul, wasn't it? The body,' I added when they looked blank.

'It was the body of DC Phil Haddon,' Mike corrected me carefully.

Julie was about to say something, but a look from him silenced her.

I carried on putting two and two together, for my benefit, if not theirs. 'While I was in France I was sent a photo of a man I knew as Paul. He'd been badly beaten up. I took this as a warning not to mess with the so-called Charles Montaigne any more. And certainly not to mess any more with Paul.'

'Mess with Paul?' Julie repeated.

'Have anything to do with him, at least. Or rather, let him have anything to do with me.'

Not surprisingly, they both looked blank.

'I'm sorry. My grandfather's still in hospital, and I'm afraid my brain's gone quite soggy. Maybe it's that bang on the head . . . The man I knew as Paul met me secretly – at a garden centre of all places – to tell me to pull out of the play and everything going on at the oast. I thought he'd taken a beating as punishment for contacting me. The two heavies admitted dealing with a policeman – presumably, Montaigne somehow discovered who he really was, an undercover officer.' To stop myself crying, I asked, 'Did you pick that up from the phone?'

Mike nodded reluctantly. 'It all tallies with what we found out. Well, obviously not just us. The team. Both Sussex and Kent police, plus Interpol. In fact, the man you called Paul had taken a tremendous risk warning you off. Someone with an organization as big as this – we believe it stretches as far as the US in one direction and Italy in the other—'

'Mafia,' Julie put in.

'—doesn't like dissent in the ranks.'

'Dear God, why didn't I put all this together before?'

'Because, as you said, you were rather busy doing other things. And I should have thought that forgetting that someone else had died might be part of some self-preservation instinct.'

Julie was inclined to take the other view, that it would have generated extra adrenalin, but I didn't want to join the discussion.

Eventually, I raised a hand to stop them bickering. 'Charles Montaigne. What's his real name? Not that it'll mean anything to me, but I don't like fakes, even when it comes to names. And another thing: how did this so-called Montaigne find out so much about me personally? I'd really like to know. There were bits and pieces only people who know me could have told him. About my father, and about my relationships.' All those postcards. I'd better hand them over as evidence. They weren't worth anything to me.

'No idea,' Mike said. 'But people who want info can charm it out of stones. Remember what is said on those war posters: *careless talk costs lives!*'

'It could have cost me mine,' I said bitterly. 'Or my soul, I suppose, if I'd actually agreed to work with him.'

This seemed a bit beyond them.

'And his name is? Montaigne's, of course.'

'He's got a number, actually. Camille Monet, for a start.'

'Spare me! That's when he's dealing in Impressionist art, is it? His real name – the one he was born with. I just need to know. Humour me.'

'Christopher Mills. French mother, English father. Bilingual. Double first at Cambridge. Brilliant man. Until he went wrong. He runs an army of forgers – you were spot on with the French Impressionists. Nice line in anything fakeable. Manuscripts, miniatures. Never soiled his hands. Always got other folk to do the dirty work – some more successfully than others.'

I nearly threw up. What if Pa was working for him? Pa and Titus? No, surely they were too low down the food chain. And even they had principles – of a sort. But Freya had definitely wanted gen on Titus. Deep breath time. Buy a moment on my own time. I popped upstairs and gathered the cards. I felt cleaner as I watched Mike stow them in an evidence bag.

Nodding as if that wrapped up one line of questioning, I said, 'Now let's talk about the good guys. I know about Griff and Morris, but I haven't a clue about what happened to Emilia Cosworth after she was taken to hospital. I know Griff would want me to send flowers.'

'I don't think we're supposed to divulge confidential health information to a third party,' Mike said cautiously.

'In her position I'd want flowers,' Julie said. 'Always assuming the hospital allows flowers – it's amazing that a simple flower should be a Health and Safety issue.'

'But—' They were going to start again, weren't they?

'So she's still in hospital and likely to need cheering up,' I prompted them. 'So the fit she had—?'

'You'd really need to talk to the medics.'

'You know as well as I do I've no idea where she is, and even if I turned up at her bedside the staff wouldn't tell me. OK, I'm being nosy. But Griff and she go back forty years, and he's entitled to know what's happened to an old friend.'

They looked around the room, I swear, as if to check for eavesdroppers. 'If your grandfather's that ill, it might be better not to tell him. Not if they were – you know . . .'

'They were friends,' I supplied. 'So she's very ill?'

'They think she's got a brain tumour,' Julie said with a rush.

'Does that mean she's going to – oh, my God . . .' All those things I'd done to provoke her. On the other hand . . . 'Is that why she's been behaving so . . . oddly?' Griff wouldn't have wanted me to speak ill of the nearly dead, so I replaced the word I wanted to use with a kinder one.

'Could be,' Julie continued. 'They say that's why Mo Mowlam was so unconventional, don't they? Poor woman.'

There was no need to reveal my ignorance by saying I wasn't sure who she was talking about; I made a note to look her up later.

'So Emilia's in hospital. And where is Charles Montaigne? Christopher Thingy? Surely, they won't let him have bail this time. He's done a bit more than diddle rich people.' I wanted to sound jaunty – I think it came out more like desperate.

'They won't. We take the murder of our own very seriously, as I'm sure your boyfriend will have told you.'

The boyfriend who was too busy sorting out the poor deprived rich to stay with me. Or even phone me, on a morning he must have known I'd be beyond scared. 'Of course,' I said loyally. 'May I ask something else? In early September there was an antiques fair in Hythe, with a stall dealing in tea caddies, writing slopes, work boxes – all very heavily and badly restored. I've mentioned it to DCI Morris, but he hasn't been able to tell me – was it anything to do with the Montaigne-Mills empire?'

The notion seemed to surprise them. They both scribbled in their notebooks and got to their feet. I didn't try to detain them. I had a phone call to make. Titus might be weird, but he was a mate – and mates, as I could have told Morris, should always be there for each other.

TWENTY-NINE

'**M**e? Work for anyone else? Specially some bugger I told you was a nasty piece of knitting! You got to be kidding, doll. In any case, the rate your Pa works, he wouldn't have time to supply anyone but me. Been lying very low, we have, since you warned us about that Freya woman wanting to nail me. Good job, considering you only went and told the fucking pigs to make sure no one took a pot shot at the old bugger.'

'Sorry, Titus. But I was really scared – the bloke calling himself Montaigne knew so much about me. And about Pa. And when they tried to kidnap Morris's daughter, I panicked.'

'I suppose you might,' he said grudgingly. 'Any road, the old geezer played the innocent – pretended to be really grateful when they turned up on his doorstep. Yes, officer, thank you very much, officer. All that crap. That Freya still sniffing about?' he asked suspiciously.

'Don't know. She's giving me the cold shoulder. Totally freezing me out.'

'Shit. Could mean she's really got us in her sights. Don't worry – nothing at the Hall to give him away,' he added kindly. 'Not any more. Send my best to Griff – actually, no. Don't want him to have a heart attack. Sorry. No laughing matter. Hey, doll – for your ears only – that guy who topped himself. Croft. Under pressure to pretend he was producing real antiques, not repro. And sell them to just one dealer. Get my drift?'

'Montaigne—? You should tell the police.'

'Fucking hell. That's really bloody likely, doll.'

End of call.

There was still no news from the hospital. Any moment I'd phone the ward myself. But they'd told Griff he was just one of a list of patients having the same procedure, so he might just be at the tail end of the queue. What might that mean? That he was worse or better than the others?

If only I could have settled to some decent restoration, but, confronted by the pieces of the Toby jug, I really lost heart and left them where they were. Perhaps while the spring-cleaning bug was still in me, I should tackle the shop, closed since it was a Monday.

Not a speck of dirt anywhere, of course, under Mrs Walker's regime. Not a single mote dared hang in the air. In fact, the place looked far better than it had for years, our previous assistant having been far too grand to so much as waft a feather duster. She'd died of heart failure. Not a good thought at the moment.

Reduced to playing Solitaire and Freecell on the computer, I intermittently checked our emails. Even an online survey would be better than nothing. I even checked the weather forecast, the latest celeb gossip and anything the screen threw up. I had mail! Yes!

And it was serious mail. It was from the guy wanting Ulysses. He wanted him now, and twenty thousand was his final offer. Pounds, if I insisted. I did. The deal was done, with a cyber handshake.

So there was another task – a useful one this time. If Ulysses was going to fly across the Atlantic, he'd travel in style. More to the point, in an acre of bubble-wrap. I might not reach Mrs Walker's standards of neat elegance, but I could pack anything so well that it'd survive being kicked round a Royal Mail sorting office.

There was nothing on the answerphone when I got back from the post office, having broken all records for the journey time there and back. I'd cut short half a dozen conversations with our nice chatty neighbours, all with time on their hands and none waiting for news of Griff.

I picked up the phone and dialled the hospital.

The line was busy.

So I did what I wanted to do anyway. I headed off to the William Harvey, so jumpy and prone to road rage that I told myself if I wanted to get to Ashford in one piece I'd better pretend I was on my driving test.

The hospital car park was heaving. It would be visiting time any moment, and people were jostling for the few remaining spaces. We circled like vultures. And at last, forgetting all about manners, I found a place and nipped in. There could have been a row, but I ran to the pay station as if my life depended on it, darted back, and began running again.

'Lina! Lina, for goodness' sake.'

I'd practically charged someone down; in my efforts to swerve, I lost my footing and would have fallen if strong arms hadn't grabbed me. Robin's. He used to be a boxer and still kept very fit.

'Long time no see,' he said mildly. I could recall the time his Adam's apple would have danced a hornpipe just at the sight of me. 'Come on, we'll have a coffee. And you can tell me all about it,' he added, peering into my face.

'I can't. It's Griff. Heart.'

'Attack?'

'Angiogram.'

'Routine. I know you two are like this,' he said, crossing his fingers, 'but you really don't need to worry. Just a test. What they do is . . .' By now he'd got me walking towards the hospital, almost as quickly as I wanted, with far more details of the procedure than I liked. Griff would be scared witless.

'There's something wrong,' I insisted. 'I have to go to him.'

He stopped by a desk and spoke to one of the women behind it. I let him get on with it. I'm sure my jabbering wouldn't have got through to her as quickly as his quiet authority. That was vicars for you. Or their dog collars.

'Hasn't got back to the ward yet,' he said, 'so panic not. And, as I said, coffee. And a sandwich, because I'll bet you didn't manage to eat any breakfast, and if you did it was a long time ago. Come on.' I'd never been vicar-talked before, but he was very good at chattering away – what sort of sandwich, did I want a cake? – to take the pain from the moment.

'What are you doing here?' I asked, able to get a word in at last as we sat down.

'Seeing a parishioner. Very near the end, so they waived the

usual visiting regulations. I gave him Communion –' he patted
a neat little case I'd scarcely registered – 'and hung on till he
died.'

'You seem remarkably cheerful,' I observed.

'Death doesn't have to be a sad thing – not when you're in
your nineties and pretty well paralysed with arthritis and you
buried your wife of sixty-five years only two weeks ago. I
can't say he willed himself to die, but he certainly didn't want
to hang about on this earth any longer.' When he saw I was
having difficulty speaking, he continued, 'I want you to be
one of the first to know that I'm leaving Bossingham. I haven't
even told the churchwardens yet, not officially. I couldn't carry
on as I was, not with Freya's job in Maidstone, so I've found
another parish. Actually, it's close to you and Griff. Near
Loose. So Freya can be a Loose Woman.' He paused so I
could laugh at a very, very old Kentish joke.

'Freya? How is she?'

He looked briefly furtive. 'You and she had a bit of a falling
out, didn't you? Her making,' he added, before I could protest,
'which she freely admits. You know – better than I – how
stiff-necked she is. You'll wait till Domesday for an apology.
But if you could, you know, turn the other cheek, she'd love
to see you. And be very grateful for a fresh face, I should
think.'

'Fresh face? You've missed something in the story, Robin.'

'Oh! Of course! She's in hospital back in Pembury. You
remember all that business about reducing maternity services
in Maidstone? Quite. And from theoretically opposing them,
she's now experiencing the problems first-hand – it's such a
schlep over to Pembury that not as many of our friends make
it to see her as often as we'd like.'

There were still a few pieces of narrative missing. 'So it's
a problem with her pregnancy? If only I'd known . . . Why
did none of her police colleagues tell me?'

'Because her overnight departure – yes, a real emergency
– left a big hole in their staffing, and I'd imagine that whoever
took over her role has been running to stand still, just to deal
with the stuff on her desk. And her in tray.'

'And probably the floor, if I know her,' I said, grinning to show there were no hard feelings. Not many, anyway. 'But she's all right? And the baby?'

'Fine. Though she's on complete bed rest. Hence the need for visitors. She's having a scan this afternoon – so I can't hang about here too long.' He gave a serene but wondering smile. 'It's so amazing what prayer can do – plus a bit of help from the dear old NHS.'

'Do you need to be on your knees and in church for prayer to work properly?' I asked, not quite idly.

'You're winding me up, aren't you? Come on, you know better than that. You can ask God for help whenever, wherever. But if you want a bit of kneeling and a bit of church, I'm happy to oblige. With or without you.'

He meant it, too. 'I could do with a shed load for Griff. Thanks.'

He got to his feet, checking his watch, then hovered.

'Do you know why Freya felt embarrassed about getting back in touch with me? You know I was only a phone call away. You should have phoned me.' I looked at him. The Adam's apple was on the move. 'She told you not to, didn't she? Robin, she's the nearest thing I have to a woman friend – I wouldn't have done or said anything to upset her.'

'It's more what *she* did or said. The thing is, she was, in her own words, grossly unprofessional – even I can see that, though I blame the pressures of the job on top of a difficult pregnancy.' He sat down again, fidgeting with someone else's empty KitKat wrapper. 'She sounded off about you, and the fact you were badgering her, in front of other people. And walls have ears. She thinks she might have mentioned stuff about you to people she shouldn't.'

'One of whom might just be an acquaintance of Charles Montaigne, aka Christopher Mills? Shit and double shit! How could she?'

'Because he was a very senior officer? You know that Morris of yours was investigating police corruption at Interpol? This guy's name came up on the radar, and now he's awaiting trial, I believe.'

'The dock'll be nice and full then.' I gave him the briefest rundown of what had been going on in Paris and back here in England. 'But maybe we shouldn't tell Freya about all this just yet. It won't do her blood pressure any good, will it?'

'I can tell her you forgive her, though?'

'Big word, Robin, forgiveness. Tell you what, if God brings Griff through all this, I'll see what I can do about forgiving Freya.' It might sound flip, but it was all I could do to make my mouth work. There was pain in my back and chest so bad that I nearly cried aloud.

'I don't think God works quite like that. Hey, are you all right? You're not, are you?'

I clutched my chest, then my arm. I was dizzy with the pain. Reeling with it. And then it stopped. I could breathe again. And then I couldn't. He tried to push my head between my knees, but that made it worse. Great yellow blobs swam across my eyes. I started to plunge between them.

Then the breaths came again. Just like that. And the pains went. All of them.

Robin was on his feet yelling. People were running towards me. I couldn't stop them, but I could stop Robin. I grabbed his hands.

'Don't you understand? It's not me who's ill! It's Griff! And I think he might have died.'

The NHS doesn't like people keeling over on their premises, so willy-nilly they were going to treat me. Furious, I sent Robin on his way. He needed to see his baby and to hold Freya's hand. Meanwhile, on a stretcher, I protested all the way to A and E, where they stuck clips and pads on me. If I twisted round, I could see the nice regular rhythm of my body on a monitor. So they tried to find other things wrong. It was only when a young Asian doctor paused to listen to what I was trying to tell them that they stopped.

'This happened to my mother,' she said with the same quiet authority as Robin, 'when my father had his heart attack. They were a thousand miles apart, physically, but she knew. I suggest we contact the cardiac unit and ask about Mr . . . Griff?'

'Griffith Tripp,' I gasped. 'He's supposed to be having an angiogram. And I'm just so afraid—'

'Oh, just an angiogram,' she said, dismissively. 'Routine.

But we'll check, anyway. Stay where you are, please.' She withdrew from the cubicle, drawing the curtain behind her.

With all those wires and things I pretty well had to. As exhausted as if I really had been ill – or perhaps it was a result of all the previous day's problems – I allowed myself to sink back on to the bed. But I couldn't switch my ears off. I tried to track what was going on by footsteps and murmured voices. If I hadn't still been attached to the monitor, I'd have got up and followed them.

The wait seemed to last forever. People came and went to the cubicles either side. There were moans and comments I tried to do more than ignore – I wanted them shut out.

At last feet stopped outside my cubicle. Dr Lal popped her head round the curtain and stepped inside, followed by a couple of people about my age, not wearing white coats but sporting stethoscopes.

'You've had a very interesting experience, Lina,' Dr Lal said. 'I wonder if you'd mind talking about it to these students.'

I sat up and started literally to tear my hair. 'I will do nothing – nothing, do you hear? – until I hear about Griff.'

She pulled my hands away, but as soon as they were free I started smacking my face. This time her grip was much tighter.

'He's fine, now. Fine. We'll talk about your anger management issues another time, maybe.' She smiled kindly. I glowered. 'Someone should have come to tell you. He's in Cardiac ICU, and he's stable.'

'ICU?' I repeated stupidly.

'Intensive care,' one of the students explained.

'But he was only supposed to be having an angiogram.' I was totally bewildered.

'He was, and he did. But even while he tried to phone you to tell you to collect him, he had a cardiac incident. A very severe attack of angina,' she added.

'Bugger me,' I said. 'So much for the cat on the roof.'

THIRTY

A pparently, in the Intensive Care Unit each patient had his or her own nurse. Griff's, a woman not much older than me, and not much bigger, emerged to speak to me. Much as I wanted news, I wanted her back there watching him.

'He's fine,' she assured me. 'Fine. In fact, he'll probably be moved to the High Intensity Unit soon. And then he'll have his bypass tomorrow and—'

'Bypass?'

'Yes. A quadruple bypass. The arteries round his heart have serious lesions – that means they're in poor condition.'

'Why? Because of the stress of rescuing me? Have I fed him the wrong stuff? Not made him exercise enough?'

She shook her head, trying to talk across my questions. 'I don't think, given your age, it's anything to do with you. Such a problem is not surprising for a man of eighty.'

'Eighty?' Why hadn't the old bugger told me?

'What happens in the operation is this . . .'

I'm not sure how much I took in. Half the time I was willing her to go back to him. Once she did break off, only to come back to tell me he was worrying about me. Since visiting was just over, all she could let me do was stand by the door and wave at him. I could speak to him this evening, she promised.

He looked tiny, lost in a huge space station of a bed, with wires and cables and even bigger, more sophisticated monitors than the ones I'd been briefly attached to. We smiled and waved. That was it until the evening. But at least he was still alive, and, the nurse assured me, once he'd got his operation over, he'd be better than he'd been for months. Years, even. She made it sound so easy.

'Just remember,' she said, very seriously, 'not to talk to him about the earlier incident. And don't mention your reaction.'

Did she think I was stupid?

'We'll deal with that in the recovery period. You must be as positive as I've been with you. And to do that, you've got to believe that I've told you the truth. No more, no less.'

Ashford isn't much of a place to kill a few hours in, but there was nowhere else to go. I just walked; if I passed anyone I knew, I didn't recognize them. I made myself eat, because I'd got to drive back home eventually. Then I walked some more. I found a bench in the late sun and texted Morris and Aidan. Then I nipped into Boots and bought some cheap make-up: I might not be as good as Griff when it came to applying slap, but I'd do my best.

As I sat in the car outlining my lips, it dawned on me for the first time that the oast house dream was well and truly over. It wasn't just me who'd not tread the boards – a lot of people, from Wine-Box Lady down, would be bitterly disappointed. How ironic that ordinary illnesses should end the show, not Charles Montaigne or whatever his real name was. Poor Emilia. A death sentence, by the sound of it – though I tried to work out a scenario for her fit that would convince Griff for tonight at least. And Griff – the only acting he'd be doing, if I knew him, was trying to convince me he wasn't in pain and that he was fine. Perhaps, if the nurse was to be believed, in time he would recover and he wouldn't need to pretend.

The car park was almost as full as it had been earlier, but I refused to panic about finding a slot. If I was to convince Griff that I was calm, I simply had to be calm. Full stop. So when I eventually grabbed a place, I did the deep breathing exercises my therapist had taught me. I pulled a face – she wouldn't have thought much of my efforts today, would she? Or last night?

Still in a spaceship bed, but now sharing the attentions of the nurse with a couple of other patients, Griff beamed at the sight of me. No flowers, of course, any more than poor Emilia could have flowers. No choccies, no anything. But I brought him what he wanted. My love. We nattered about the Toby

Jugs, and he gave a little whoop of pleasure when I told him about Ulysses and his next journey.

'A nest egg, dear one. I wanted you to have a nest egg. Just in case.'

'But—' Was that why he'd splurged on those designer clothes? But he didn't want questions, that was quite clear, so I shut up. For some minutes we just sat without saying anything.

'Have you heard from Morris?'

'A text. He's got full-blown flu, bed, can't keep anything down, hopes he hasn't passed it on to either of us.'

'Poor man. That's what happens when you work every hour God sends – your immune system takes a battering.'

'You sound like Pa!'

'Oh dear. But you could have done with Morris to hold your hand, my love.'

'I've got Tim the Bear for hand-holding. In fact, he's predicting Morris will produce yet another wildly expensive bear with stiff fur and hard paws.'

'Tim's probably right. When will you tell Morris you don't like posh teddies, only cuddly ones?' He looked at me with narrowed eyes. 'You ought to be straight with him, dear one. Straighter, at least. For your sake. Happiness never comes from half-truths.' He coughed. 'I ought to have said this before, but I was afraid of losing you. Now you might lose me, I must try. Dear one, your life is wrapped up in old men. Me, your Pa, Titus – even Morris is old enough to be your father. Your only woman friend is – let us say, not good at friendship. I've made you into a middle aged lady – I've taken away your youth.'

'It wasn't much of a youth,' I managed. 'And if it hadn't been for you, the chances are I'd be dead by now – dodgy drugs, dirty needles . . .'

He couldn't deny it, but his mouth became stubborn. 'We must redress this. If the operation fails, you will have to redress it on your own. I have to say it, my sweetest Lina. I have to. You do understand, don't you – everything?'

I took his hand and kissed it, not letting it go.

Eventually, he asked, trying to sound casual, not wistful, 'Any news of Aidan?'

'Bad news about his sister, but good for you – he'll be on the first plane after her funeral next week. He promises you the pampering of your life. And Robin – I ran into him earlier – tells me that Freya and the baby (can you call it a baby at this stage?) are doing fine, and that he's popped you on his prayer list. I still think knees-bent-in-church prayers might be better than muttered-under-your-breath-on–a-motorway prayers.'

'I'm happy with either,' he said, squeezing my fingers.

He didn't mention Emilia, and neither did I. And if he had, I'd probably have lied through my teeth and said she was fine and being as rude to the medics as she had been to the cast.

We sat in silence while the hands of the clock moved round. Then, just as I was about to leave, he pulled me back. 'I had such a funny turn today, Lina. Did anyone mention resuscitation or anything?'

I shook my head. 'Not a word. Now, I can't see you till tomorrow evening, remember – and even then you probably won't know I'm here, they say. But I will be. Right beside you.'

'Of course you will. We'll get through this together, dear one. I promise.'

'We'll get through this together,' I agreed, desperate to be telling the truth.